FAMILY MATTERS AT BLACKBERRY FARM

BLACKBERRY FARM SERIES - BOOK FOUR

ROSIE CLARKE

B
Boldwood

First published in Great Britain in 2025 by Boldwood Books Ltd.

Copyright © Rosie Clarke, 2025

Cover Design by Colin Thomas

Cover Images: Colin Thomas

The moral right of Rosie Clarke to be identified as the author of this work has been asserted in accordance with the Copyright, Designs and Patents Act 1988.

All rights reserved. No part of this book may be reproduced in any form or by any electronic or mechanical means, including information storage and retrieval systems, without written permission from the author, except for the use of brief quotations in a book review. This book is a work of fiction and, except in the case of historical fact, any resemblance to actual persons, living or dead, is purely coincidental.

Every effort has been made to obtain the necessary permissions with reference to copyright material, both illustrative and quoted. We apologise for any omissions in this respect and will be pleased to make the appropriate acknowledgements in any future edition.

A CIP catalogue record for this book is available from the British Library.

Paperback ISBN 978-1-78513-129-5

Large Print ISBN 978-1-78513-130-1

Hardback ISBN 978-1-78513-128-8

Ebook ISBN 978-1-78513-131-8

Kindle ISBN 978-1-78513-132-5

Audio CD ISBN 978-1-78513-123-3

MP3 CD ISBN 978-1-78513-124-0

Digital audio download ISBN 978-1-78513-125-7

This book is printed on certified sustainable paper. Boldwood Books is dedicated to putting sustainability at the heart of our business. For more information please visit https://www.boldwoodbooks.com/about-us/sustainability/

Boldwood Books Ltd, 23 Bowerdean Street, London, SW6 3TN

www.boldwoodbooks.com

1

CAMBRIDGE, ENGLAND, MARCH 1943

John Talbot stopped outside the florist in King's Parade and looked at the display of gorgeous spring flowers, daffodils, snowdrops, anemones, violets, and great bunches of ever-lasting blooms that had been dried over the winter. He hesitated, not sure what he wanted, because he was about to do something that aroused conflicting emotions in his head. It had cost him some sleepless nights, but now he'd made up his mind. He was going to ask Lucy to be his wife.

Lucy Ross was a nurse, just as his beloved Faith had been – his darling sweet Faith who had died during the birth of John's son. Faith was John's first love; he'd fallen for her at first sight and they'd planned to wed. Tragically, she'd been brutally attacked by her uncle – a cruel man John had despised and disliked – and her baby had come too soon; she'd died alone and in pain, and John could never forgive himself because it was his fault she'd been pregnant, unmarried, and alone. Jonny had survived, because Lizzie, his brother Tom's wife, had found Faith in time to get help for the baby, though it had been too late for Faith. John had been torn apart by his grief, blaming himself for the death of the girl he loved, no matter how many times his family told him that he wasn't to blame.

Did John have the right to ask another girl to be his wife? His doubts had haunted him for a while now. He'd first met Lucy when she'd nursed him in Addenbrooke's Hospital after his plane had crash-landed, breaking his ankle. Lucy was young and pretty, though older than Faith had been when they'd met, and he was almost sure that she loved him. At the time, John had been in love with Faith, but when Lucy had nursed him for a second time he'd realised he liked her, found himself confiding in her.

He hadn't spoken much of his feelings for her, although they'd been out often these past months since his return to duty in the RAF. The war continued and every man was needed and expected to return to duty as soon as they healed. John's physical wounds, caused when his plane was shot down over enemy territory, had healed after many months of pain; but the mental strain of returning from a long stay in hospital to the knowledge that Faith had died in such an awful way, had never left him.

When he was flying on a mission, as an invaluable navigator guiding the crew in their deadly mission of bombing enemy territory, then, just for a while, John could forget his grief. He was no longer the young dreamer who had fallen so madly in love with Faith Goodjohn, but he did love Lucy, too, in his way. And Jonny needed a mother.

John's mother was looking after his eighteen-month-old son and he knew the boy was well cared for and loved, but John's mother was getting older and his father was very ill. Arthur Talbot didn't have long to live and John knew that was a terrible burden for his mother to bear. She shouldn't have the worry of a toddler on top of all she had to carry. Jonny was a part of the wonderful girl he'd loved and lost. She would want John to provide a good home and a loving mother for their son – and John loved the boy. It had taken him a while to come to terms with his grief and find that deep well of love within him for his son, but now he had, and Jonny's future meant everything to him.

John took a deep breath. He would do it. He had decided the previous night when he'd learned he had a twenty-four-hour pass. Lucy had agreed to meet him this morning and they would spend the day together. So, what would be suitable? Should he buy a huge bouquet of flowers – or a small posy?

John walked into the shop. A young woman came through from the back carrying an armful of gorgeous white flowers that had a wonderful perfume.

'Could I buy a dozen of those lily of the valley please?' he asked.

'Oh, these were a special order,' the girl said. She must have seen his disappointment, because she added, 'I could let you have a small posy. I always order some extra just in case there is any damage when they arrive, but these are all perfect.'

'Thank you, that will be fine,' John said. Lucy would be pleased whatever he gave her, though he wished it could be a red rose.

* * *

Lucy looked at herself in the mirror. She was an attractive girl with a sweet smile and wide grey eyes, her hair dark and glossy. It was shorter than she really liked at present, but she'd had it cut in a moment of impulse because when it was long it was heavy on her neck if she put it up in a twist for work, and she'd been in trouble with sister because some strands kept falling down. Her dress was red with tiny white flowers scattered across the flared skirt and it had a squared neckline and little puff sleeves. None of which would show under her dark coat, but the coat was a good one and the best she had. It would come off when they went for lunch.

John had told her he was taking her somewhere nice and she'd got the feeling that this date was something special. Was John going to ask her to marry him? Lucy felt a little flicker of nerves in her tummy, though whether it was excitement or anxiety, she couldn't tell. She had been in love with him for such a long time now. The first occasion they'd met, he'd been in Addenbrooke's Hospital, because of a minor injury to his ankle. She'd felt something even then, but he'd talked about his girlfriend and she'd had to laugh at herself and pretend she just liked him as a friend. Then, a year or so later, John had been brought back to her hospital after serious injuries, and he'd talked to her about his life. She'd sat with him in the long hours of the night, letting him tell her of the nightmares that haunted him. Lucy hadn't been able to stop herself falling more deeply in love with him – but the dreadful thing that had happened to Faith hung like a dark shadow over them: between them.

It hadn't surprised Lucy when John had turned to her as he wrestled with his grief. She'd nursed him and he'd come to trust her – perhaps he even sensed her feelings for him ran deeper than she dared let him see – but, whatever the reason, it was Lucy he sought whenever he had free time. She knew he didn't go home much, even to see the son he loved, because he couldn't bear to be near where Faith had died.

'They all keep looking at me – as if I might do something stupid… Oh, I don't know,' John had told her once when she'd questioned why he didn't visit his little boy more, his anger and frustration pouring out of him. 'I don't want pity, Lucy. I want—'

'You want your beloved Faith back,' Lucy had said, her heart wrung with love for this man and sympathy for his grief. 'I wish it was possible, John, I truly do – but you know it isn't. You have to think yourself lucky you still have your son... think about Jonny and love him. He needs his father.'

For a moment, he'd looked angry, but then he'd flopped back on the grass. It had been late autumn then. They'd been sitting by the River Cam, watching the punts float by, propelled by young serving men on leave, sometimes with a girl, sometimes not.

'I'm sorry. I shouldn't have said—'

'Yes, you should,' John had sat up and smiled at her, his melancholy gone. 'You are the only one who dares. You are good for me, Lucy. Thank you for putting up with me.'

'Well, I have nothing better to do...' Lucy had teased and he'd laughed and his mood had gone, just like that. He'd taken her punting on the river and then they'd had tea and he'd walked her home, kissing her goodnight. It was a proper kiss and for a moment Lucy had let herself cling to him.

Since then, they'd kissed several times on their frequent outings, sometimes with passion, often as friends. Lucy believed that John thought of her as a good friend, that he wasn't sure of his feelings, but that he'd realised that he needed a mother for his son. Lucy loved children and she would willingly be a mother to John's darling little boy. She'd only seen Jonny once, but he was very like his father and her heart ached to think of his mother's tragic death. Yet something pricked at her, because she wanted to be loved for herself and she wasn't certain John truly loved her. He liked her, cared for her, and would be a kind and gentle husband – but was that enough?

Sometimes, Lucy's heart rebelled and something inside her said 'no' – she needed John to love her as she loved him, with all her heart and no shadows. Yet life wasn't like that. In her role as a nurse, Lucy had seen terrible injuries since the war had begun and she knew that lives could change irrevocably through no fault of one's own. John was one of the war wounded, even though his scars were mostly inside. Perhaps the mild affection he offered her was all he had to give.

Was it enough for her? Lucy sighed as she picked up her coat and slipped her lipstick and purse into the pocket. She still didn't know what her answer should be if John did ask her...

'You look beautiful,' John said as they met outside the nurses' accommodation. He presented her with the little posy that smelled lovely as she held it to her nose. 'It should have been a big bunch of lily of the valley, but they only had a small one left.'

'It's lovely,' Lucy said and tucked it through the buttonhole in her coat. John offered his arm and she took it. 'Where are we going today?'

'That hotel by the river,' John said. 'The Garden House, I think they call it. I've never been, but I've been told they do good food – and we can walk in the gardens through to the river afterwards.' He smiled at her. 'It's a bit on the chilly side, but that coat looks warm.'

'You've only got your uniform...'

'I'm never cold,' John said. 'I was brought up on a farm and always outside. And, in peacetime, my job as a plasterer is normally in cold unfinished buildings, so I'm used to it. Not like you nurses, all tucked up in a warm hospital.'

'Oh yes, with all the bugs that are going around this time of the year,' she said, hugging his arm. She sniffed her posy. 'That lily of the valley smells gorgeous.'

'I was lucky to get it; they were a special order.' He smiled at her. 'I'd like to buy you something nice, Lucy – what would you like?'

'Nothing. I'm happy with my posy.' She looked up at him. 'I hope they do good food here. I'm starving.'

They had reached the lovely old hotel. John held the door for her to enter. What he really wanted to buy her was an engagement ring, but he wasn't sure she would say 'yes' when he finally worked up the courage to ask her.

* * *

'So that's it, Lucy.' John held her hand as they sat on a bench by the river later that afternoon. 'I know it isn't the most romantic proposal, and I know it is a lot to ask, but you understand my situation. I have a son and I'm asking you to be his mother as well as my wife. I'm not sure how it fits with your plans for life, Lucy. Do you want to continue nursing after the war?'

'I think so...' Lucy looked at him thoughtfully. It wasn't a very romantic proposal, but John was being honest with her. 'Obviously, I couldn't do full-time – but I might do part-time as a district nurse or a surgery nurse at a general practice. It would mean leaving Jonny with someone for a few hours, but not all day, every day.'

'If we lived nearby, Mum would have him, but if you want to live near your family, we could find someone suitable...' John said vaguely. 'I know I'm being selfish asking you to give up a job you love. I've wrestled with this for a while and I'll understand if you say no, Lucy.'

'Thank you for being honest with me, John,' Lucy said carefully. She'd known all this anyway, but he'd been careful to spell it out for her. 'Tell me, is it just because you want a home and a mother for Jonny...?'

'Oh, God no! I've been a clumsy idiot,' John exclaimed. 'I loved Faith very much and I shall always remember her, but you must know I care for you deeply, Lucy? I wouldn't have asked you if I didn't. We've become good friends and I trust you – think of you with affection. You make me laugh and there's been times when I thought I would never laugh again. You understand me, made me feel life was still worth living – and I love you for it.' He squeezed her hand. 'I do love you, Lucy, please believe me. I think we could have a good life together – have more children, if you'd like that... I want you to be happy.'

So he'd said the word love. Lucy didn't doubt that John loved her – but not quite in the way she loved him. Was it enough? Could she make it enough? Yes, his love would grow stronger with the years, wouldn't it?

'John...' She held his hand between hers, looking up at him. 'Yes, I will marry you. You must know that I love you very much. I just want you to be happy and live with you all my life.'

'And you will,' he promised. 'Once this damned war is over...' He looked into her eyes. 'I wish it was over now so that we could be together all the time.'

'I can't marry you yet, though,' Faith said. 'I have my duty, too. They desperately need nurses for the field hospitals overseas, and I've been asked if I will apply. It will be a tour of just six months and when I get back, I can take my exams to be a ward sister – that means I'll find it easier to get the work I want after we marry.' She looked up at him. 'It means your mother would have to continue caring for Jonny for a few more months. Would she do that?'

'I am sure she will – and if anything should happen to me, they will help you raise Jonny,' he said and leaned forward, kissing her gently on the lips as Lucy protested at the thought of anything untoward happening to him. 'Thank you, Lucy. I promise you won't regret this. I'll make you happy, my love.'

'You do,' Lucy replied and raised her head for his kiss. 'All I want is to be with you, as soon as we can.'

'It's what I want, too – a home of our own, all of us together.' John carried her hand to his lips and kissed it, smiling. 'Shall we go to the pictures now? I'm not sure what's on, but at least it will be a bit warmer in there.'

He stood up, pulling her to her feet. Lucy laughed and took his arm and they set off leisurely towards the town, in harmony with each other.

2

BLACKBERRY FARM, MEPAL, APRIL 1943

Lizzie Gilbert gazed down at the face of her beloved son as he lay in his cot. Arthur was just sixteen months old, two months younger than his cousin, Jonny Talbot. Did he look a little hot or was she worrying for nothing? Young Arthur Thomas Gilbert, as they'd eventually had him christened, had been grizzling most of the night. His beautiful little face was a bit flushed, but Lizzie couldn't see any spots or blemishes, and he'd swallowed some of his milk and a little sweet rice pudding at breakfast.

Young Arthur had been named for the man who had taken Tom Gilbert as his son, even though he wasn't his own, marrying his mother, Pam, despite her illegitimate child and giving them both his gentle love and care. Young Arthur was normally a healthy boy and had grown fast during the first nine months of his life. Needless to say, he was a favourite with his grandparents, Pam and Arthur Talbot, though they also had another grandson. Jonny Talbot's mother, Faith Goodjohn, had died after bringing him into the world from a cruel twist of fate, and care for him was shared between Lizzie and Pam, with a little help from other female members of the Talbot family: Susan and

Angela, the boys' young aunts, and Jeanie, Artie Talbot's wife of a few months. Arthur and Jonny were cousins but, being brought up together, were almost as brothers, equally loved and cherished.

Pam had taken on the care of the little boy without hesitation, because her son was a serving officer in the RAF and couldn't make other arrangements for her grandson. She loved the child, but, unfortunately, her husband's health had taken a turn for the worse towards the end of the previous year and, although Arthur senior was still living and doing what he could on the farm, that didn't amount to much. These days, he spent a lot of time sitting in the kitchen, watching as Pam carried on her usual work, and Lizzie knew the worry about him was taking its toll of Pam. She never said a word of it, other than to often ask if Arthur needed anything, but she still had all her work to do, plus the care of a small child, a daughter of eleven, soon to take the exam that would decide which school she would attend – and another about to take her exams for her chance of a place at teaching college. Susan had been studying hard and everyone thought she would pass her exams with flying colours, but Angela was another matter. Inclined to be lazy when it came to schoolwork, the family feared she would fail her tests and be sent to the secondary modern school in Chatteris. It was a decent school, but her mother had hoped she would follow her sister to Ely High School and go on to college.

Angela loved animals and Lizzie knew that Pam had tried to interest her in becoming a vet, or at least, a veterinary nurse, but she was bored by the idea of years of study and insisted she would be a farmer's wife like her mother. No amount of persuasion made Angela change her mind, but she was very good at looking after little Jonny, so Pam had given up nagging her about her homework. She had far too much to do taking care of an ailing husband, who refused to give in and still went out every night to look at the animals before bed, and all the other tasks that fell to her.

* * *

Young Arthur let out a wail of misery. Lizzie recalled her thoughts and picked him up, feeling to see if his nappy was wet. It was perfectly dry and his little body felt warmer than she liked. It was no good, she would have to take him to their family doctor in Sutton – a village only a mile or so away as the crow flies, but the road that led straight to Sutton had been absorbed into the aerodrome which stretched up the small hill and across several acres of what had once been prime farmland. Now you had to go the long way round, through another village called Witcham, up to the Toll and then back into Sutton – which meant she would be gone for more than an hour, and that was if she was lucky.

The surgery at Sutton was run by just one doctor – Doctor Parker. His small waiting room was usually packed with patients; there were chairs against the wall along three sides of the room and as one patient went into the consulting surgery, another would take his seat and everyone moved up. No one ever tried to jump the queue. You just went in and took the seat at the end of the line and no matter how long it took, the doctor always saw every patient who had the patience to wait for his or her turn. Occasionally, he would be called out urgently to a very sick patient and those waiting just sat on in the expectation of his return. Some glanced at the clock on the wall and fretted because an important task awaited them, but most were happy to sit and chat. Only once had Lizzie known the doctor's wife to come out and tell them to come back that afternoon at three when the next surgery would be held; that had been when the doctor had taken his patient to hospital himself, because there was no ambulance available and by doing so had saved a life. When the villagers spoke of Doctor Parker, it was with reverence, because he was a saint.

Lizzie was fortunate that she had a car she could use herself. It was Tom's. He'd changed his truck for a car to make it better for his wife and son and Lizzie had learned to drive so that she could get to her hairdressing salon in Chatteris without waiting for buses. She had appointments that morning and she would have to ring the girl who worked for her and tell her that she might be late. Either Janice, the girl Lizzie employed to run the salon in her absence, would wash and set the customers' hair for them or they could return later. Little Arthur came first. Normally, she might have left him with Pam, but her mother-in-law had too much to do already. So she made a quick call and then got the car out, putting Arthur's carrycot on the back seat.

As she approached the farm gate, just up the road from her house, Lizzie saw her brother-in-law, Artie, getting his tractor out and lifted a hand as she was about to pass, but he waved her down. Reluctantly, Lizzie stopped.

'I'm taking Arthur to the doctor's,' she told him as he came to her window. 'He has a bit of a fever.'

'Jonny does too,' Artie said. 'Can you wait a minute while Jeanie brings him out? She was going to take him, but Dad needs the car. He has a dentist appointment in Ely... but Mum wants Jeanie to drive him in, because she says he isn't up to driving. Could you take Jonny, too?'

'Yes, of course I can,' Lizzie obliged and, when Jeanie appeared with Jonny in her arms, Artie opened the back door, sliding Arthur's carrycot along the seat and sitting Jonny beside him.

'Are you sure you can manage both?' Jeanie asked, looking anxiously at the two babies. 'Jonny is getting heavier. He has been whimpering most of the night, but Pam isn't sure what is wrong with him – his nappy is clean so it isn't a tummy upset.'

'Little Arthur is the same,' Lizzie replied. 'I didn't know Jonny was unwell – it must be some sort of a fever going round.'

'Susan is at school today,' Jeanie said. 'Most days she studies at home, but her big exam comes up soon and they wanted to go through her work with her and give her some last-minute coaching. Otherwise, she could have come with Jonny.'

'I will manage,' Lizzie said, smiling at her. 'I can't say how long I will be – it might be all morning if the surgery is full.'

Jeanie nodded. 'Yes, I know. I visited last week and I was hours. Artie was annoyed, because he needed me on the land, but I had a problem and it was a good thing I went, because they've cleared it up…'

Lizzie nodded, glanced at the two little boys on the back seat, and then drew away from the farm. Both were grizzling, having been disturbed by the voices and the sound of the tractor in the background. Unable to hush or comfort them, Lizzie drove along the winding road through the next village and turned right into Sutton. She turned right again soon after, up by the ancient and beautiful church to the High Street, where the doctor's surgery was situated. She parked at the top of the incline leading down to the house and surgery, which was set a few yards back from the road.

Lizzie took the folding pushchair from the boot of the car, then reached into the car and lifted Arthur out. She strapped him in and then picked Jonny up. It was going to be difficult manoeuvring the pushchair down the incline to the doctor's surgery with Jonny in her arms. Pausing, she wondered whether to put one baby back in the car when she felt a firm hand on her arm. She glanced round swiftly and saw a face she knew well as he owned and ran the local butchers.

'Oh, Mr Goodman, I didn't see you there—'

'I could see you were struggling, Mrs Gilbert. Please, allow me to carry Jonny for you. He is getting to be a fine lad – and big for his age.'

'Yes, he is,' Lizzie said. 'Time flies, doesn't it? It seems only a few weeks ago – but it is eighteen months since his mother died…'

'Such a tragedy,' he said, and then, seeing the shadows in her face. 'Have you heard from Tom recently?'

'Yes, only last week. He is still training recruits at the moment and a bit fed up with it. You know Tom – he would rather be in the thick of things…'

'Yes, I imagine so.' Mr Goodman smiled. 'I was too old when the war started to be considered for the army – and they seem to think being a butcher is an important job.' He made a wry face. 'However, I am now a sergeant in the Home Guard – or, as everyone calls us, Dad's Army.'

'Oh, well done, you,' Lizzie said. 'I sometimes wonder with all the fighting men stationed overseas – or most of them – who is going to defend us if Hitler invades.'

'I don't think we need to worry too much,' he said as they reached the doctor's surgery. 'I believe Hitler had a chance to invade when the battle of the skies was going on. For some reason, he didn't launch his invasion force – and, believe me, he had one waiting. We can only be thankful he hesitated. I think now he has his hands full fighting on several fronts at once and he hasn't the strength of armies needed to invade us.'

Lizzie nodded. They entered the surgery and discovered only three patients ahead of them. 'Oh, that is good,' she exclaimed. 'I have appointments waiting for me in Chatteris, but boys are feeling poorly and there was no one else to bring them.'

He nodded, then looked thoughtful. 'I know Arthur Talbot isn't too clever these days. I hope you won't think me too forward, Mrs Gilbert – but my wife, Dot, would happily help to look after your little boy – or your nephew – if needed. As you know, it's our misfortune that Dot and I were unable to have a child.'

'I didn't know,' Lizzie said. 'That is upsetting for you both.'

His eyes shadowed with private grief. 'We had hoped for three or more – but it wasn't possible. So Dot would be glad to give a hand any time. She spends far too much time at home alone.'

'That is so kind,' Lizzie said. 'I will speak to Pam and hear what she says, but there are times when I'd be grateful to leave Arthur with someone I could trust.' She smiled at him as the first in line was called in to surgery and they all moved round one seat. 'I often take him with me to the salon, but if we're doing perms or strong colourants, the air isn't too pleasant for him. Pam always offers to have him, but she has so much to do at the moment.'

'That is what I thought...' He nodded. 'Just a suggestion if it suits you, Mrs Gilbert.'

Lizzie thanked him and, after a few moments, moved up as the next patient was called; they were going in at a good rate that morning and with luck she would get to Chatteris for her first client after all...

* * *

'Doctor Parker didn't think it was anything too dreadful,' Lizzie said as she carried the cots into the large warm farm kitchen. 'He says it is just a little chill, but to watch for any red patches or sudden rashes and to take them back if that happens.'

'Thank goodness for that,' Pam said and Lizzie thought she looked tired. 'I don't think it is nappy rash or the croup. I was a bit worried about scarlet fever, because Susan said two girls at her school went down with it, last week, and... well, you never know, though she is fine herself...'

'Oh no, we don't want that,' Lizzie said, horrified, because the illness could be a killer, especially where babies were concerned. 'I haven't seen any redness on their skin – and I changed Jonny in the car after we came from the doctor.'

'Then we can stop worrying for a while,' Pam said and smiled at her. 'Have you got time for a cuppa – or must you leave at once?'

'I need to get on, I'm afraid,' Lizzie said, 'Are you sure you can manage little Arthur as well...?'

'As well as big Arthur and Jonny?' Pam laughed. 'Put it like this, Lizzie. I'd rather have them all and see some of my jobs left undone than lose one of them.'

'Oh, me too,' Lizzie said and sighed. 'I sometimes wonder if I should employ another assistant and give up work for a few years...'

'No, don't do that, love,' Pam said. 'It's only now and then it gets difficult. We'll talk this evening. Come for your supper and we can discuss it then.'

Lizzie agreed and left. She enjoyed her work as a hairdresser and she was good at it. Fashions changed in hairstyles as swiftly as clothes and if she took time out, she wasn't sure she could catch up again. She would prefer to keep working – and maybe Dot Goodman might be the answer. She would talk to her mother-in-law that evening. Pam's opinion meant a lot to her and if she thought it a good idea, Lizzie would call on Mrs Goodman and ask for her help.

Sighing, Lizzie thought that things could be so much easier if her own mother still lived in the village and would be happy to help with the children, but she wasn't. Mrs Jackson only grudgingly acknowledged her daughter and was never loving or affectionate towards her. Lizzie wasn't sure why she bothered to visit March – the town a few miles beyond Chatteris, where her mother had chosen to move. Lizzie was sad that this grandma never seemed pleased to see Arthur or his mother. Instead, she bore a grudge and always succeeded in making Lizzie feel guilty. However, there was no mending it and she pushed the idea from her mind as she drove the few miles to her salon, parked her car and entered the premises just as her customer arrived; it was a permanent wave and colour today and worth the trip, as this lady always ordered the best. Lizzie also had two trims and sets – and then her assistant would finish up for the day. Janice was a real find; she could trust her to open and close the shop, and with the cash in the till. Without her, it would have been impossible to carry on with young Arthur's arrival.

3

'Now, not a word to Pam about my being short of breath in the dentist,' Arthur Talbot gave his daughter-in-law, Jeanie, a straight look. 'I don't want her worrying for nothing. It isn't the first time it has happened and it won't be the last.'

'I know. I've seen you a couple of times, when you were walking the fields – and when you insisted on driving the tractor while I spread the muck down the fen. I haven't told Pam and I won't – but do you need to speak to the doctor again, Dad? He might give you something to help...'

'I doubt it,' he replied with a frown. 'They told me there was nothing to be done, Jeanie love. I've a bit of time yet, but not as much as I'd hoped. I've been doing what they told me and resting – but, if I'm honest, I'm better out on the land than under Pam's feet with nothing to do but drink tea.'

'She'd worry more if you didn't rest a bit, Dad.'

'I know – and it's for her sake I'm trying to take it easy. You young ones will be fine – even Susan and Angela. Angela is a bit young to understand, but I think she knows, though she just looks at me and says nothing. She tries to help her mum more these days and she'll make a good farmer's wife. Like me, she isn't much for the book learning. If she can count her change, read a book and write a letter she'll do – but Pam wants better for her. Can't blame her, but I think Angela knows what she wants even if she is only eleven.'

'Perhaps she will surprise us all and pass her exams,' Jeanie said as she left Ely and they began to pass fields and then the heavily guarded airfield at Witchford. It seemed busy that morning, with planes flying low over the main road on their journey to who knew where. It was a sight and a hazard the locals had become used to. They had another airfield at Mepal at the top of the hill – well, in Sutton really; the two villages were only separated by large fields, most of which were now occupied by the RAF and its planes, though the crews came from all over: Australia, New Zealand, America, Canada, as well as Britain.

'She might, but it won't change her mind. Angela isn't going to college if she can help it...' He laughed softly to himself. 'She will give some young lad a run for his money once she's wed.' Arthur shook his head and his smile dimmed. 'Pity I shan't be here to see it – but I've had my share of the good things.'

'We none of us want to lose you,' Jeanie said softly, and to cover her emotion, 'Do you need anything from the shop in Sutton? I think I'll just pop in and get a couple of things – Artie needs some shaving soap if they have any and I'd love a new pair of stockings. Not that I'll get them, but I could try...'

'Try that new shop further along the High Street,' Arthur suggested. 'He sells all sorts, mostly workingmen's things, but you never know. You should have gone to the shop on the hill in Ely. Miss Lavender always has nice stuff. I buy presents for Pam there – or have in the past...'

'I tried last week. She didn't have any – or so she said. I think she keeps her nylons under the counter.'

'It was silk stockings when I was young.' Arthur chuckled. 'Most girls just draw a black pencil line down their bare legs these days.'

'And it smudges...' Jeanie said, wrinkling her nose. She entered Sutton, turned left at the church lane and then right, deciding to try the new clothes shop as Arthur suggested.

To her surprise and delight, she was able to buy two pairs of nylons in a tan shade and was beaming all over her face when she came out.

Arthur wasn't in the car. Jeanie felt a shock of fear. Where was he? Was he all right? Her heart raced and then she saw him leaning on a wall, talking to an old friend, and smoking his pipe. Pam would frown if she knew, but Jeanie would never tell.

She left the car open for him to get in when he was ready and walked up to the general shop, where she bought the other items she needed. When she came out, Arthur had driven the car and parked outside, saving her the extra walk.

Knowing he wasn't supposed to drive with his heart condition, she waited for him to shift over to the other seat but didn't say a word to chastise him. Arthur Talbot was a grown man; he didn't want folk fussing after him as if he was a baby.

The word 'baby' lingered in Jeanie's mind. She hadn't told anyone the reason for her visit to the doctor's the previous week. She had taken a test into the surgery the next day and was waiting to learn the result. If she was right to suspect herself pregnant, that was going to cause more problems. They already had two young babies in the family, a third would only make everything more difficult – as well as the need to find another new land girl to take Jeanie's place on the farm...

* * *

The medicine the doctor had given Lizzie seemed to have quietened the two babies and they were asleep on the sofa when Jeanie entered the kitchen. Pam looked at her, relief in her eyes as she saw her husband following behind.

'Everything all right then?' Pam asked, pushing the kettle onto the hot plate to finish boiling as she prepared a tray for tea. 'Docky will be another hour yet, Jeanie, if there's anything you need to do before we eat?'

'Is Artie back yet?'

Pam shook her head.

'I'll go up and change into my working things then and check on the cowsheds. I'm not sure if Artie cleaned them. He said he would so that I could take Dad into Ely but—' Whatever she continued to say was lost when they heard the roar of a motorbike outside and looked at each other.

'John?' Pam wondered aloud. 'Or Tom?' Both sons had been known to borrow a motorcycle from friends to get home if they only had short passes. 'John...!' Pam cried as her youngest son walked in wearing his RAF uniform, the trousers clipped with cycle clips to stop them flapping in the wind and a soft flying helmet on his head rather than his smart cap, which would probably have blown off had he worn it. 'Oh, it's lovely to see you...'

'It's a flying visit,' John said with a grin as he took off his helmet, his fair hair tousled, his nose and cheeks red from the breeze. 'Lucy has a few days off work, so I said I'd take her to see her parents. I need to be back by eight this evening. I'm meeting her and we're borrowing a car and driving through the night down to Sussex, a seaside town called Hastings. We've arranged to meet to give them the news...' He paused, looking from Pam to Arthur and then to Jeanie. 'We're engaged...'

'That was quick,' Pam said, a look of anxiety in her eyes. It didn't seem long since Faith had died after giving birth to John's son. Most of the family had now met Lucy, when he'd brought her for a quick visit the previous Christmas, and she seemed a pleasant girl, but more direct than Faith; a little harder, in Pam's opinion. 'Are you sure about this, John?' she asked more hesitantly.

'Faith has gone and Jonny needs a mother,' he said, not sounding like Pam's son at all. She knew the war had changed him but wasn't sure she liked this new John as much as the innocent, loving boy, who had been so eager to join up at the start of the war. 'Lucy says she needs another six months in her job, possibly overseas, and then she can change position – to a practice nurse, if she wants. So we'll probably get married in the autumn, before Christmas anyway. I'll look for a house – or ask Artie to let me know if he hears of anything.'

'Jonny is being well cared for here,' Pam said, her voice a little sharper than she intended, because she felt defensive, though didn't know exactly why she should.

'I know that, Mum,' John said. 'But, don't you see, the longer he stays with you, the harder it will be when we take him away…?'

'But… is this what you truly want? You loved Faith. Lucy is a nice girl and I don't doubt she'd make you a good wife – but…' Pam drew a breath, then, 'Don't marry in haste because of Jonny. You might regret it one day, John.'

John sat down with a sigh, running his long fingers through his cropped fair hair. 'Please, Mum, don't give me a hard time over this. It was difficult enough to convince Lucy. She is the one hesitating, not me. I know I'll be lucky to get her.' He lifted his head and looked at his mother, their eyes meeting. 'I know it isn't long since Faith died and I haven't forgotten her. I never shall. Faith was my first love and had she lived, my last – but she didn't. It wasn't my child that killed her – but her death makes me responsible for him, and I know what I need to do for the future.'

'John is right,' Arthur said in his quiet voice and everyone looked at him. It wasn't often he voiced his opinions, but when he did, Pam usually listened. She was listening now and sat down at the kitchen table, looking at her husband. 'The longer you keep him, Pam, the harder it will be to give him up. I know you'd keep him all his life, but John is his father and it's his decision. If he wants to marry Lucy and she is willing to look after the boy, then we have to let Jonny go.'

Pam was silent, digesting his words. 'I know Jonny belongs to you,' she said at last, looking at John. 'I was just asking if you were sure this was what you truly want. Is it what Lucy wants or have you pushed her into it?'

'I may have persuaded her,' John said. 'That job at Addenbrooke's is killing her. They've been so busy... there are extra units in the grounds now, temporary accommodation, and the nurses are rushed off their feet with wounded men.'

'She is obviously needed where she is,' Pam said, but a frown from Arthur made her pause, before continuing: 'and in the meantime – who looks after Jonny?'

'I am hoping you will continue to for the time being, Mum,' John said. 'I know you have far too much to do, but I can't put him with strangers... or I'd rather not.' He paused, looking anxious and uncertain. 'I was hoping you would congratulate me and tell me to bring Lucy to see you as soon as possible for a celebration...'

'Well, of course we're pleased if you're happy,' Pam said. 'As far as Jonny is concerned... Well, it would be nice if Lucy could visit sometimes and get to know him. Otherwise, she might have trouble when you do take him.'

John nodded. 'That was the other thing. When we've visited Lucy's parents, I hoped we might stay here for a couple of nights. Lucy thinks the same as you. She says it will upset him if he is taken from the person he sees as his mother and given to a stranger. She wants to get to know him gradually but didn't like to come without an invitation.' He pulled a wry face. 'She kept me guessing for a while, Mum – but she loves me. Like you, she was afraid I was still hankering for Faith. I managed to convince her that I do care for her... love her. Not in the same way but... Lucy is easy to be with, Mum. She is caring and a wonderful nurse. She will make a good mother...'

Pam nodded, pushing a cup of tea and a piece of her pound cake in front of him.

John bit into the cake and smiled. 'I always know I'm home when I eat your cake.'

A wail from Jonny had him on his feet. He walked to the sofa where his son was lying next to Tom and Lizzie's son, bending to pick him up. Raising him high above his head, he laughed as Jonny's wail turned to chuckles. He obviously hadn't forgotten his daddy, even though John wasn't often home.

'He's heavy,' John said with a laugh and took him on his knee, offering him a tiny piece of cake, which Jonny chomped on with glee.

'I've got a house lined up for you, John – if you want to be this way,' Arthur said, bringing all eyes back to him once more. 'I knew you'd want a home for the boy. I wasn't certain Lucy was the one – but she's a nice girl. I liked her. I thought you might prefer to be in Chatteris, as a lot of your work is that way. Once the war is over, you'll go back to your job as a plasterer, I expect?'

John nodded.

'Well, there is a good house for sale in Chatteris – and there are several doctors in the area, and a decent bus service between

Chatteris and March for Lucy. It would mean you'd find a baby-minder there rather than bringing Jonny to your mother – but Lucy might prefer Sutton. I've got a house there you could have once I give the tenants notice – about six months should do it. It isn't as big or as modern as the one in Chatteris, so it would be best to let Lucy see them both and decide whether or not either suits her.'

'I'll talk to Lucy,' John promised, 'and thank you, Dad. I didn't say anything before, because I wasn't sure Lucy would ever agree.' He smiled ruefully. 'When we marry, she says she'll take a few weeks off to get to know Jonny, and then find a part-time job.'

'That sounds very sensible.' Pam smiled. 'It's not that I don't like Lucy, John. I want both of you to be happy...'

'I think we shall be,' he said and looked at his father. 'That is enough about me – now tell me about the family news. Has Tom been home lately?'

4

'You could have knocked me down with a feather,' Pam said when sitting alone with Lizzie that evening. John had left just after three, promising to return in a day or two with Lucy. Everyone else had work on the farm, finishing up the milking and bedding the animals down for the night. 'I thought they were just friends...'

'Did you?' Lizzie asked. 'I suspected John was thinking of getting married, if only for his son's sake. I know you love Jonny – but he is your grandson, not your son, Pam. And you do have a lot to do. At the moment, Jonny is content in his playpen most of the time, but soon he'll want to be everywhere and into everything. You will get very tired, Pam – which is why I am thinking of asking Mrs Goodman to look after Young Arthur sometimes when I need to work.'

'Dot Goodman...' Pam looked at her in silence for a moment and then sighed. 'She is a nice lady, Lizzie. I used to know her well years ago. She's a few years younger than me, but went to the same school. I remember when she married. I thought she would have a big family, but she couldn't – or he couldn't; I'm not sure which.'

'I've said hello to her in the street, seen her shopping in Ely on market days, but can't say I know her. Do you think she would be a good babyminder for me – and perhaps Jonny, too, if they decide to live this way...?'

'I suppose that will be Lucy's decision,' Pam said, looking reflective. 'Oh, I knew it must happen one day, Lizzie, but I didn't realise it would hurt so much. You know I'm always willing to have little Arthur, don't you?'

'Of course I do, Mum,' Lizzie said. She looked on Pam as a mother and loved her dearly. 'I just thought sometimes – if you needed a little break or it seemed there was just too much to do...'

'Yes, it does feel that way occasionally,' Pam agreed. 'I would like to get Arthur to the sea this summer, if he is up to it. We haven't had a holiday for years and if—' She broke off, a little sob in her throat. 'I won't think about it, Lizzie. Ask me first if you need to leave Arthur with someone, but otherwise, I expect Dot is as safe as you'll get. I don't know if she has any experience with nappies or feeding young children...'

'Mr Goodman says she has looked after her sister's children in the past when needed – but now they are grown up and in jobs...'

'Well, it sounds as if she would be a help to you, Lizzie.'

Lizzie smiled. 'In that case – and only if you can't manage him, then I will ask her...'

'Yes. If Arthur's condition deteriorates...' Pam's face reflected her sadness. She seldom mentioned his illness to Lizzie, but it was always there in her heart and mind. 'I don't want to lose him —' Pam caught back a sob. Lizzie would have comforted her, but she shook her head as they heard the men's voices outside the door.

'You reckon I went on the high land too soon then?' Artie was saying as he walked in with his father and Jeanie behind them. 'I thought it was dry enough...'

'That's the trouble with the heavy land,' Arthur replied. 'Tom would have left it another couple of days and then you'd have had a better crop.'

'Tom is never here when he is needed...' Artie sounded annoyed. He didn't like being reminded that his elder brother was better at farming the heavy land. 'Oh, hello, Lizzie. How is your son?'

'He is fine,' Lizzie said. 'Doctor Parker gave them both a special medicine and it seems to have done the trick. It wasn't anything serious, but you can't take risks with young children, can you?'

'Wouldn't know. I'm not a baby man,' Artie replied in a disgruntled tone. He missed the sharp look his wife gave him, but Lizzie didn't. It confirmed what she'd been thinking about her sister-in-law. Jeanie hadn't said a word, but there was a look in her eyes, especially when helping with one of the babies. Lizzie was almost certain that Pam had noticed, too, but they hadn't discussed it. Jeanie would tell them her news when and if she was ready.

'I'd best get home,' Lizzie said. 'Susan is doing her revising at mine. I left Arthur sleeping, but he might wake up and she needs peace and quiet to do her homework.'

'Yes. Tell her to come home when she's finished. I'll put her meal into the warmer to keep it nice for her,' Pam said as Lizzie got up to leave.

Lizzie nodded. Susan had made herself some toast and

marmalade at hers, but she would probably eat her mother's dinner later when she was ready.

* * *

Walking home in the dusk, Lizzie thought about her husband. Tom's letters were usually frequent, but she hadn't had one for more than a month. That didn't mean anything was wrong. Tom was often busy while he took a unit of men to different parts of the country, some of them top-secret locations, where they all underwent a course of training of various kinds until they were passed as fit for service. Her husband didn't give her details of the exercises or locations, but he did tell her funny stories about the various recruits and the antics they got up to.

'Put a group of young lads together, take them from their homes and families and give them a rough time – and you've got a recipe for trouble,' he'd told her on his last leave, laughing at an incident at their base. 'You can't teach them all the dirty tricks in the book and expect them not to use them when they get in a drunken squabble down the pub – problem is, the locals get the worst of it and complain, so my lads end up in the cooler for a couple of days, even though they did what I'd taught them to do very well...'

'Dirty tricks, Tom?' Lizzie had lain looking up at him in their bed. 'I thought you always fought fair?'

'Before the war,' Tom had replied. 'War is different, Lizzie – it is evil and the men we're fighting are devils. You can't imagine the atrocities – and I don't want you to; so our men have to learn to defend themselves and to know when to attack first.'

'I know, Tom – just testing. I don't want you to change too much...'

'I shan't change towards you, but war makes you harder.'

It was true. Lizzie had seen that for herself in John. She'd spoken to him briefly; he'd told her of his engagement to the young nurse Lucy. Lizzie couldn't help thinking of Faith, who had died in her house. She'd never forgotten or stopped regretting that she hadn't been there to help Faith. If she hadn't gone to work that day, perhaps her friend – for Faith had become her friend – might still be alive.

For a moment as she went in, Lizzie shivered, remembering, but then she heard laughter and entered her kitchen. Susan's schoolbooks were spread out over the kitchen table, but she was standing, looking into the face of a young flying officer from the Sutton/Mepal aerodrome. They were both smoking – something Pam would frown upon – and there was a small bottle of beer and a larger bottle of lemonade on the table. The airman had a half-full glass of shandy in his hand and Susan's glass was empty.

'Oh, Lizzie...' Susan blushed as she saw her looking at them. 'Jerry just called to see me and we had a glass of shandy...' The expression in her eyes was begging her not to tell Pam.

'Is there any left?' Lizzie asked. 'I could just do with a glass of shandy.'

'Enough for a weak one,' Jerry Mancetti, the young New Zealander pilot, said with a grin. 'Susan thought you wouldn't mind – and I have to get back in half an hour. I didn't have long enough to take her anywhere...'

'Susan knows what she wants,' Lizzie replied and accepted the glass, drinking a mouthful. It was more lemonade than shandy but pleasantly cool. They must have stood the lemonade in cold water for a while. 'Has Arthur woken at all, Susan?'

'No. I looked on him five minutes ago and he was sleeping.'

'I'll just check...'

Lizzie left them alone in the kitchen. Her son was sleeping, just as Susan had said. She smiled and sat on the edge of bed, giving them time to say whatever they needed to say, drinking her lemonade slowly and thinking. Susan had been out with more than one airman recently, to the pictures or for a walk, a drink or, her favourite, dancing. She didn't seem to favour any of them but enjoyed going out. Lizzie hoped it stayed that way for a while, because Pam had her heart set on Susan passing her finals and getting a place in teaching college.

Hearing the back door open and shut, Lizzie returned to the kitchen. Susan had put the used glasses in the sink and was washing them in warm water and soda. She looked round and smiled at Lizzie.

'Thanks for not making a fuss. It was just a chance to talk and have a drink.'

'Did you get your revision done?'

'Some – enough,' Susan smiled. 'To be honest, I keep going over and over the same stuff. I'm ready for my exams. I shan't fail, Lizzie – Mum just worries I might.'

'You know best,' Lizzie said. 'I haven't seen Jerry before. Have you known him long?'

'For a few months – but I was too busy with my studies. I like Jerry a lot, but I don't think it's love.' Susan gave her a puzzled, questioning look. 'How did you know Tom was the only one for you, Lizzie?'

'I didn't at first,' Lizzie admitted. 'I liked him, wanted him to love me, but he never said anything. I flirted around a bit, but none of them kissed the way he can...' Lizzie giggled, Susan catching onto her mirth so they both laughed. Then Lizzie's laughter faded. 'Things went a bit wrong for us and caused a lot of pain on both sides.'

'That's why you went to London?'

'Yes. I had to get away and I thought our chance had gone –

but then Tom came after me and when he kissed me... I knew that was it,' Lizzie said. 'I'd been breaking my heart for him, but I was too stubborn to admit it. I've never looked at another man since.'

'I wish that would happen to me,' Susan said. 'I thought I loved someone and then I discovered I didn't, or he didn't anyway – so now I don't know what to think.' She sighed. 'Besides, I have to go to college and become a teacher before I can think of marriage.'

'It would be easier that way,' Lizzie said without thinking.

'Do you mean I could marry and still do it?'

'I don't know if that would work for you...' Lizzie knew she mustn't put ideas in Susan's head. Pam would never forgive her. 'I think they've relaxed the rules for teachers regarding marriage – but you might have children and that could put a stop to your ambitions for years.'

'That is what Mum says...' Susan grimaced. 'I know she is right – but when a kiss is wonderful...' Her cheeks were pink again. 'It makes me wonder what it is like to – well, you know...'

'The one thing your mum wouldn't like is for you to be pregnant before you were married,' Lizzie said quietly. 'You don't have to be a teacher. You could work with me at the salon or whatever you wanted – but tell your mum if marriage becomes more important, Susan. Don't hurt her that way.'

'Oh, I wouldn't. I dare not...' Susan laughed. 'It's just I can say things to you I can't to Mum. And I do wonder about – well, making love. Does that make me a bad girl?'

'Oh no, not in my book.' Lizzie's eyes sparkled. 'I wanted Tom to make love to me long before he got round to it – but...' She gurgled with laughter. 'I can tell you this, Susan, the man who makes you wait is so worth it...'

'You're wicked, Lizzie Gilbert,' Susan said on a gasp and they both started laughing. 'I'd better get home or Mum will worry.' She gathered up her books into her satchel and then gave Lizzie a hug. 'I'm so glad Tom married you, Lizzie.'

'Me too,' Lizzie said and hugged her back. 'Remember if you're worried, you can always talk to me.'

Lizzie's smile faded as the young girl left. It seemed ages since she'd seen Tom and it would probably be months before he got leave, because he'd told her in his letters that he was very busy just now. She just hoped he was safe and well...

5

It was early May now and the weather had been wet and cool for the beginning of spring, though that morning, the sun had come out from hiding behind heavy clouds, and was doing its best to cheer the atmosphere of shock and gloom overhanging the men who had just suffered a resounding defeat.

'My God, sir,' the young recruit said, laughing ruefully and offering Tom his cigarette packet. 'When they came through those trees shooting at us, I thought it was for real and we would all be killed.'

'Had it been the real thing and not an exercise you would all be dead,' Tom replied, no answering smile in his eyes as he refused the offer of a smoke. 'They took us by surprise – where were our scouts? Why didn't they let us know where the enemy was?'

'Lazy buggers were probably having a fag rather than doing their job,' Private Walters replied, dragging deeply on his cigarette, and watching as the two groups who had been shooting blanks at each other a moment ago now relaxed, talking, sharing food and fags.

'Or dead,' Tom said harshly. 'So what have you learned from this lesson?'

Private Walters looked at him uneasily. 'Double the number of scouts and pick the best men for the job.'

'Your best men have already been sent out and have not reported back – now what do you do?'

'I suppose we should have had more guards around the camp.'

'That might have helped,' Tom said. 'What else? Come on, private. We were camped and had not yet moved off in search of our quarry. They stole a march on us, and attacked at dawn. What more could we have done to avoid a bloody slaughter?'

'I don't know, sir.' The soldier looked uncomfortable. 'I would expect my officer to tell me what to do—'

'You lost your officer in a skirmish yesterday and you have to get the men to safety, but you haven't given up on attacking the supply dump yet – what *do* you do?'

'The senior soldier would take command and make a plan...'

'Yes – so you're it, Private Walters. I'm waiting for your orders, sir. What would you have done differently?'

The young soldier stared at him for a moment in silence, then nodded. 'Instead of camping last night, I would have pressed on, sending regular teams of scouts out – and, if we got close enough to the enemy, make our attack... hope to surprise them.'

'Good!' Tom looked at him with approval. 'That is exactly what ought to have happened. Making camp was predictable and laid us open to an unexpected attack before we were awake.' He grinned. 'Right, Acting Corporal Walters. I'll see about getting you that promotion. Now, go and tell the men to break camp. We're all going on a twenty-mile hike back to base camp.'

'But, sir...' Walters looked at him and then nodded. 'I suppose that's the punishment for losing the skirmish?'

'Yes. You're beginning to think for yourself.' Tom saluted. 'I'll recommend the promotion when we get back – and I believe you are nearly ready for active duty.'

Acting Corporal Walters laughed and walked off, a swagger in his stride.

Tom strolled over to congratulate the sergeant in command of the winning squad. He saluted Tom, knowing that he was merely here as an observer and to report on the men's progress. He had taken no part in the mock battles, though he had followed team B and left his junior to watch team A. Tom had given no advice to team B, but he had a feeling team A had been guided by the team supervisor.

'Well done, sergeant,' he said and saluted. 'You did well today – a dawn attack was a surprise. I wasn't sure you would try it, though it was the obvious thing. Team B made a mistake – they should not have camped when their scouts did not report back. I suspect you have them nicely trussed up?'

Sergeant Hodder smiled smugly. 'They didn't even split up and we heard them talking and laughing. I don't think they took it seriously until we pointed a rifle at their heads and addressed them in German. I think one of them actually thought it was for real then. He tried to shoot me, but one of my men grabbed his rifle. I'm afraid he got a few bruises...'

'That is the object of these exercises,' Tom said. 'Some of them need to be taught the hard way. Play about now at your peril. When it is for real, they will wish they'd listened and learned. So well done – and you have the transport home. Team B will run it...'

'Poor devils,' Sergeant Hodder remarked as Tom walked away.

'He's a right bugger, isn't he?' a soldier standing next to the sergeant said to him. 'I bet he didn't give his team the least help – not like us...' He smirked cockily.

'Keep your mouth shut on that one, Jinks. If Captain Gilbert got wind of it, he'd come down on us like a ton of bricks. He may seem a bugger to you, mate, but there's no one I'd rather have leading me on a dangerous mission...'

'He doesn't though—'

'I told you to shut it – that man is one of the bravest I know. I've been told how he carried a wounded friend home for days and he's been in the thick of it from the start. He'd rather be there now, but they need him to train idiots like you who don't know how lucky they are.' Sergeant Hodder glared and strode off, leaving the private to stare after him and then spit on the ground.

* * *

Private Jinks didn't like to be spoken to that way. He might not have the best mind for tactics, but no one could master him with a knife – and he could sneak up and cut a man's throat before he knew anyone was there. He was only in this bloody lark because he'd been in prison, awaiting trial for a triple murder charge. Someone had come to the prisons and a whole bunch of men like him had been plucked from their cells, taken to an army camp, sworn in, given food, baths and a uniform, and begun to train for the Dirty Squad, as the men had fondly named this bunch of cut-throats and thieves that were now pretending to act like soldiers.

Jinks sometimes wondered what was in it for him, more than the fact that he was alive and not dead at the end of a rope. If he'd been close to a town, he might have scarpered. While he was at home in the dark in the stinking back alleys of cities like London and Glasgow, he was like a lost lamb out here in the wilderness. He wasn't even sure where they were. They'd been taken on a ship for a while, but he'd been sick; he had no idea whether he was still in Britain or some outlandish place he'd never heard of.

Sooner or later, he'd be given leave – and then he would go AWOL, but until then he had to keep his nose clean. He wiped the snot from his nostrils on his uniform as an officer barked an order at him and he went reluctantly to help pack up the camp before being conveyed back to their base. He couldn't wait to put all this behind him, and he had a few scores to settle before he left – with a few of these bleeding officers for a start. Ordering him about like a piece of excrement. Oh, he'd have a bit of fun before he finally disappeared for good...

* * *

Tom was ready for a bath and then a drink in the officers' mess when he reached camp with his band of sorry losers. The hike was always the punishment for losing and it both humiliated and exhausted beaten men. However, once back at the camp, Tom had spoken to them, telling them that they'd fought well, although they'd lost to better tactics.

'Tomorrow we shall discuss what we should have done and we will learn from our mistakes,' he'd told them. 'In the meantime, I have arranged for a round of free drinks for you all at the bar. Don't give up, just decide to do better next time.'

He had heard the faint cheer from exhausted men and smiled. They would have to suffer a lot more before they were ready to join the ever-growing group of men who were winning a secret war. These men in training now would, if they were good enough, join an elite band of soldiers who made unexpected attacks deep into the heart of enemy territory, inflicting damage in lightning raids that were seldom heard of and yet did huge damage, both to the supply dumps and weapon factories they were aimed at, as well as pricking the ego of an enemy who believed themselves superior. Superior numbers they might have, but important infrastructure and secret hideouts had been destroyed, leaving the enemy bewildered by this kind of warfare. Their victories seldom made the newspapers; they were suppressed, because that further confused the enemy. As yet they couldn't decide whether these were random attacks by a few stray soldiers who got lucky or the highly strategic raids they actually were. No one had really heard much about their secret army.

Tom preferred it that way. He never told anyone how often he had been on one of the more daring raids. His presence would never be announced until they were underway, and was never spoken of afterwards. When men returned from these raids – if they returned at all, and inevitably some didn't – they were so firmly bonded they never spoke of what happened, even to wives, lovers, or mothers.

Tom had his drink in the bar. Another officer – a great friend, Shorty – one of the men he'd worked with on his very first raid – was to lead the mission they were planning for the last batch of trainees. Tom had asked for the mission but been refused. He'd been told he would be given leave once these new men were ready – a leave of two months, after which he would return to active duties.

He wasn't yet certain what awaited him in the future, but preferred not to dwell on it. For the moment, he had a job to do with some of the worst and hardest men to break into his ways that he'd ever encountered. Tom knew that at least a third of them were the dregs of criminal society, pulled from their prison cells, given the chance to redeem themselves and serve their country. A few of these men had shown real promise; some were surly but good fighters – and a few, only a sprinkling, would never make it. Tom already had four in mind. He wouldn't trust them an inch, but they would have one last chance – after that, the regular army could have them or they could go back to the condemned cell. It was their choice. One last test... he smiled coldly, a smile his wife and family would never see. He'd planned it for the following weekend – but in the meantime, he had a seventy-two-hour pass and he intended to spend it with Lizzie, even though he would need to travel through the night both ways to make it there and back in time.

* * *

'Tom!' Lizzie gave a shout of joy as he walked into the kitchen and discovered her feeding their son at breakfast time. She stood up with Arthur in her arms and went to him, to be enveloped and embraced in a gentle hug that held them both. 'It is so good to see you. I wasn't sure when to expect you.'

'Lizzie love...' Tom kissed her. 'I swear you look lovelier every time I see you.'

'I look a fright,' Lizzie said but laughed. Her hair was sleep-tousled and her face free of all make-up, her nose probably shiny. 'But I'm so happy you're home, if only for a few hours.'

'Yes, not long enough, but I'm lucky to get it. Most of the men I'm working with haven't had a pass for months and they probably won't get one either.'

Lizzie gave a little shiver. She didn't ask questions these days;

she didn't want to know. 'I've rescheduled my work for today and tomorrow,' she said. 'There was nothing Janice couldn't do, so I will be at home with you for as long as you have.'

'I'll take the night train back tomorrow,' Tom said and smiled. 'How have you and the boy been?'

'He had a bit of a fever last week, but he's over it now,' Lizzie told him. 'I had a couple of sleepless nights then, but I'm all right.'

'You look a little tired, but beautiful...' Tom touched her cheek lightly. 'It looks as if it will be a nice day, Lizzie. We shan't stay indoors. Let's take a picnic somewhere – by a river – and just relax for a few hours.'

'That is a lovely idea, Tom,' Lizzie said. 'We'll make it a real holiday.' She smiled at him. 'If you pop up and see your mum, I'll pack us some food.'

'We might be able to buy something out – fish and chips or—'

Lizzie laughed. 'I've got plenty of stuff ready cooked, and your mum made us some of her pasties. We can get fish and chips on the way home and bring them for everyone, if you want...?'

'That sounds good,' Tom said. He kissed her again, then his son. 'I'll go and have a word with Mum and Dad – shan't be long, Lizzie.'

She nodded and continued to feed young Arthur his breakfast as he protested noisily at the delay. These days of being all together and doing little except talk, kiss and make love were the very best. They didn't come often but were to be treasured. Lizzie knew she was lucky. A lot of the men were fighting overseas and home leave was almost impossible. Tom was safe training his men in the wilds of wherever... at least for the moment. It wouldn't last forever. She lived with the knowledge that he might be required to fight again, but tried not to dwell on it. For now, she had a day of pleasure to look forward to and she would make the most of it.

6

Lizzie and Tom took his car, Arthur on Lizzie's lap, and drove into Ely, the nearby cathedral city. It had a small town and a marketplace, which was busy every Thursday with the stalls that attracted folk from the surrounding villages. If you drove down Forehill and then kept going, you could reach the river and the quayside, but if you went down Backhill, you could get to the boatyard easily. Here, there were small motorboats and punts for hire in normal times; these days, it was just the punts and rowing boats, because of fuel shortages.

However, the owner of the boatyard came to greet them with a smile on his face. 'Tom Gilbert!' he cried and offered his hand to shake Tom's. 'It's wonderful to see you – and yes, I do have a motorboat for you. I don't get enough fuel to run the business, but I manage a little for my friends.'

'Thanks, Frank,' Tom said. 'I thought it would be good to find a peaceful spot down the river. How far can I go?'

'I filled the tank, so it is up to you,' his friend said and smiled at Lizzie, who was holding her son in her arms. 'That's a fine lad you've got there, Mrs Gilbert.'

'Thank you. His name is Arthur Thomas,' Lizzie said, holding him up to be introduced. 'And he weighs a ton!'

They all laughed.

Tom took their picnic baskets, his son's pushchair and a rug on board the boat and set them down and then came back for his son. 'Can you manage to climb on board, Lizzie?' he asked as she hesitated.

'I think so...' She was wearing a flared cotton dress and knitted cardigan, plimsoles on her feet. Frank offered his hand and she took it but stepped quite firmly down onto the deck of the small boat. 'It's ages since I went on one of these...'

'Enjoy.' Frank said and stepped back, lifting a hand before going into his house.

'This is a surprise,' Lizzie remarked as she went to stand by Tom at the steering wheel. 'I thought we would just walk to wherever—'

'I thought we'd find somewhere quieter downriver, further than we could if we walked.' He looked at her. 'Is it all right for you?'

'It's lovely on the water.' Lizzie held her face to the sun. It was early May now, but the weather had settled for once and was really warm, almost summer.

Tom had placed the pushchair next to his feet. It was secure and half in shade so that the baby wouldn't get too hot. Lizzie stood next to him as he steered the boat into midriver and set off downstream. It was a slow, meandering way to travel, peaceful, disturbed only by the swish of the water displaced to either side and the cry of a bird.

Tom had taken off his jacket and was in his shirtsleeves. They passed the quayside and the gaggle of geese and ducks that frequented the shallow water there, went on towards the Cresswells, bypassing the houses and pub, and leaving the town behind.

'It's like being in another world,' Lizzie said as she stood with his arm about her waist. 'Almost as if we are the only people left in the world...'

'That's what I always felt when I took a boat out alone,' Tom said, smiling down at her. He steered easily with one hand, tall, relaxed, confident. 'Just you and me and Arthur... and them.' He nodded ahead of the boat.

Lizzie laughed as they saw a family of swans approaching. There were three cygnets, gliding in the parents' wake, their serenity only slightly ruffled by the wash of the boat.

Tom continued to take the boat further downriver from Ely until they reached a spot that looked inviting. Willows overhung the water's edge, shading and enclosing a flat grassy patch of bank. Tom steered the boat alongside the bank just up from the idyllic scene and moored it to a post put there for the purpose; they were not the first to use this spot, but, on a weekday, and during a time of war, it would not see many visitors.

He jumped onto the bank and Lizzie handed him their picnic things and, when he'd spread the rug, Arthur's pushchair. He placed the baby on the rug in the shade of the willows and then came back to give her a hand, but she made a little leap and he caught her in his arms.

'All right?' he asked as she looked up at him, laughter in her eyes.

'Fine...'

He leaned in and kissed her. 'This is what it is all about – what I think of when I'm not with you.'

Lizzie smiled, her heart catching. He looked so wistful that she saw for a moment what lay behind the confident mask he showed to the world. 'Is it awful, Tom? I know when you're fighting it is... but the rest of it?'

'I'm fortunate,' he said, the shadows banished. 'The men I'm training will be lucky to see home again. It's just that I miss you like hell – and everything I loved at home. I hate it that we've had hardly any married life together. How many times have I taken you on holiday, or even to the pictures?'

'It's true we haven't had a lot of time together,' Lizzie replied, 'but I treasure the hours we have all the more for it.'

'I'm so lucky...' Tom settled himself on the rug as Lizzie suspended a bottle of lemonade and two bottles of pale ale in a fishing net to let them cool in the water beneath the hanging willows. 'One of the officers I work with – his wife left him. She couldn't stick all the lonely nights and days. Found herself a bloke who won't be called up – in a protected job.' Tom laughed harshly. '*He* won't be protected from Reg when he gets leave...'

'She couldn't have loved him much,' Lizzie said, coming back to sit beside him. 'I get fed up sometimes being on my own, but I have my work and Arthur – and your parents. Pam is like a mother, sister and friend all wrapped up in one. I go to the pictures with Susan now and then, and Jeanie and I get on well.' She laughed. 'I think she is having a baby, but I'm not sure she's told anyone yet, so don't say anything.'

'I shan't,' Tom promised. 'Have you heard from John lately?'

'He is getting married... to that girl Lucy. You haven't met her, but she came to the farm last year... she has been twice now.'

'Married?' Tom's eyebrows rose. 'Best thing for John – but Mum won't like it – she thinks Jonny is hers.'

'She loves him. We all do – he and Arthur are like brothers.' Lizzie smiled. 'What else can I tell you? Oh, I'm doing well at the salon, but it's a rush in the mornings sometimes...'

'I know you keep busy,' Tom said, reaching out to caress her bare arm now that she'd taken off her cardigan. 'But you deserve some fun, Lizzie. When I get the chance, I'm going to take you somewhere nice for a holiday. Where would you like to go?'

'I haven't thought about it,' Lizzie replied, lying back to feel the sun on her face, her discarded woolly under her head. 'Cornwall or Devon perhaps... or Scotland. I've been told it is very pretty up there – lots of wide-open spaces...'

'Sounds good,' Tom said. 'But I want you to have fun – go on a shopping spree, go dancing, to a nice show on the pier...'

'No good going shopping without lots of coupons,' Lizzie smiled as he bent over her. 'I think we'll have to wait for that one until the war is over, Tom. It surely can't go on forever?'

'It won't,' he said grimly. 'One side or the other will gain an advantage. It just has to be us...'

Lizzie saw the expression in his eyes, and reached up to kiss him, putting her hands to his face. 'Let's forget about it all,' she whispered. 'We've got all this peace, all this gorgeous seclusion, let's make the most of it...'

Tom laughed and took her at her word.

* * *

'Well, we've been lucky,' Pam said later that evening when they took fish and chips home for the whole family. 'A visit from John last month – and now Tom. Was it lovely by the river, Lizzie?'

'Gorgeous,' Lizzie told her. 'So peaceful on the boat and Tom found us a lovely place to moor.' She laughed. 'We all had a little paddle, and Arthur enjoyed kicking his legs in the water.'

'You never took him in the water!'

'We did and he loved it,' Lizzie said. 'I dried him with a spare nappy and he soon warmed up in the sun. We were so lucky to get such a warm day, Pam.'

'We'll pay for it,' Pam replied. 'You'll see...' They both laughed and then looked at Tom and his father talking together. 'I'm glad he got home... both of them.'

Lizzie nodded. She didn't need to say anything. They both knew that Arthur was gradually getting weaker.

* * *

'Dad isn't so good,' Tom said as they were getting ready for bed. Arthur was already sound asleep, bathed and read to by his adoring daddy. 'He thinks he hasn't got much longer. He asked me to take care of Mum – and John's boy, if anything should happen to him. He knows you'll look after young Arthur, and you and Jeanie will see Mum is all right – but, after the war, when things settle, he wants to make sure Mum isn't alone.'

'She won't ever be that,' Lizzie told him. 'I'm not sure if she will want to carry on at the farm forever, but she'll always be near us – and with us, if she chooses.'

'Thanks, Lizzie. That's what I promised Dad. He thinks Artie will probably want to take over the farm and house, but some of the land is mine and we'll share the yard.'

'Is that what you want, Tom? When it is all over? I know it was good while your father and mother were at the farm...'

'The land I shall own is enough for now,' Tom replied, looking thoughtful. 'When things are settled and I have the time, I'll consider a second income – a small business of some kind. Not sure what at the moment, but George wants to set up a motorcycle repair business... that's my friend, not my cousin George. I might think of something similar.'

Lizzie smiled. Pam's nephew, George, had come to stay with them at the farm after his mother died. At first, he'd been a bit awkward, uncertain of his place and always in mischief. He'd settled down after the first few months and was beginning to be helpful on the farm, when he was summoned to go and visit his other aunt, Pam's elder sister. He'd been gone for ages but they were expecting him back any day now.

'George wants to work on the land with you when he leaves school, Tom,' Lizzie said. 'He didn't want to visit his aunt, but she insisted that it may be his last chance, so Pam said he should go. He has missed school because I don't think any lessons were prepared for him. Susan says she will coach him to catch up when he gets back.'

'If I know George, he couldn't care less if he is behind with his schoolwork, but he won't like it that he missed two new calves being born.' Tom smiled at her as she yawned. 'Tired, my love? Come to bed and we can talk until we fall asleep.'

Lizzie climbed in and snuggled up beside him. 'Pam told me that Frances isn't coming back to Blackberry Farm. She likes it where her husband's family are and so she has applied for land work there.' Frances, their land girl, had married a guard from the Mepal airfield and gone off with him for a holiday to his parents' home, but she'd extended her leave three times and had now decided she wasn't returning, as her husband had been transferred to another base.

'Dad has applied for another land girl,' Tom said, his arm around her as he pulled her close. 'He says Frances wasn't the most reliable, so he isn't too bothered. I just wish there was no war and we could go on as before...' He sighed and tightened his hold on her.

'It's a pity you and Artie couldn't just share Blackberry Farm, instead of dividing the land, and go on as always.'

'I don't think that would work, Lizzie. We get on better these days than we used to, but then I'm not around much. When I'm back full-time and Dad is not here – I think there might be arguments. It is probably best the way Dad has split it up. After all, I'm not his son. I am very lucky he is leaving me the high land—'

'Don't say that! Arthur loves you as much as Artie. I sometimes think more...'

'And that, my darling, is the problem,' Tom told her with a kiss on her nose. 'He has always favoured me and Artie resents it. That is fair enough, because I'm not Arthur's blood, though he treats me as if I am. Artie doesn't often show his resentment, but it is there. We both know it and I think Dad is aware of it. So he gave Artie the land in Sutton, the fenland, and me this land here in Mepal. The yard we share and the house is Mum's – until she decides what to do with it, but, of course, she would never tell Artie and Jeanie to leave. They were going to move, but then they didn't... I think Artie decided he would take over when Dad goes.'

'But the house is your mum's to do with as she wants.'

'Yes – but I can't see her turning them out,' Tom said. 'So unless she wants a smaller place – or if Artie does decide to move to Sutton when the land is divided, I suspect they will go on as they are for a while, anyway.'

'Maybe that's for the best, at least until you can come home, Tom.'

'Yes. As long as Mum is happy with the situation, I don't give a damn,' Tom said. 'I can work for whatever we need.' He chuckled softly. 'Besides, I have a wife with her own business. I could be a kept man...'

Lizzie laughed and kissed him. 'I'll put you in reception. My trade will double overnight.'

7

John and his girlfriend, Lucy, arrived at the farm the following afternoon. It was their second visit in a month, because John was keen for Lucy to get to know his son. Tom was on the verge of leaving to catch his train in Ely, so their meeting was brief.

'I wish I'd known you were here,' John said, shaking his elder brother's hand. 'I'd have come yesterday. I spent the day in Cambridge, because Lucy only had a few hours off in the morning, but I could have come for a quick visit later. It is so good to see you, Tom, and we so seldom get the chance to talk.'

'Let the women talk for a bit and come outside,' Tom invited. They went out into the yard together, John offering his brother a cigarette as they stood looking out at the flat fields around them. At the top of the hill above the farm, a plane was taking off from the aerodrome. 'How are you finding it, John?'

'OK,' John replied. 'A bit bloody awful, if you want the truth. I've lost a lot of friends lately—'

'I know the feeling,' Tom said; he hesitated, then, 'Are you sure about Lucy – will she look after your son if you don't make it?'

'We've discussed it and she says she will love him for my sake even if I should be killed...' John ran his fingers through his fine blond hair; it needed a cut and was beginning to wave. 'I know Mum thinks I'm mad to marry so soon after Faith – but she can't have the responsibility of a young lad forever, Tom. She may think she is strong, but we thought Dad was...'

'Yes, I know why you're worried. You love your son – just as I love Arthur. If anything happened to me, I'd hope you'd keep an eye on things for me, even though I know Lizzie would cope.'

'Well, of course I would if I could,' John said. 'Artie would too, I expect – but Arthur is Lizzie's son. I wasn't sure I had the right to ask Lucy – because if I didn't come back one day, it would be hard expecting her to bring up Faith's child. But she is the one for me now, Tom. I know it.'

'Good, we all just want you to be happy. I will keep an eye on your boy, if you want,' Tom said. 'Lizzie agrees. If you have any doubts, make me and Lizzie joint guardians with Lucy... should the worst happen.'

'And if you don't come back?' John asked bluntly.

'If Lucy couldn't look after Jonny for any reason, Lizzie would bring him up with Arthur; they are almost as brothers now. Just a thought for you, John.' Tom threw his cigarette down and ground it out with his heel. 'Dad isn't good, is he?'

'No. I hoped the doctors were wrong, but you can see he is fading... I can't help even if I had time. I was lucky to get a forty-eight-hour pass.' John frowned. 'I wouldn't know where to start on the land... and Artie buggered the top field again this year, so Dad says. Went on it too soon and its gone down hard as a rock.'

Tom laughed. 'So that's why he's been giving me funny looks. Well, he'll see a difference in his crop, but you can't tell him. I have tried, John, but he's got all the work. He's the one Mum and Dad rely on for now. I can't and won't say anything to upset him.'

'Artie never takes notice of me,' John said and then laughed. 'Best get back in or Lucy will think I've done a runner.'

'And I have to get off too or they will think I've gone AWOL.' Tom laughed. 'You do your best to survive, John. I think I'm going to need your support when all this is over.'

John raised his brows, then nodded. They had always got on and both had suffered from Artie's moods in the past. Although John and Tom would defend their brother from others, they had learned to tread carefully around him.

Together, they went back into the kitchen: Tom to say his last farewells, and John to take Lucy upstairs so that she could help him bathe his son and put him to bed.

* * *

Pam looked at Lizzie when they'd all left later that evening. 'Well, what do you think?' she asked. 'Lucy is pretty, though nothing like Faith – and she seems to care about John. She says she wants to look after Jonny, and she plans on visiting when she has time, so...' Pam sighed. 'Oh, Lizzie. I do wish Faith had survived. I have nothing against Lucy, but I'm not sure she's right for John...'

'You mustn't think that way,' Lizzie said. 'Honestly, Pam. She seems a genuine girl. I am quite certain she loves John – and she will grow to love his son. If she seemed nervous around him, it was probably because she knew we were watching her. She needs time alone with him, time to bond, as you have.' Lizzie smiled. 'The trouble is, he thinks of you as his mum, Pam. I imagine he will take a while to adjust when they finally take him away.'

Pam got up to put the kettle on. She was restless and upset but knew she was probably being unfair to Lucy, just because

Jonny had started screaming when Pam handed him over to her. She'd seen an expression of... Was it annoyance or disappointment? Pam wasn't certain. Jonny had stopped screaming as soon as his father took him.

'It's the same for me,' she confessed. 'I've had him since he was born and it's like he's a part of me. I know I have to let go, Lizzie, but it's like having the heart torn out of me. I don't know how I'll bear it if—' She broke off and turned away, biting her lip. What Pam couldn't bear to say was *when* she lost Arthur. If she lost John's son, too, it would tear her apart – yet she had no right to keep him. When John had a wife and they were ready, the boy must live with them; it was only right, but it was just too hard.

'I know, Mum. It isn't fair on you, or Jonny. You've formed a bond. When he had no one, you stepped in. If you hadn't, I'm not sure what would've happened to him. I would've taken him, but it might have been too much with my own baby to nurse. John is lucky his son had you – and perhaps he isn't giving a lot of thought to your feelings, Mum. I expect he is just thinking of Jonny's future.'

'I imagine he thinks it will get too much for me and perhaps in a few years it might be. I'm in my fifties, Lizzie, and when Jonny is eighteen, I'll be more than seventy – if I am still here. That wouldn't be fair to any of us, I suppose. John is doing the right thing, but I just hope he isn't doing it for the wrong reasons. I would have preferred that he courted Lucy for a couple of years to make sure – and I could gradually tell little John that I am his granny not his mum.'

'It would have been sensible,' Lizzie replied. 'But – if he loves her and wants to make sure of her. I mean, we none of us know these days...' Lizzie faltered, looking sad. She could see that Pam was upset at the thought of losing little Jonny but knew she would come around in her own time, because she was always fair. 'We have to give Lucy a chance.'

'Yes. I know, Lizzie. We are lucky to still have them both – so many fine young men have been lost already...'

Lizzie nodded. 'They won't take him for a few months, because Lucy is probably going overseas to nurse and when she gets back, she has to sit those exams to become a nursing sister. She has time to get to know John's son – and us. I thought she was a bit shy. After all, she is stepping into Faith's shoes and that can't be easy for her, Mum. Lucy knows that John loved Faith and would have married her if she hadn't died. Perhaps she loves Jonny but still feels herself an outsider. We must try to make her feel welcome. Once we all know each other better, things will improve.'

'Yes, I expect so.' Pam smiled at her daughter-in-law. 'I'm so glad I've got you, Lizzie. To be honest, I'm not sure I could carry on without your support...'

'Oh, Mum,' Lizzie said, her eyes shining with tears. 'I love you and I'll always be here for you – just as you are for me.' They moved together and hugged, then laughed as they heard Artie and Jeanie's voices. 'You've got the hungry workers to feed now – and I'm going to get back and put Arthur to bed, after I bathe him. He'll be a bit grizzly because of missing his daddy...'

They nodded and smiled to each other, Lizzie stopping to speak to Jeanie and Artie on her way. They seemed a bit quiet, but Jeanie asked if Tom had gone and then went in when Lizzie confirmed it. Artie stopped, hesitantly.

'I was hoping to have a word with Tom...' He frowned. 'There's never time these days. I suppose you don't know when he'll be back?'

'He says he thinks he is due a longer leave soon, but I don't know when.'

'Let's hope it's harvest time then.' Artie ran his fingers through his short dark hair. 'How the bloody hell I'm going to manage unless we get another land girl...' He met Lizzie's startled look. 'Jeanie hasn't told you then? She's pregnant...'

'That's wonderful, Artie,' Lizzie said and saw his look of exasperation. 'Isn't it?'

'It would be if I didn't need Jeanie on the land,' Artie said with a sigh. 'Frances isn't coming back and God only knows if we'll get another girl in her place.' He shook his head. 'This farm normally provides work for three men, Lizzie – and there's only me to do it. It was hard enough with Jeanie helping, but when she has to pack up...'

'Surely they will send a replacement for Frances?' Lizzie frowned. 'You can't manage alone, Artie. You need to hire someone – if not an able-bodied man, someone who can drive a tractor, and a couple of land girls.'

'What I need is Tom here,' Artie grumbled. 'He's the only one who knows how to farm the heavy land. Even Dad isn't sure. If it were up to me, I'd sell it and buy more fenland.'

'Tom loves this land,' Lizzie said, looking across the fields to her home. 'You need to talk to him about it, Artie. He'll help you.'

Artie nodded and went in, but she could see he was in a mood and nothing she'd said had helped him.

8

CAMBRIDGE, ENGLAND, MAY 1943

'Your mum doesn't like me,' Lucy sad when John took her out for a meal the next day. 'She doesn't think I'm good enough for you.'

'Oh, Lucy, don't be daft,' John said and reached for her hand, giving it a squeeze. 'Mum is very attached to Jonny. She has had him right from the first and... well, she thinks of him as her own. I wish I'd been in a position to make my own arrangements for him then, but I wasn't – and I still wouldn't be if you were unwilling to have him when we marry.'

'He's yours, John,' Lucy said and when she looked at him, the love she felt for him was in her eyes. 'Of course I'll have him and love him. I would now, but I ought to get my promotion to sister and then I'll always have a living if I need to return to nursing.'

'You won't, unless you want to,' John promised. 'Once this damned war is over, I have a partnership to go back to – and it will be a good life.' He smiled at her. 'Dad promised me a house of my own and it doesn't have to be near Mum – we can live in Chatteris or one of the other villages.' He saw the doubts in her eyes. 'If I should be killed, Tom and Lizzie will help you get settled and look after you both. You liked Lizzie, didn't you?'

'Yes,' Lucy admitted with a smile. 'Please, don't even think of what happens if... I want us to be together, John. You have to keep your head down. Don't be a hero. Just come back to me.'

'You bet,' he said, his fingers entwining with hers. 'I'd give it up in a heartbeat for you. I do what I do because I have to, Lucy – we all do. None of us wants to be a hero, but we don't have much choice at the moment.'

'I'm not sure about that,' Lucy said and laughed. 'A lot of my patients can't wait to get back out there once we've patched them up.'

'Braver than me then,' John quipped. 'I thought it was a great lark when I joined, Lucy – and I love the flying part. I even enjoy what I do, navigating and getting us home by the safest route – but the rest of it...' He shook his head. 'I don't enjoy the fact that when I say we've reached our destination, the bomber lets our load go – and only God knows what harm it does. We see sudden fire and we know we've hit the target and we make for home – we don't see the shattered homes and the injured people, the hospitals and the factories, the lives we've ruined.'

'You can't think about that, John,' Lucy told him. 'It's not your decision to bomb a certain city or an area – other people make those decisions. You simply follow orders.'

'I know. We all tell ourselves that, but it gets harder to justify – at least it does for me. I just wish someone would kill Hitler and call a halt to this carnage on both sides.' It had been reported that an attempt on Hitler's life had been made and failed earlier in the conflict and John believed that, had it succeeded, it would have brought the war to a finish.

'I've seen the devastation indiscriminate bombing can cause to the people caught up in air raids,' Lucy said. 'The burn cases are the worst – and they did that to our people. They've tried to destroy us, John, so I think they only have themselves to blame if we retaliate. I am proud of you for what you do – so don't let yourself feel guilt, my love.'

'I know what you say is true...' He smiled at her. 'Where did all this come from? We don't want to waste our time talking about the war. After this evening, I shan't see you for a while. We've got a lot of special training on...' He hesitated, then, 'I might be moved elsewhere.'

'We both might,' Lucy replied. 'Write to me if you can. When you ring the nurses' accommodation, I'm not always there – and I may be seconded to another hospital for a while...' She hesitated, then, 'It is possible that they might need me to go overseas, John. They've been round again, urging us to come forward – and it is only for six months. The nurses at the Front have to be changed regularly, because it is too much of a strain; some can't even last their six months, though others stay on. I've said I will go if I'm needed. If it happens, I'll write and let you know.'

John looked at her. 'And you told me not to be a hero...'

'Oh, I'll be as safe as houses,' Lucy said and laughed. 'Most of the nurses say it is fine, just harrowing – but, as you said, it has to be done. Besides, I'm not happy with my work – my ward sister has it in for me.'

'I know...' John hesitated as though he wanted to say something important, then, 'You are important to me, Lucy. I love you very much. I want you to be my wife.'

'I know that,' Lucy said and smiled. 'I wouldn't have said yes if I didn't know you love me. You deserve to be happy, John – we all do...'

* * *

John was thoughtful as he went to catch the last train back to his base that evening, his leave over. He'd noticed the slight strain between his mother and Lucy and been sorry for it, particularly as it wasn't like Pam to hold back. John's mother always took people to her heart and made them welcome. She'd taken her sister's boy George in, even though her family had treated her badly when she'd needed their help as a young woman. Why couldn't Pam take to Lucy?

It was because she didn't want to give Jonny up. He faced the thought that he'd repressed, realising that he hadn't taken his mother's feelings into account when he'd made his plans for the future. There was never any question in John's mind that he would one day take his son into his care; he owed it to Faith and to Jonny. He just hadn't realised that it would upset his mother so much – and at a time when she had enough grief to cope with.

It was a problem and John wasn't sure what to do about it. As an RAF officer and flying almost round-the-clock missions, he'd had no option but to leave his and Faith's child with his family, since Faith's mother wanted nothing to do with the boy. It had seemed the natural thing to do – but he hadn't reckoned with emotions.

If he could be there, talk to his mother, make sure that Lucy got time alone with Jonny... but there was a war on. Despite what he'd told Lucy, John knew he would be flying more dangerous missions in the weeks to come. So far, he'd been lucky. John had seen so many of his friends go down in flames and it was happening all the time. In truth, he couldn't commit to his own child until the war was over. Perhaps he should have waited until the war was finished to think about marriage... but would that be too late? If Jonny had bonded so much to his grandmother that it couldn't be broken...

It was an uncomfortable thought. Faith would expect that her son would be brought up by his father. Pam was a loving woman and no one knew that better than John, but she was too old to be the mother of such a young child; he needed a young woman, like Lucy, to give him the kind of childhood John wanted for him.

He felt like a traitor to the mother he'd always adored. It was wrong to inflict pain on her and he knew it would be devastating when he took Jonny away – whomever he married. John didn't think it was Lucy his mother disliked; there was nothing to dislike in her. She was a good nurse and a kind, loving girl. No, it was the idea that Lucy was taking Jonny away that was upsetting her.

He sighed as he saw his train about to leave the station. He ran after it, taking a flying leap on board and slamming the door as the whole thing jerked and shuddered before starting to pick up speed. Finding a seat in the corner of an empty carriage, John sat down and closed his eyes.

He didn't know what was right and what was wrong at the moment. Yet something inside told him that he had to fight for his son. Faith would expect it. John thought she would approve of Lucy – they were both nurses and both passionate about their work, and life.

Oh, God! Why did Faith have to die like that? John felt the constant ache in his heart. He was never going to forget her. She was so beautiful and she'd entwined herself in his heart from the first time he saw her. He loved Lucy. Yes, he really did, but not in the same way. John had been young and innocent, eager for life, when he fell in love with Faith. The man who had asked Lucy to marry him was not the same person. His youth and innocence had fled and sometimes he felt old... and helpless.

Was his mother right after all? Was it too soon? Should he have waited longer before speaking to Lucy? John wished he knew – but Lucy was the only other girl he'd ever met who had touched his heart. Surely, he was doing the right thing? If there was no war, he was sure they could be happy together, all of them.

Drifting into sleep as the train chugged through the night, John's features relaxed at last. Some problems were just too difficult. He'd prepared the ground, now all he could do was let life take its course.

* * *

Alone in her tiny room, Lucy sat on the edge of her bed and cried. She cried every time John departed after his all-too-short leaves. It hurt so much to know that she might not see him again; he risked so much night after night and she knew there was no training course. John told her things like that to make it easier for her, but it never did, because she knew. Lucy picked up on all John's feelings – his fear, his grief, and his love for his son. She knew every mood, because she loved him. No other man had ever come close to touching her heart in the way John did, which was why she'd said yes, even though she knew he would never forget his first love.

Why hadn't John's mother liked her? Lucy didn't understand. She'd sensed right at the start that Pam didn't want her there and it had been worse on their second visit – though Pam had tried to hide her reluctance to give the baby to Lucy. Then he'd started crying and wouldn't stop until John took him.

Was Lucy an idiot to plan a future with a man who had a child by his first love? She had agreed, because she loved John and when he'd asked her to marry him, she'd known it was what she wanted. Marriage to a lovely man, lots of children, and a happy home with dogs and friends. It was all there in her head, pictures of their home; a nice garden to grow flowers and food, all the details of how she would make it comfortable – a place of warmth and love that would take away the sadness from his eyes. John had lovely blue eyes, unlike his brothers who were both dark.

Lucy liked children. John's son was beautiful. She was sure she could learn to love him, given the chance – but would John's mother hate her for it? She knew John had always been close to his mother, by the way he spoke of her, and she didn't want to spoil that relationship for them. All Lucy needed was to be accepted and welcomed.

John was set on going back to his part of the country after the war. He had a business and a home all set up – but was village life what Lucy wanted? She'd become used to living in Cambridge and enjoyed the shops and the cinemas – the busy streets. It might be all right, if she made friends – but... there were so many ifs.

Getting up, Lucy went to wash her face in cold water in her basin. She was a practical girl and she knew there was no use in torturing herself just because Mrs Talbot hadn't liked her. It would have made her feel so much better if she'd been welcomed properly, but, perhaps, she was asking for too much, too soon – and perhaps Faith's shadow would always be there. Lucy had the feeling that she'd been measured and found wanting.

Oh, well, tomorrow was another day, and she had a decision to make. Did she want to be posted abroad to nurse wounded men? If she agreed, it would mean that she would not see John for six months.

Perhaps that would be a good thing? It would give them both time and breathing space and perhaps she owed it to herself to be more sure that marriage to John was right for her.

9

Tom mentally reviewed the men he'd been training, ticking off in his head those that had already passed the extreme tests he'd set them, men he knew would give their all for the mission; men who would fight as a team and knew how to bond together and win. Not many had fallen by the wayside this time. Unfortunately, Stanley, Blackwall and perhaps Jinks would need to be sent back to their units – of course that meant prison and perhaps the noose for Jinks, unless he was sent to the Front as a fighting man. Tom crossed them off in his mind; they'd failed 40 per cent of their tests for fitness and mental alertness and that was the worst thing to fail. A man penetrating into the heart of enemy territory needed his mind on the job 100 per cent.

Tom frowned as he went over the last four men to qualify. Private Hanley was eager and willing, but not as fit as he ought to be for a young man. He was thoughtful and a good team player, which meant Tom would like to include him, especially as he was good at fixing anything without the benefit of a workshop. That was very handy at times when on a mission, because equipment had a habit of breaking down when you were miles from home. So maybe yes for Hanley – but he'd been hanging around with the other three and Tom suspected they were up to something he wouldn't like.

Jinks was undoubtedly the ringleader, a bad influence on the others. He was tough and a bully, not bad traits in men who needed to be able to kill without the blink of an eyelid – but you saved your aggression for the enemy, not your comrades. Tom had seen a scuffle between Walters and Jinks and he'd had to step in and give them both a night in the cooler. They both knew it wasn't permitted to fight among themselves. He'd noticed dark looks between the two on more than one occasion and guessed who was to blame. Not that Walters was completely innocent either. He'd been in prison awaiting trial for grievous bodily harm and was no stranger to violence, but he'd responded well to training and his promotion to Corporal Walters had now been confirmed on Tom's recommendation, which might or might not be the cause of the friction between the two.

Hard men, the lot of them, but Tom would have trusted them with his life – which was the real requirement for the work they did. All of them but Jinks, Blackwall, and Stanley. He'd seen them in a huddle and wondered what Jinks was planning. He would be the one to instigate whatever he was up to, but the other two were followers – and that was one reason they'd failed their tests and would be going back to a fighting unit. They needed initiative, that in itself wasn't a bad thing. Jinks had initiative in spades, but he also held a grudge.

Tom frowned as he reached his decision. The three of them were out; he couldn't risk them. It was a pity because Jinks had the skills needed for the job – but he was a viper and couldn't be trusted.

The men were all going on one last ten-mile run. After that, he would be giving most of them the good news. Tom would join them for the last part of the exercise drill. He couldn't run the whole way these days because of his old war wound; it didn't stop him doing most things, but now and then it played up and was giving him hell right now. So he would follow on the motorbike, go back and forth, and watch for cheating – because none of them were beyond getting a lift part of the way, if they thought they could get away with it. Tom grinned. That was called initiative, and although he gave them a tongue blasting if he caught them out, he approved. When you were in hostile territory and had only your wits to rely on, you did whatever you had to, to get in there, do the job and then get out.

Satisfied he'd made the best decision he could, Tom called the men to order and told them where they were destined to run that day and what he expected of them.

'It's results day,' he told them and someone made a jeering sound and a couple of others laughed. 'Do your best and some of you might just make it if I scrape the barrel...'

'Yeah, we all know who...' a sneering voice muttered.

Tom ignored the taunt. He knew who had spoken. Tom didn't insist on brass buttons being polished, but he wanted 100 per cent loyalty from his men. He had made the right decision.

* * *

'Bloody Gilbert,' Jinks muttered as his cronies set off at a jog, keeping pace with him, while others, more enthusiastic, hared off, determined to get back to base in the first group. 'I'd like to wipe the smile off his face.'

'He ain't as bad as some of them,' Stanley said. 'But he does make us run for bloody ever... or thinks he does.' He grinned at his companions. 'Good thing you hid them bikes, Jinks. We can cycle most of the way and then hide them again.'

'I'd just as soon run it,' Blackwall said. 'No point in cheating, it won't help when we get out there.'

'I've no intention of going wherever they think they're sending us,' Jinks said. 'If you two play your cards right and give me a hand, we'll get our own back on Gilbert and a couple of other bloody officers and then scarper.'

'What yer talking about?' Blackwall asked, staring at him. His eyes narrowed in suspicion. 'If you mean what I think, I want nothing to do with it. That's desertion and they'd bloody shoot us on sight.' He gave Stanley a shove. 'Don't get involved—'

'Mind yer own business and clear off,' Stanley muttered.

'Suit yourself.' Blackwall set off at a run, leaving the other two to retrieve the stolen bicycles and pedal after him. He saw them coming and took a dive into a ditch to avoid being mown down, but they didn't bother to come for him.

After they'd gone out of sight, he got to his feet and started to run. He was behind the rest and would probably be last in, which meant he might not get selected, but he'd rather that than get involved in dirty business.

Hearing the sound of a motorbike, Blackwall glanced over his shoulder and saw it was Captain Gilbert. He kept running, but the noise of the engine was cut and then his officer was beside him.

'Why are you last, Blackwall?' he asked.

'Slow and daft, sir,' Blackwall replied with a grin. He hesitated, then, 'I don't know much, sir, but I reckon you should watch your back tonight...'

'Jinks and Stanley?' Captain Gilbert said and Blackwall nodded. 'Right. Hop on the back, Blackwall, and hang on tight.'

Blackwall looked at him and then grinned and climbed on, holding onto his officer's uniform. He was shocked and then exhilarated as the bike was turned and they headed across country at what felt like high speed, skidding through fields and over a shaky wooden bridge until they came to a small wood. Here the bike was brought to an abrupt stop, almost unseating him.

'Right, get off, Blackwall and head through the woods and you'll find yourself in the front group of runners; there's a path that takes you back onto the planned route. It's easy enough to see if you look. Find it and get there with the others and you might still get your chance.'

'Thank you, sir.' Blackwall laughed as the bike shot off back the way it had come. He set off as fast as he could.

Within twenty minutes, he found the path that the other runners were following and saw a small group just ahead. He put on a burst of speed and caught up with them, feeling pleased. Maybe it was cheating – or perhaps just initiative. He hadn't planned to cheat, so maybe that's what you did, just took the chance that presented itself. He would remember that in future.

* * *

Tom saw the two men on the bikes ahead of him. He put on speed, passed them and cut across their paths, causing them both to ride off the track and fall off in the long grass at the side. Switching off the engine, he parked the motorcycle and stood waiting for them to pick themselves up.

'Bloody hell!' Jinks spluttered, incandescent with rage. 'You might have killed us – crazy bugger!'

'I'm the enemy, Jinks,' Tom replied. 'I've stopped you escaping – what are you going to do about it?'

'I'll bloody kill you…' Jinks came at him in a fury. 'I was going to do it tonight when you'd had a drink but now will do…'

Tom wasn't surprised when Jinks went for a weapon; it was forbidden to carry them unless on a mission, but it was expected of a man like Jinks. Tom's hand was out in a flash and he caught the arm meant to strike him, seeing the flash of metal as Jinks' knife stabbed with his left hand. Tom hadn't anticipated the left-hand hit, but Jinks was good with either hand. His free arm drove forward, but Tom jerked his captured hand back brutally, making him scream in pain as the wrist broke. Yet even in pain, he struck Tom in the side, his knife going through the uniform and scraping flesh. Tom winced and brought his boot up, kicking him in the crotch and hearing another cry of anguish.

'Help me, you bugger,' Jinks screamed at Stanley as he staggered back and was sent crashing to his knees. Tom pulled the knife from the body armour under his uniform that had prevented it going deep and held it as he turned to face the second man; the point was just tipped with red.

Stanley held up his hands in surrender. 'Not me,' he said, jerking his head at Jinks. 'He's a flaming madman. Don't want any part of this—'

'OK, on your way then, Stanley,' Tom said.

'What about you, sir? He wants to kill yer and another two of the officers. He was telling me what he wanted me to do – but I ain't crackers.'

'Oh, I don't think Jinks is going to give me any trouble now,' Tom said and smiled. 'No, I'm not wounded, thanks for asking, Jinks. Your knife hardly went through my combat vest.' Seeing the fury in the other man's eyes, Tom nodded. 'Yes, I've been wearing them for a while now, just in case you tried anything.' He bent down and jerked Jinks' arm back, making him scream with pain as he handcuffed him at the back. 'In future, learn to go for the eyes or the throat if you want to survive. Sorry for the lesson, Jinks, but be glad I wasn't the enemy. You would be dead now.'

Jinks mouthed a stream of profanities at Tom, which made him grin.

'Get running then,' he said and went to pick up his motorcycle, watching as Jinks struggled to his feet, hampered by his hands being cuffed behind his back and the pain of a broken wrist. 'No, I won't help you. You can complete the course and I'll escort you. Make a break for it and I'll catch you. If I have to knock your head off to make you see sense, I will. I doubt if you've completed one course honestly, well, this time you're going to.'

Jinks staggered forward, cursing and bellowing, but it didn't help him one bit. As he ran, awkward and in pain, stumbling to his knees more than once but forced to get up again, he learned for the first time that he wasn't as clever as he'd thought.

'I'll sodding kill you,' he hissed as he stumbled on.

'Not where you're going,' Tom said. 'You had the chance, Jinks. You could have fought for your country and won your freedom – now you're headed right back where you came from.' Since he'd had a death sentence hanging over him, Jinks would not have long to dwell on the chance he'd wasted.

'Bastard,' Jinks muttered between his teeth. 'I hope you rot in hell!'

* * *

'Yes, I did make this man run all the way with a broken wrist,' Tom said as he addressed the weary soldiers, who had been lounging around after their long run, but all straightened up at his approach. They had been drinking water and relaxing until they saw him and then a buzz of astonishment broke out.

Most of them hadn't believed Stanley when he'd told them Captain Gilbert had broken Jinks' wrist when he attacked him. 'I did to this traitor what the enemy will do to you – except that they will probably just shoot you. Unless of course they decide to torture you for information. It is a lesson to you all not to get caught.' Tom handed Jinks over to the corporal who had accompanied him. 'This one goes in the cooler but he can see the doctor now. Tomorrow he will be returned to the prison who sent him to us. He failed...' Tom's cold eyes swept the other men who were holding their breaths and waiting. 'Jinks was the only one to fail this time. Two others were close to being sent back, but they proved one thing to me today – they have loyalty, and that is still the most important thing. For everything you've learned, and now that you've all seen how bloody and brutal things can be for real – it's your loyalty to each other that makes the difference in the end.'

A ragged cheer came from the thirty or so men gathered, most of whom still looked stunned, as if they hadn't expected to pass. Or perhaps it was the reality of what their training officer had done to Jinks that made them look at him differently. They'd always thought him a bit of a bastard, firm but fair, but now they knew Tom Gilbert could be the Devil himself when he chose.

'So, this evening you all get free drinks all night, on me,' Tom said and suddenly the ice had gone and he was the officer they'd thought they knew, his eyes smiling. 'Tomorrow, you will all be briefed. You'll hear that from Major Carlton in the morning. So drink, have a good time, but don't be late for your briefing – which is at eleven-thirty sharp.'

'Three cheers for Captain Gilbert!' a voice rang out from among the relieved and now happy men. 'Wish you were coming with us, sir.'

'So do I, Corporal Walters,' Tom said with a grin. 'You were bloody hard work, but you're one of the best squads I've trained.'

All the men laughed then and split up, drifting off towards the showers and the canteens. Tom walked away, a smile on his face. He just had some paperwork to finish up and then, he hoped, he would be getting that long leave he'd been promised.

'Captain Gilbert, sir!' Tom looked round at the soldier who had approached. 'Major Carlton would like to speak to you in his office... now, sir.'

Tom repressed a sigh and nodded. He'd wanted to have a look at the slight wound Jinks had inflicted, which was sore but not too painful, and he needed a drink.

'Thank you, sergeant,' Tom said and turned towards the officers' area. He approached the line of huts used for briefings and official meetings and knocked at one of the smaller ones.

'Enter...' Major Carlton was behind his desk. He looked up as Tom came in and then stood, offering his hand. 'Ah, Gilbert. Finished for the day? I hear you had a bit of excitement?'

'Nothing I couldn't handle, sir.'

'In your own distinctive style as always...' Major Carlton smiled. 'We take a risk with these hard men, Gilbert, but they are needed – and, shall we say, expendable...'

Tom caught back a flash of anger. 'I wouldn't use that word, sir. They are good men – hard, yes, but prepared to fight for their country – even if most of them are criminals. I believe they deserve their chance.'

'And you've given it to them. If they've survived your training, Captain Gilbert, they are ready for anything. You are not our only instructor, but you are our best. It is for that reason that I am reluctant to ask, but are you prepared to go on this mission with these men?'

'Yes, sir.' Tom spoke without hesitation. 'I've been asking for another chance.'

'I fought to keep you here,' Major Carlton admitted. 'However, the officer who was to have led group B has been taken violently ill and will be in hospital for the foreseeable future. Your name came up in discussions. I told them you were badly injured on your earlier mission and might find it hard to keep up under certain circumstances, but no one else has the right amount of experience. I promise you; you will get that long leave when you return.'

'Thank you, sir!' Tom saluted sharply.

'No need for formality, Tom. I'm sorry – but we've lost some good men recently—' He faltered, then, 'I'm afraid your friend didn't make it back this time... none of them did. Seems they were expected, walked into a trap. We don't know how the enemy got the information, but we're looking for a leak this side of the Channel.'

'Shorty didn't make it?' Tom flinched. Shorty's death was like a blow to his guts and he felt as if he were winded. 'Has his wife been told?'

'Yes, of course. I'm sorry to give you this news on top of the other.'

'That's the job you get for holding rank, sir,' Tom said, though he wasn't really sure what he was saying. The knowledge that one of his best friends had been killed hurt more than this man could possibly understand; he didn't train his men; he just gave orders. Tom and Shorty had trained together, fought together and made it back alive – but this time they had not been together, and Shorty had died.

'Well, go and take some time for yourself,' Major Carlton said. 'You've earned it.'

Tom saluted automatically and walked away. His eyes felt

sore, as if they wanted to cry but couldn't. He thought of Lizzie, his beautiful wife, and Arthur, his wonderful son, and prayed that he would hold them in his arms again. Yet despite his regrets that his promised leave was postponed, there was a raging anger inside him, and he knew that a part of him was ready. He didn't yet know for sure where they were going, but if it gave him a chance at revenge for Shorty's death, he would take it gladly...

10

'Are you certain about this?' Matron asked, giving Lucy a hard, piercing stare that would have made her shudder had she done anything deserving a reprimand. 'You are one of our very best nurses and I'm not happy to lose you...'

Lucy's resolve almost faltered, but she kept her face expressionless as she said, 'I understand they are desperate for good nurses in the field hospitals – and I received the leaflet asking for volunteers... the lady was most insistent that we are needed.'

'Yes, yes, I realise that,' Matron snapped. 'I suppose you think it's brave and patriotic to volunteer? Have you thought of the dangers, nurse? You are so close to taking your exams to become a ward sister – and we need our nurses as much as they do over there.'

'I know...' Lucy hesitated, then. 'My brother, Nick, was injured overseas and he told me how much he and the other men appreciated the nurses who looked after them when they were first wounded. I really do think I am needed there...' She wavered under Matron's stare, but to her relief the older woman nodded and smiled.

'Good for you, Nurse Ross. You stood your ground. I just wanted to make sure you understood what you face. Several volunteers have been so shocked and upset, they've begged to be sent back almost as soon as they get there. While the conditions are not as bad as they were for us in the Great War, they are still pretty basic for our nurses. I dare say you've read all the information, so you know what you're in for.'

'Yes, I do. Thank you, Matron. Will you recommend me?'

'Yes, I must,' Matron replied. 'We've been asked to recruit more nurses willing to serve overseas. I believe you girls are very brave and I wish you luck. I will let you know when your orders come through.'

'Thank you,' Lucy said again and, when Matron nodded, she took her leave, feeling a bit shaken now that she'd finally done it.

Lucy was thoughtful as she walked back to the wards. Her decision had been made after John had rung her to tell her that he was definitely being posted elsewhere – he thought abroad. It had been on her mind ever since her brother had been invalided home and told her of his experiences.

'I would have died if one of the nurses hadn't got me through it, Lucy,' Nick had told her. 'She was an angel – sat with me all one night, talking to me when I just wanted to die, because the pain was so bad. I couldn't have done it without her.'

'I'm glad she was there,' Lucy had told him, giving him a fierce hug. 'I don't want you to die, Nick.'

He'd grinned and hugged her back. When the woman came to Addenbrooke's, distributing her leaflets, Lucy had felt called to volunteer. Lucy had been unhappy in her present job for a while. Now, with John being sent abroad, it seemed the right decision. Her posting would be for six months and then she would be sent home. If John managed to get home, they could marry, so it would make no difference to their plans.

Lucy felt her doubts return. She'd been happy to promise she would care for Jonny, but after a few visits to the farm, Lucy had begun to wonder if she'd been too hasty. She felt that Pam Talbot resented her and it had made her realise that she would not want to visit the farm without John by her side. It was so unfair, because her parents had welcomed John with open arms, even though they had pressed her to take her exams before the wedding.

Back on the ward, Lucy reported to Sister Morris. She nodded and looked annoyed, then told Lucy to get on with her work. 'You ridiculous girl! What difference do you imagine you will make out there?' She shook her head. 'Doctor's rounds will be starting soon and this ward looks a mess, Nurse Ross. Get it cleaned up before you start imagining yourself as Florence Nightingale!'

Lucy nodded, repressing the resentment that Sister Morris often made her feel with her sharp remarks. It was this nurse, a woman in her forties, and a dedicated practitioner, who had made her think she might be happier as a practice nurse. It was true that the senior nurses needed to keep good discipline on the wards, but it was surely not necessary to take their grudges out on the younger nurses, and Lucy knew she wasn't the only one to suffer. She'd seen at least two probationer nurses in tears after being reprimanded by Sister Morris' spiteful tongue.

Lucy soon forgot Sister Morris's harsh words as she began tidying beds and making the patients comfortable. Her present ward was filled with elderly ladies and new mothers, who had been moved from the maternity ward after giving birth. Most of them were smiling and cheerful, even one old lady named Edith, who was unlikely ever to see her home again. She looked up as Lucy approached her bed and smiled.

'Has the ogress been on at you again?' she whispered. 'Miserable old so-and-so, isn't she?'

Lucy couldn't help laughing, though it caused sister to look across at her sharply. 'How are you feeling today, Edith? Is the pain in your chest any better?'

'Yes. That nice young Doctor Norton was here earlier, and he prescribed a new medicine for me; it has worked a treat.'

Lucy smiled, because Doctor Norton was in his fifties, but to Edith they were all young, because she was ninety and very proud of it, just a few days off her ninety-first birthday. She was very anxious to get there and beat the sickness that was gradually robbing her of life.

'Don't you go flirting with him, you wicked woman,' Lucy teased as she smoothed sheets and plumped pillows. 'He has got a wife and two children. We don't want him running off with you.'

Edith gave a cackle of laughter and then choked. Lucy held out a glass of water for her to sip. 'You'll be the death of me, girl!' Edith chortled. 'Run off with me – that's a good one. Mind you, there was the time when he might have, and with my good will…'

Lucy laughed and gently lay her back on the pillows, before passing on to the next bed. Edith liked a laugh with the nurses, even though Sister Morris didn't approve. She'd told Lucy that the patients needed to be quiet and not to chat with them, but it wasn't in Lucy's nature to pass by without a little joke when she knew it was what Edith looked for.

'She's a right one, isn't she?' the next patient remarked. A woman in her early forties, Mary had just given birth to her sixth child, all of them lusty boys – except that Mark, the last one, wasn't quite as strong as they'd thought when he was born. Mary should have been thinking of going home any day now, but Mark was having difficulty with his breathing and they'd had to put him in a little oxygen tent. Mary couldn't understand it and told everyone that her five boys were all as healthy as could be.

'Edith has had a hard life,' Lucy told her. 'She lost her first husband in 1914 and brought up four children alone. Then she remarried when she was in her sixties and her children grown up. She and her husband were going to retire to the seaside in a little cottage, but then he died of a lung fever... or that's what the doctors told her. She has no one now, because her son lives in Australia and two of her daughters died in an air raid. She doesn't know where the other daughter lives because they quarrelled years ago when Edith got married for the second time.'

'That's rotten,' Mary said. 'Makes you realise how lucky you are. My old man is on the railways in a safe job and I've got five boys at home. My sister, Kirsten, is looking after them until I get home – and she wants to know when that will be, because she says she has a home to go to...'

'Well, ask her if she can be patient for a bit longer,' Lucy advised. 'Doctor needs a bit more time to discover why Mark is ailing – but if you have to go, he will need to stay here.'

Mary sighed. 'My old man says to stop here with the baby and don't listen to Kirsten. She doesn't have kids to worry about and her husband is fighting overseas.'

'Well, she's better off looking after your boys then,' Lucy said and smiled. 'Is there anything more you need, Mary?'

'I'm all right, nurse. Just like a bit of a moan now and then.'

Lucy nodded and moved off to the next bed. She was just finishing her line of beds when the two doctors and their entourage arrived. Sister made an urgent gesture to her to finish quickly and Lucy did so, not quite tucking the last corner straight in her hurry.

She collected a trolley of used bits and pieces and took it out to the sluice room to scour and cleanse everything, before going back onto the ward. The doctors were about halfway down the line when she saw one of them beckon to her.

'Nurse... Ross?'

'Yes, Doctor Boyce?'

'This patient was telling me you are the best nurse on the ward.' Lucy started to smile at Edith but saw Sister Morris glare at her. 'She says you always make her smile.'

'I try, sir...' Lucy faltered under the eagle eye of her superior.

'Well, keep it up. Edith says she is feeling better and I'm sure that is down to you rather than our medicines.'

'Thank you, Edith,' Lucy replied and she did smile now. 'But I think the medicine has picked you up.'

'Well, something has,' the doctor said, looking pleased. 'Keep it up, Edith, and we shall get you to your hundredth birthday, let alone your ninety-first...'

He grinned at her and moved on. Edith winked at her behind Sister Morris' back as she followed the doctors. Lucy smiled but knew she would catch it later, when the doctors had gone.

* * *

'John...' Lucy was breathless when she got to the phone in the nurses' accommodation that evening, having run all the way down the stairs. 'I wasn't expecting you to ring me this evening – is something wrong?'

'Yes and no,' John replied. 'I'm fine – but I've just been told I'm being posted tomorrow. It means I shan't be able to come and see you before I go.'

'Oh, John, I'd hoped you would get another leave first.'

'I know, so did I,' John replied. 'I'm sorry, Lucy, but there is nothing I can do. They need some of us in a new location – I can't tell you where or why, but it is a new phase of the strategy and I've been picked together with about a dozen others.'

'I've applied to go overseas and been accepted – but it is only for six months, so it won't affect our plans to marry – if you get leave.'

'You won't be able to visit Jonny...'

'I know and I'm really sorry, but I need to do this... Besides, I don't like visiting without you, John. I am sure your mum resents me.'

'No, it isn't that,' he said. 'She is just reluctant to give Jonny up – and perhaps it is better this way. We'll visit together once we're married and then take him. She'll accept it then.'

'Yes, perhaps—' Lucy gave a little sob. 'I love you so much, John. Please take care and come back to me.'

'I promise. I love you, too, Lucy. As soon as we both get leave at the same time, we'll get married,' John said.

'Yes, we will,' Lucy agreed. She heard the pips as his money began to run out in the phone box. 'Take care, my love.'

'I love you, Lucy. Please don't forget that when we're apart...' John sounded a bit desperate as he replaced the receiver.

Lucy heard the click at the other end and hung up. She walked back up the stairs to her own room and sat on the edge of the bed. Tears stung her eyes. Were they destined to be together as man and wife – or would the war tear them apart forever?

11

Pam heard Jeanie being sick in the toilet. She'd been struggling with sickness for a couple of weeks now and that must be the reason for Artie's worried looks. He had been overwhelmed with the work since his father was unable to help and they'd lost Frances. They had applied for a new land girl, but as yet no one had been sent.

'I've got the kettle on,' Pam told Jeanie when she came into the kitchen looking pale and drained. 'Sit down, love. I'll make you some lemon barley later and you will find that helps a bit first thing – at least I did with mine.'

'Oh, Mum,' Jeanie said with a little wail. 'I never thought having a baby would be like this... I feel sick all morning, every morning.'

'Some women are worse than others,' Pam said with sympathy. 'It should get better in a few weeks, love.' She stared as Jeanie headed for the door. 'Where are you going? You can't work like this...'

'I haven't cleaned the milking shed,' Jeanie replied. 'I can't leave that for Artie on top of all the rest. It's too much for one man, Pam.'

'George is doing it,' Pam replied. Her nephew was back home and keen to help once more. 'He had a day off school for something or other – and he was keen to help, so Artie told him to muck out the sheds and scour the milk pans.'

'In that case, I will sit down,' Jeanie said and sank down into one of the wooden rocking chairs with a big cushion at her back. 'George is really helpful. It is a pity he isn't a bit older. He could leave school and work full-time on the farm.'

'I've no doubt he will as soon as he is fourteen,' Pam said. 'I've told him I want him to stay at school until he is sixteen, but he says there is no point because he wants to be a farmer and he would rather work than study. I feel it is taking advantage of him, but Arthur says leave him be and let him decide for himself.' Pam sighed. 'I suppose I should be thankful he isn't old enough for them to take him in the army.'

'George is one of the few lads I've spoken to recently who isn't interested in joining up,' Jeanie said. 'He is fascinated when the airmen come for tea and tell us about their exploits, but he says he would still rather be on the farm.'

'I know he was disappointed he'd missed Tom's visit, because he wants him to teach him how to farm the high land,' Pam said with a smile. 'He heard Arthur complaining that Artie doesn't know what he's doing with it and said he would learn so that he could help.'

'He's nine going on twenty-nine,' Jeanie laughed. 'I'll give him half-a-crown to spend for doing my job.'

'He'll be thrilled with that – his other aunt never gave him even sixpence to spend when he was with her. He says he won't go there again... won't tell me why, but I think she nags him.'

'She didn't want to look after him when his mum died. I don't know why she insisted on having him for a holiday.'

'George says he would rather be here looking after the animals,' Pam said. 'Arthur says he's got the makings of a farmer... I wish—' She broke off and sighed. 'No, I shan't say it. No good in wishing for the moon.'

She bent to take some baking from the oven just as the kitchen door opened and Arthur entered, followed by George. A strong scent of cows followed the boy as he went to the sink and washed his hands and arms up to his elbows, his shirtsleeves rolled right up.

'I've made some rock cakes,' Pam said, setting them on a rack to cool. 'And the tea is just brewed...' She glanced at Arthur, who had sat down in his chair by the fire. He had his pipe in his hand, but, even as he popped it in his mouth, she knew it was empty; Arthur was no longer allowed to smoke, even if he could get his favourite tobacco, which was almost impossible these days. 'Cup of tea, love?' she asked, noticing how tired he looked. His illness was gaining on him fast and her heart caught with pain. 'Where is Artie? Is he coming?'

'No. He took a load of muck down the fen to spread,' Arthur said. 'Has the post come, love?'

'Yes. There are two for you by the mantel clock, love. I think one might be from John.'

'You didn't open it?'

Pam shook her head.

'You should...' He picked them both up and handed her John's letter, opening his own official one and scanning it. 'At last!' He smiled as everyone looked at him. 'We are getting two new land girls – Betty Smith and Olive Rainer. I think they both come from London or big towns, not country girls. That should make life a bit easier for Artie – they've both had training but no experience on a farm yet, so he will be able to show them our way of doing things.'

'Thank goodness— Oh!' Pam's relief turned sharply to worry as she read John's letter. 'John is being posted to a new job so says we shouldn't expect to see him for some time – and Lucy is being posted abroad, too, so she won't be able to visit... They will get married next spring now if they can...'

'That is a nuisance for them,' Arthur said with a frown. 'It leaves you with Jonny on your hands for longer than you thought, Pam.'

'I don't mind that bit,' Pam replied. 'I wish John hadn't been sent off somewhere – he doesn't say where, but you can bet it is overseas...'

'Well, our fly boys won the Battle of Britain in the air,' Arthur remarked. 'I suppose they need them elsewhere... might be anywhere, Mediterranean probably or the Far East. There is no good us guessing.' He shook his head. 'I wonder if Lucy applied so she could be near him...'

'That isn't likely, is it?' Jeanie said and laughed as George reached for a hot rock bun. 'Watch your fingers, George.'

'It's delicious,' George said and then blew and waved his hand in front of his mouth as the cake burned his tongue. He went to the sink and got himself a cup of water. Then came back and proceeded to eat the still-hot cake.

'I'm glad we'll have two new girls,' Pam said. 'We will give them Tom's old room – we'll have to bring the camp beds down from the attics.'

'I should leave one bed in the attic room,' Jeanie suggested. 'Just until you see if they get on well enough to share.'

'Yes. You didn't like sharing with Nancy much, did you?'

'She gave me the creeps,' Jeanie admitted. 'A lot of girls like their own rooms, but you need to keep John's free – in case he or Lucy do visit...'

'Yes,' Pam agreed and passed John's letter to his father with a sigh. 'I just wish this war would be over and our boys could come home for good.'

Arthur looked at his wife anxiously. 'The new girls will be a big help for Artie, but they will make a lot more work for you, Pam. You have enough to do looking after John's son...'

'I will be able to help Pam more once I stop working on the land,' Jeanie said. She hesitated, then, 'We've decided not to move into our house when it is finally ready, Dad. Artie says he'll let it and I can have the money for myself – and we'll stay here, make it easier for Mum.'

Pam looked at her. 'Oh, Jeanie, that is so thoughtful – but are you sure you don't want to move into your lovely new home? It has all been done up for you and it will never look the same if it is let out...'

'Artie says if we want to move in the future, he'll have it done again, but he thinks we should stay here and I'm happy to stay.' She looked at Pam. 'If you want me, Mum?'

'You know I do, love.' Pam smiled at her fondly. Jeanie had become like another daughter to her since her marriage to Artie. 'But I can manage if you'd prefer your own home. Susan will help while she is here and Angela did the washing-up for me last night, bless her. I had to do a bit of it again, but don't tell her...'

'Susan will be at college later this year,' Jeanie reminded her. 'Angela will learn, but she is a bit young to do ironing and things like that.'

'Yes, she is, though it is what she wants to do. She is like George, wants to leave school as soon as she can.'

'I could leave now?' George said hopefully, but Pam smiled and shook her head.

'No, you have to go to school, love. We're grateful for your help about the place, George, but you must have your school years – just as Angela must.'

'Why did you get a day off at your school and Angela didn't at hers?' Jeanie asked curiously.

'We didn't have enough teachers, because Miss Smith left to get married and Mrs Peters was sick – so they closed the school until Monday. They should both be back by then.'

'What is it coming to?' Pam said with a shake of her head. 'Most of the teachers were men, of course, and they all went off to fight. I suppose we have to be grateful the schools could stay open at all.'

'Angela has to travel to school now,' Jeanie said. 'Lizzie took her into Chatteris today, didn't she?'

'Yes. Angela likes that – and she doesn't have to get up quite so early if Lizzie takes her.' Pam smiled fondly. 'I was disappointed she didn't pass her exam for the High School but she is happy so I shan't nag her. I've told her she will need to be up at six if she marries a farmer, but she says that will be fine, because she'll be doing things she likes rather than boring old school.' She shook her head. 'Not a bit like Susan. She is all for making a better life for herself...'

'Susan is like her mother,' Arthur said and chuckled. 'Pass me one of those rock cakes, Jeanie, love. I just fancy a nice cake for a change.' He picked up his paper and folded it as he liked. 'Churchill says we're winning and the tide is turning. That man is an inspiration...'

'Was that at the thanksgiving for the Allies victory in Tunisia?' Pam asked and he nodded.

'I reckon it shocked them when the RAF used those new

"dambusters", the bouncing bombs – they never thought we could touch their dams in the Ruhr,' he said.

'That was marvellous,' Pam murmured.

'It did a lot of damage,' Arthur said, nodding and looking pleased. 'There was a time when I thought we would lose this war, but now I believe we've got them by the...' He gave a little cough, remembering his company. 'Pass me that cake, love. I'll eat that and then I'll go up and have a little rest before I help with the milking.'

'I'll do that, Uncle Arthur,' George said. 'Me and Jeanie together.'

Arthur nodded and went out, taking his cake with him. They heard his slow tread up the stairs. Pam looked at Jeanie, her eyes brimming with tears. She held them back with a struggle. Crying never did any good and it certainly wouldn't make Arthur feel better. He never said a word to her about his feelings. Except now and then to assure her that she would be all right after he'd gone – something she didn't want to hear. If he was afraid of death, he never gave a sign of it, but the knowledge that it couldn't be long was breaking her heart.

'I think I'll try one of the cakes,' Jeanie said to break the silence. 'I'm feeling a bit better at last. Hopefully, I can keep it down.'

'I'll make that lemon barley,' Pam said with a smile. 'I knew as soon as I spotted the lemons on the market, they were just the thing. You could have knocked me down with a feather when he said the price, but I was lucky to get them. Haven't seen one for ages, even on Pancake Day.'

'I think a few more ships have been getting through lately,' Jeanie told her. 'The convoys for the Atlantic run are so huge that some of them have to get through, and they have air support when they get a bit nearer home and I read the tonnage sunk has reduced by more than half...'

'We're winning the U-boat war. I read that bit too. It's because they quashed the trouble in North Africa last month and can now bring more ships and aircraft to the Atlantic.' Pam said; her thoughts deflected from Arthur for a while. 'I'm glad none of my boys are in the navy. It's bad enough to have one in the army and another flying dangerous missions.'

'At least Tom is safe enough in his training job,' Jeanie said. 'You don't have to worry about him, Mum.'

'No...' Pam shook her head. Lizzie had received a letter from Tom that she believed meant he was going on another mission, but as neither Lizzie nor Pam was too sure, they were not telling the rest of the family. There was no point in upsetting everyone for no reason.

* * *

It was half past four when Pam went up to the bedroom she had shared with her husband ever since their marriage. George and Jeanie had gone out to the sheds to do the evening milking, but Arthur would be annoyed if she didn't wake him in time to at least help fill the churns.

The curtains had been drawn to shut out the early-summer sunshine, but she could see the shape of Arthur's body lying on his side, the eiderdown pulled up over him. He'd taken off his boots but was still dressed and clearly asleep. Pam hesitated, not wanting to disturb him, but then something made her reach forwards and touch his cheek. The shock ran through her as she felt his ice-cold skin.

'Arthur? Arthur, no—' Pam's heart caught with pain as she

bent over him and saw that his colour had gone and his skin was marble-white. He wasn't breathing and he must have just gone in his sleep – some hours ago by the feel of him. 'Oh, Arthur my love...' Pam's tears spilled silently down her cheeks.

Why hadn't she been with him? She should have been here by his side, instead of downstairs carrying out her everyday chores. Arthur had slipped away quietly in his own way, never making a fuss, and she hadn't realised today was the last time she would see him alive. Regret and grief swept over her. Had she told him she loved him enough? Did he know how much he'd always meant to her – how grateful she was for all he'd given her these past years?

She sat down on the bed, reaching for his hand, just holding it. Would he know she was here grieving? Was it possible for the dead to know – to see how they were missed?

Pam wasn't aware of time as she sat there quietly by Arthur's side, telling him in her mind how much she loved him and would miss him. Of course he must know it, had always known it, because they'd been happy together. They'd had a good life, filled with children, laughter and fun despite all the work. Yet it hadn't been long enough. It could never be long enough. Pam knew that the years ahead would be lonely without Arthur. But she was lucky. She had a lot of family and much of it here with her, whereas some women had no one – all their loved ones taken in some form by the war. She had grandchildren and would have more – but there would never be another Arthur. Pam would never set another in his place.

She gave a long shuddering sigh as she accepted the loneliness. She would make as much of her family as she could, but there would always be this need for Arthur inside her.

'Mum, are you up there?' Pam heard Lizzie's voice and then

Tom's wife came into the bedroom. 'Mum – what is it?' Lizzie approached the bed cautiously, and then gave a little gasp. 'Oh, Mum. I am so sorry.' Lizzie sat on the bed and put her arms about her. Pam leaned into her and the tears she'd held inside came thick and fast.

'He just said he was going to rest...' Pam sobbed. 'He didn't say he felt worse... nothing. He was pleased the way the war is going. Just smiled at us and said to wake him at four... so I let him rest...' She raised her head, the grief in her eyes. 'I love him so much, Lizzie.'

'I know. We all know what Arthur meant to you,' Lizzie said. 'He was a lovely man, Pam. We all loved him, and we shall all miss him – but it is hardest for you.' She gave Pam's shoulders a little squeeze. 'I'll always be here for you, Mum. Tom knows I will look after you.' She smiled into Pam's eyes. 'You've looked after us all and you will go on doing that, because it is you – but we will look after you, too.'

'Yes, I know,' Pam said and took a big handkerchief from her apron pocket to blow her nose and wipe her face. 'At least he was peaceful, at home with us all.' She sighed. 'I suppose we have to get a doctor and all the rest – but I don't want him taken away, Lizzie. He rests here in the parlour, until we follow him to the churchyard.'

'They won't need to take him away; it was expected, Mum. The doctor will confirm that so you can keep him here with us until the last.'

Pam nodded and stood up. 'We'd better go down, Lizzie. There are things to do. Will you ring the doctor for me and I'll tell the others...?'

Lizzie nodded. Pam looked calm and in control. She would continue because she had to, but Lizzie could see the change in her already. The light that told you she was a happy woman because she was loved by a good man had gone. Now her eyes were dull and unseeing. Lizzie wasn't sure if that light would ever return.

12

'Typical,' Artie muttered to Jeanie, as five days later, they filed into church behind the coffin, borne by six bearers, the rain sheeting down. 'Why does it always rain on days like this?'

Jeanie shook her head. She knew Artie's anger was fuelled by grief. He'd wanted Tom and John here with him so they could help to bear Arthur's coffin, but they were unreachable, and so he'd left it to strangers, walking instead with Jeanie, just behind his mother who had Lizzie's arm to support her. Susan and George walked behind, with Angela firmly in the middle. She hadn't stopped crying since her mother had told her and was inconsolable, which Jeanie thought made things all the harder for Pam.

Susan and George looked white-faced but dry-eyed. Jeanie knew her eyes were red, because she'd cried a lot since her father-in-law had died. Arthur had been so quiet, sitting in his corner, but he'd been the rock on which everyone depended. Artie felt lost without his father's guiding hand. He would never admit it and yet she knew it was true and, although he was stony-faced now, he had cried by himself behind the cowsheds.

She'd heard him but left him to weep, because it was his way. Artie felt things as much as any of them but didn't like to show it.

Jeanie knew her husband was worried about managing the farm alone. Yes, they now had two land girls, who had arrived the day before, looking and feeling like fish out of water when they realised that a funeral was to be held the next day. This morning, they'd been up early, volunteering to do all the milking and work in the yard. Artie had spoken to them briefly and then left them to get on with it.

Jeanie and Lizzie had stayed close to Pam, knowing how much of an ordeal the day would be for her. A small reception would be held in the village school, which had closed for a few days' holiday due to staff shortages again. Pam had done much of the cooking, but several friends and neighbours had contributed so that she hadn't been given too much work. Although, Jeanie knew Pam was best kept busy rather than sitting around and crying.

* * *

It had upset Jeanie that neither John nor Tom had been reachable when they tried to contact them to let them know about their father's death. Lizzie had done the telephoning and been told that Captain Gilbert and Lieutenant Talbot would be informed and given leave when it was possible.

'It means John has already left for his posting – and Tom must have gone on one of those missions he never talks about,' Lizzie had told Jeanie when they discussed the arrangements in private. 'It was the worst possible time, but I suppose it doesn't make much difference – neither of them could do anything.'

'Pam might have been comforted by their presence had they

been able to attend the funeral,' Jeanie had said. 'But you are right. None of us can really do anything to help her. Pam has to cope with his loss in her own way.'

'Yes, I know, and she will,' Lizzie had replied. 'I wish Tom could have been here for the funeral. I know he will regret it so much.'

'Yes, of course he will,' Jeanie had agreed. 'This rotten war has a lot to answer for, Lizzie. If it hadn't been for the war taking them both away, Arthur's condition might not have shown up so soon.'

'We can't know that,' Lizzie had said. 'Hearts are funny things. You can be fine one minute and drop down dead the next. I heard about that happening to a young RAF officer. He passed his medical in the morning with flying colours and dropped down dead playing tennis in the afternoon.'

'That is dreadful,' Jeanie had said, shocked. 'How could he possibly have been thought fit and then die just like that?'

Lizzie had shrugged. 'We all knew Arthur was ill, but I don't think even Pam expected it yet.'

'I am sure she didn't,' Jeanie had agreed. 'I was shocked. I mean he looked tired but...' She'd shaken her head, because they were all still reeling from the shock. Arthur's death had not been unexpected, but it left a big hole in the family.

* * *

Singing hymns and listening to prayers and the sermon helped a bit, but it was a sombre group that walked to the school, where a tea had been prepared by willing helpers. That was the thing about living in a village, the women all came forward to offer practical help, which had been gratefully received in this instance.

Pam was still quiet, shocked, not quite functioning in her normal way. She got up in the mornings and cooked breakfast; the ironing and cleaning got done with a little help from Jeanie, Susan and Lizzie. Even Angela had done her share of the washing-up without complaining – but there was a stillness in the big kitchen. Always, it had hummed with life, movement and laughter, cats in front of the fire, and kettles boiling, but now, somehow the sounds were muted. Everyone spoke in soft voices.

Her gaze followed Pam as she greeted friends of her husband at the reception. She was gracious and polite, but her deep laugh and wicked looks of enjoyment were missing. It was as if she moved in a sort of fog, only half with them. Jeanie's heart went out to her.

She'd asked her mother and her sister, Annie, to come, but Annie was working on the wards at Addenbrooke's and Jeanie's mother had declined.

'I'll come another day, when Pam is feeling better,' she'd told Jeanie. 'Give her my love – but tell her Terry isn't too well at the moment so I can't leave him.'

Terry was Jeanie's brother and he'd lost a leg in the war. He'd recovered from his wounds and found a desk job in his father's building firm but still had days when he wasn't well enough to work; he'd lost his wife from a gas explosion but had his daughter, Tina, who was a bundle of mischief. Tina had stayed at the farm for a while but now lived with her granny, grandad and father in London.

'Mum looks so pale,' Artie said in Jeanie's ear as she sat down at one of the small tables with a cup of tea and a salad sandwich. 'I've tried to help, Jeanie, but she just smiles and pats my hand... I can't get through to her.'

Jeanie looked at her husband and saw the depth of his concern. Artie didn't often show his real feelings, even to her, but he loved his mother and he was worried now. 'She needs time to grieve. She'll come back to us when she is ready,' Jeanie whispered. 'They were together a lot of years.'

'Not long enough,' Artie said fiercely and she saw the anger there; it was his way of dealing with his grief. 'He wasn't old. I didn't know he had a heart problem until it was too late. I wouldn't have let him do all the stuff he used to do.'

'We none of us knew until last year,' Jeanie said. 'It isn't your fault, Artie.'

Artie scowled. 'I can't stand any more of this,' he hissed at her. 'I'm going back to the farm – I want to see how those girls are getting on. Don't like leaving them alone on their first day. And I'll see if Dot Goodman is all right with the kids...' Mrs Goodman had stepped in to look after Arthur and Jonny while everyone was at the funeral.

Jeanie nodded. 'Do you want me to come?'

'No, you stay here and support Mum. Tell her I had work to do, she will understand.'

'All right.' Jeanie watched him go. He hated all this stuff. The church part was OK but not the tea party afterwards. Artie could be really good company when he was in the mood, but at other times he went into his reserved mode and there wasn't much she could do or say, so she didn't try; he would get over it and apologise later. Besides, his father's death had cut him hard. Perhaps harder than it would his brothers, because Artie would miss his father's company every day, while they had busy lives serving their country. It was true Artie's job was safer than either Tom's or John's, but, in some ways, it was even harder to be the one who stayed home and kept things going.

'Pam is doing so well,' Lizzie said, coming up to her with a glass of sherry in her hand. 'I didn't get you one, Jeanie, because of the baby. I can if you'd like?'

'No, thanks, I'll stick to my cup of tea,' Jeanie said. 'Unless, I might have an orange squash if there is any...'

'I think there's some of that concentrated orange juice. Mabel Greene is a diabetic and she says they give her loads more than she wants so she made a couple of jugs up for us.'

'It looks as if George found it...' Jeanie nodded at the young lad, who was munching a sausage roll and had a glass of the orange juice in his hand. 'At least he is enjoying himself.'

'He was sniffling all through the service,' Lizzie said. 'I gave him a hanky, but I could hear him. He was fond of Arthur and will miss him.'

'We all shall,' Jeanie sighed. 'I hope those land girls are good at their work, because Artie needs them to be.' She placed her hands on her gently swelling belly. 'I wish I wasn't having this one just yet...'

'Oh, don't say that, Jeanie,' Lizzie begged. 'It's the babies that make it all worthwhile. We have to struggle on whatever, because of the children.'

'I do want my baby, but we weren't ready yet.' She made a face. 'Artie is getting used to it, but I know he isn't over the moon at the idea of being a father so soon.'

'He will be when it gets here,' Lizzie comforted. 'I wouldn't be without my little Arthur for the world – and John's son is a sweetie, and so will yours be, Jeanie, whether you have a boy or a girl.'

'The nurse I saw says I'll probably have a boy,' Jeanie replied. 'Something about the way I'm carrying it; all nonsense of course, but it would be nice for Artie if we have a son to carry on the farm.'

'Will you stay on at the farm now? There doesn't seem much point in your moving to a house of your own – unless you would rather?'

'I think Artie wants to stay for now and I've told Pam that we will. Artie wishes he could talk to Tom about things – the way the land is divided... I mean, it isn't quite the same as working for your father.'

Lizzie frowned. 'I know Arthur spoke of leaving the land to Artie and Tom – but won't they go on as a joint thing... farm it all together?'

'Perhaps until the war is over, but Artie has ideas of his own and he hates the heavy land. I think he might put it all down to grass and have cows and sheep on it rather than crop it next year.'

'But Tom says that is the best land they have...' Lizzie looked concerned, but Jeanie just shrugged.

'Well, we are only the wives,' she said. 'The men will settle it between themselves – when they can...'

'Yes, of course, and now isn't the time to think about it.'

'No – but the lawyer is coming tomorrow,' Jeanie said. 'You should try to be there, Lizzie. As Tom's wife...'

'I'm busy at the salon,' Lizzie replied. 'I didn't know he was coming. I suppose I can read the will later if I want to; it won't concern me.'

'No – although Arthur gave you your house, didn't he?'

'Yes, he had it built for us,' Lizzie said. 'I think Tom has been left some land and everything else is divided between Pam and Arthur's children.'

'Yes, well, it might not be that straightforward,' Jeanie said but shook her head as Lizzie looked at her. 'We'll talk about it another time. I only know a bit. Artie has glimpsed the will and he says Arthur made some changes recently...'

'Oh, well, as I said, it only concerns me for Tom.' Lizzie nodded and wandered off to talk to some other friends.

Jeanie frowned. She felt a bit uncomfortable with some of

the things Artie had suggested recently, but they would all know more after Arthur's wishes were made known.

* * *

Pam sighed as she got into her bed that evening. It was only nine o'clock but she felt tired out. Her day had been long and strenuous, fighting her desire to give into her grief as she went through the motions of greeting and thanking friends and relatives. It all seemed so endless and so pointless, but she knew life had to go on. The farm wouldn't run itself and Jeanie wasn't feeling her usual self, so she couldn't just leave her to get on with it – the land girls had to be fed and to be told the rules. They weren't strict, but she needed them to behave properly and she'd heard about some girls who had been rather loose in their behaviour in the neighbouring village. Someone had to hold it all together and that was her, even though she felt like lying down and letting it all go on without her.

Jeanie had been very quiet after the funeral. She'd pleaded a headache and gone up to her room. Come to think of it, Lizzie had been a bit odd – giving Artie a few strange looks. Pam hoped they hadn't fallen out. Now was the time they all had to pull together if the farm was to survive and prosper.

Pam knew Arthur had changed his will after he learned he hadn't got long. He hadn't discussed it with her, but she wasn't that worried about it. He'd always said that the farm was her home and she would receive a small cash sum and an income; it was all she needed – but she knew Artie was ambitious. Although Tom wasn't Arthur's natural son, Pam knew her husband had loved her first boy as his own and Arthur had planned on giving him the three fields in Mepal, but... She shook her head. Tom wouldn't let it bother him either way. The house had been put in Lizzie's name so that was hers and Tom's – and he would find a way to make a living whatever happened.

Oh well, they would know what was going to happen to the farm in the morning when the solicitor came.

* * *

'It was your husband's intention to leave the land between Tom and Artie, with some property going to yourself and some cash and a house in Sutton for your son, John, because he had no interest in the farm. At that time, the farm was doing well and there was a surplus of money in the bank, which would have come to you...' Mr Carraway stopped and looked from Pam to Artie. Jeanie was caring for Jonny, deliberately sitting away from the kitchen table. Lizzie had gone to work, Angela and George to school, and Susan was up in her room reading. She didn't want to hear the will read.

The lawyer went on, 'Apart from some small bequests to Susan and Angela, the remainder of your husband's property now comes to you, Mrs Talbot – for the period of your lifetime. After that time, the land in Mepal goes to Tom Gilbert, the fenland to Artie Talbot, a house and one thousand pounds to Mr John Talbot... and a sum of five thousand pounds was also to have been yours, Mrs Talbot, but that is no longer available as it has been eroded to keep the farm going this past couple of years. The difference in profits means that there is now only around one thousand pounds in the farm accounts – that was how it stood last Christmas when Mr Talbot confided in me. It may have altered a little since then.'

'What—?' Artie exploded. 'He can't have done that? He promised us the land. It was just the house and yard I wasn't sure of...' He looked angry. 'That isn't the will I was told about...'

'No, because your father didn't want a copy of this one. He asked me to keep it and signed it last Christmas.' The lawyer looked at Pam. 'Mr Talbot felt that as his savings have gone back into the farm to keep it going this past few years, it would leave you with too little to live on, Mrs Talbot. Therefore, he made you the owner of the farm for your lifetime to protect you. Your sons will inherit what he intended in time, but for now it is yours. You cannot sell it, of course...'

'I wouldn't wish to,' Pam said, stunned. 'I had no idea things had got so difficult. He always seemed to have everything under control...'

'It is the war, Mrs Talbot. All the restrictions have caused a loss of profits. Your husband does own some houses, most of which are let at the moment – and one of them is in your name; it doesn't form part of the will, but I understand you haven't been told of it. You could sell that one if you wished...'

'Where is it?' Pam asked. She'd never known much of Arthur's business; there had been no need; she had all she wanted.

'In Chatteris,' the lawyer told her. 'It is rented, but only for a pound a week – not enough to provide an income, which is why your husband made the changes. You could give the tenants notice to quit and sell – but it might not make what it could be worth after the war. No houses are selling well at the moment. I believe Mr Talbot considered selling a couple of properties to replace the cash sum but found he couldn't do it until after the war as he would get less than he'd paid.'

'So if Mum owns everything, what do we get?' Artie asked, a sharp note in his voice.

'He offers you his love and hopes you will forgive him for making these changes, but he believed that his sons would understand that it was necessary.'

'So... nothing.' Artie stared at him. 'I'm expected to just carry on for years for the same paltry wage...'

'Artie!' Jeanie cried but subsided as his angry look shot to her. 'It's your mum...' Her last words were hardly audible.

'He gave me his word. I've done all the work – stayed when...' Artie shook his head, then stalked out, leaving silence behind him.

Jeanie got up, placed Jonny in his cot and came to sit next to Pam. 'He doesn't mean it,' she said in a small voice. 'He just has big plans for the future.'

'It is a shock,' Pam said. 'It isn't what I would have chosen, but at the moment I don't see what else we can do. Everything is tied up in land and property. Arthur put his money back into things, because he wasn't keen on keeping it in banks. Five thousand pounds would have made me secure – but without it...' She shook her head. 'I can't see that we have a choice, Jeanie. We have to carry on and make a success of the farm for all our sakes.'

'Artie will – of course he will,' Jeanie said. 'He is shocked, that's all...'

'Yes – and I know his father did promise him his own land. It isn't fair, Jeanie – but you do have the house in Sutton he bought you.'

'The rent we shall get is about the same as yours in Chatteris,' Jeanie told her. 'Not enough to live on, even if...' She sighed.

'I will look into things – see what could be sold and if it is viable but I think we may have to accept that Arthur did the right thing. I don't need much. Once the profits are back to normal, perhaps – but that can't be for some years. I know Artie has the right to be angry. He has worked on the farm all his life and done a lot of extra work recently; he should have some reward for it but...' Pam sighed and closed her eyes.

'I'd best be on my way, Mrs Talbot,' the lawyer told her. 'If you need more advice, I can call and see you – on your own perhaps.'

Pam opened her eyes, forcing a smile. 'I believe I understand it all, Mr Carraway, but I have to think about it carefully – for the sake of my family.'

'Yes, I do understand. It was not what Mr Talbot planned – but the war has taken its toll on everyone.'

'Yes, it certainly has.' She shook hands with him and he left.

A silence fell and Jeanie looked at her uncomfortably.

'Please don't be angry, Pam. I couldn't bear it if we fell out...'

Pam looked at her then, seeing the tears in her eyes. 'I'm not angry, Jeanie. How could I be? I feel sad that Artie has to wait to own his land, but I'll do what I can. I'm not sure what at this moment...'

'You shouldn't have to do anything,' Jeanie said. 'Artie was just disappointed. He will get over it.'

Pam nodded but didn't reply. Artie had always been the most difficult of her sons and he'd made his feelings clear. She understood his disappointment and his anger, but it still hurt. Her heart was still reeling from the loss of Arthur and the last thing she wanted was any squabbling over land or money. It was a pity Arthur had changed his will, but he had and Pam didn't know what to do to make things better. She wished with all her heart that Tom was home so that she could talk to him about it.

Pam had very little money of her own, just a few pounds she'd saved from time to time. Arthur had always given her whatever she wanted or needed – and he'd bought her that house in Chatteris, not even telling her. Would she get a fair price if she sold it? Pam's brow furrowed. Even if she did manage to sell it, it would probably only be a couple of hundred pounds. Artie could buy a few acres of his own with that – but how could she give it to him when there was John and the girls to think of? Susan and Angela had a small trust fund each, which Arthur had set up when they were born. He'd paid money into them each year and it looked as if the girls would have something like a thousand pounds each, but not until they were twenty, which meant in two years Susan would get hers but Angela would have to wait much longer. It was a decent sum, but normally she would expect to pass on anything she had left herself to her daughters; the boys would, after all, have land and a house each. Arthur had probably intended his daughters to have a house when they married. He'd expected his prosperity to continue and to provide for them when he was ready.

After years of never having to give a thought to money, Arthur had suddenly been thrown into stormy waters. The war had made things difficult on the land, reducing profits to almost nil this past year. He'd still had plans for investing in more land but then his illness had hit him... Why, only two years ago he'd bought that land near Chatteris for the pigs and...

Pam frowned as she tried to recall what the will had said. She picked it up and reread the details; there was nothing about the piggery...

Getting up, she went through to the parlour and sat down at Arthur's desk. It was an oak rolltop and he'd loved it, because of all the little drawers and pigeonholes inside. The first thing she saw as she opened it up was a parcel addressed to her. Pam stared at it for a moment, her heart racing. She reached for it with a trembling hand and opened the large brown envelope. There were some deeds and a letter. As she began to read, Pam's eyes filled with tears. Arthur spoke of his love for her and his pride that she'd given him her trust all these years.

The second sheet was different and Pam was puzzled as she stared at it. It was a list of items of silver, jewellery, furniture, clocks, and at the end, a parcel of land.

Arthur had written something as a footnote, but her eyes were too full of tears to read it for a few moments; when she did, she caught her breath sharply.

> *I put the house in Chatteris and that land for the pigs in your name, Pam love. I told Carraway about the house but not the land, because I used money that hadn't been through the bank and he is a bit of a stickler for the law. You know I like to dabble a bit and there's always a few quid goes in the back pocket. Haven't been able to do that much since the war, but I've been putting a bit of stuff by for you for years, just in case. You know my great-grandfather got cheated of a lot of money over his father's estate, by lawyers, and so I've always tried to put a little out of the way. I've collected a few nice pieces in the attic – silver and a few paintings, some porcelain and stuff, worth two or three thousand. You won't be able to sell it at the moment, because of the war. Wait for a few years and sell a bit at a time when you need money. Also, Grandfather Talbot's furniture is stacked in the big barn; it's all wrapped up in tarpaulins, so the boys don't know what is there. Not sure what that would fetch; it was decent stuff but out of fashion so might only be good for firewood. I haven't looked at it for years and can't quite remember what he had, but it was old. Might be worth something one day.*
>
> *Lastly, my dearest Pam, I don't want you to break your heart for me, and I know you will. Try to remember how good it all was, my love, and know that I wouldn't change a thing.*

Pam bowed her head as the sobs broke from her. It was just

like Arthur to do something like this, and after a few minutes, she began to smile through her tears. Arthur had always liked to keep his cards close to his chest and he'd managed to surprise her – but if he'd left her provided for with these extra sources of income, why had he changed his will?

That puzzled her for a while. Pam couldn't see why he'd done it – unless he'd thought it would hold the family together. If so, it was ironic that it was far more likely to tear them apart.

The ten acres of land on which the piggery stood would fetch around five hundred pounds if she sold it now – and the animals would be worth a hundred or two. Pam sat frowning over it for a while, wondering what to do for the best. It wouldn't make up to Artie for the 200 acres of prime fenland he'd expected to be his – but if he had it, and kept the piggery going, it would bring him in a small private income that he could use as he saw fit.

Artie was like his father in that he wanted to do more. Arthur had never been just a farmer; he'd always had a bit of business going on, and some of that money was never declared on his tax accounts. Just as he'd slaughtered a pig now and then for his family and friends that the Food Ministry knew nothing of, so his extra dabbling was just that, his little secret. Even Pam hadn't known about most of it.

The house in Chatteris would go to her daughters when she no longer needed it – and whatever was in the attic... Well, she didn't know what that amounted to yet and she would do as Arthur said and sell something now and then when the time came.

She thought about Tom. Pam tried not to have favourites of her children, but Tom was special. She wished that he was home so she could talk this over with him. Yet she couldn't ignore Artie's claims. Yes, he would inherit some prime land, but he was impatient – and the wages farm labourers received were small. Not that Artie hadn't been given his share one way and another. All the boys had been given extra money by their father when he'd had plenty to spare...

The thoughts went round and round in Pam's head. She could continue to live on the farm and the income would be enough to support her and her family, without the money from the pigs. In a way, it wasn't fair to either John or Tom, but Pam knew she needed Artie to keep things running. It was hard enough to do all the work even with their land girls and if Artie was sullen and resentful, it would make life unbearable for them all.

Her mind made up, even though she was sure Arthur wouldn't have approved, Pam decided that she would give Artie the land to use as he wished, either to farm for crops or continue with the pigs. Those already on the land must be sold, because they belonged to the farm and the Ministry would want to know where they were – but Artie could buy his own pigs if he wished to continue with them or plough it up...

She put the deeds and letter back into the desk and locked it, just as Jeanie came in. Pam saw at once that her daughter-in-law had been crying and stood up to go to her.

'Jeanie love, what's the matter?'

'I had a row with Artie,' Jeanie sniffed. 'He behaved so badly, Mum, and I told him so. We had a big row and he's gone off on the tractor. Says he has to feed those damned pigs!'

'He will get over it,' Pam said and blew her nose. 'We all will, because I can't see we have much choice...'

'You've been crying too,' Jeanie said. 'Artie didn't mean to hurt you, Mum – he just has big plans. He wants to be rich...'

'Well, in a way, he is,' Pam replied. 'That land will be his one day – and you have the house. He can find ways of making money, just like his dad did.'

Jeanie nodded and sniffed. Pam held out her arms and they had a hug.

'It's only money, love,' Pam told her. 'We'll find a way round it – all that matters is we stay together as a family.'

'I know...' Jeanie wiped her eyes. 'Artie knows that really, Mum.'

'Yes, of course he does.' Pam smiled. 'We'll work something out. You'll see.'

13

John lay on his bunk thinking about the last letter he'd had from Lucy. She hadn't got her posting yet, but she'd expected it any day. Her letter had been loving and emotional, because they didn't know when, if ever, they would see each other again. Neither of them could be certain of returning home and her feelings had spilled over in her letter.

I love you so much... please come back to me...

He felt an aching need inside, a longing to be with her, and realised that she'd become far more important to him than he'd thought. Yes, at first, he'd thought of her more as a friend, but his feelings for her had changed gradually and now that they were unable to meet regularly, he understood how much he'd come to rely on her cheerful smile and her warmth.

'Letter for you, sir...' John came out of his reverie as the airman entered his room. 'It was marked urgent – but it looks as if it was posted over a month ago.'

'Urgent?' John swung his legs over the bunk and stood up to

take the letter. He swore as he recognised his mother's handwriting. There was only one reason she would mark her letter urgent.

He tore it open as the airman departed, scanning the brief lines that told him of his father's death.

I know it probably won't be possible for you to come home, John, but I've sent it urgent delivery just in case...

John cursed, sitting down on his bunk again as it hit him. His father was dead – and buried by now. He'd known that it might not be long, but the blow had taken all the breath from him. John hadn't always seen eye to eye with his father. Arthur had wanted him to work on the farm with his brothers, but John had never wanted that and he'd found himself a job with a builder, learning to be a plasterer. In the end, his father had accepted it and they'd been on good terms – and now the loss of the gentle man he'd known all his life was like a knife thrust into his heart.

John's eyes watered as he read the letter again. His mother must be going through hell. He wished he could have been there to comfort her, to be with his son, and part of a loving family, grieving together. John cursed the war for his being far away when he was needed.

A knock at his door made him shove the letter into his trouser pocket. It opened and his friend, Gordon, stood there. 'Just to let you know the briefing has been put forward. You're wanted now. Seems they've got a job for us...'

'I'll come,' John said, reaching for his uniform jacket. 'Any idea where or what?'

'Not yet, but I think it is a big one. There's a buzz going on...'

'Right, on my way.' John nodded to his friend. There was no time to dwell on his grief. He wondered briefly if Tom had made it home, but doubted it. His last letter had said he was going to be busy – it was their code for going into action. It would just have been Artie and the girls...

John left the barracks, which was a row of hastily erected wooden huts, and made his way to the tent where the briefing was to take place. The air was warm, the sun shining, a pungent smell of some flower drifting on the slight breeze. It had come as a surprise to John to find himself in Cyprus, but it was a pleasant enough place to be; the camaraderie among the forces stationed here was good, and the weather was great.

As he walked into the tent, John immediately sensed the air of excitement and knew something big was on. Gradually, the space filled with men and then the officer walked in and looked at them.

'Well, it's about time,' he said and everyone sat up straighter. 'Our navy has been on the receiving end too often in recent months – but this time the shoe is on the other foot and we've been given news about an enemy convoy due to come our way. So this time we're going to give them a taste of their own medicine...'

A cheer rose from many throats as the map was rolled out and the briefing began. A large convoy carrying food and weapons was being sent out to German bases in the Aegean islands.

'Our job has previously been mainly to defend our convoys from attack,' the officer went on, obviously elated by the chance to strike an enemy convoy. 'This time we've had advance warning and we'll be waiting for them.'

John listened as the briefing went on. It was good that they had a chance to attack rather than defend for once, but he felt no enthusiasm. All he could think about was Lucy and whether she'd got her posting yet, and his mother, at home, grieving for her husband.

The prospect of sinking merchant ships gave John no feeling of elation. It was just more death and destruction – and he'd seen enough of that to last him a lifetime. His stomach churned and he wished himself a thousand miles away, but even as he rejected the mood of eagerness, he listened and observed; he had a job to do and he would do it, though he took no pleasure in it. Shooting down an enemy pilot intent on sinking a ship friendly to the Allies gave him a feeling of a job well done, but the men in those ships destined for a watery death were not all monsters and John's gentle nature was disturbed by the shouts of glee he heard as the meeting broke up.

Take-off was scheduled for 2 a.m. the next day and the strike would hit the convoy around dawn. It was going to be a bloody business, because the convoy would have its own fighter aircraft to defend it.

Back in his own quarters, John sat down and wrote two letters. One to his mother and one to his son. He would include the letter for Jonny in his mother's and ask her to give it to him in the future if he didn't make it back.

His letters done, he considered writing to Lucy, but he'd written to her the previous day and there was nothing to say. Both Lucy and John knew there was a possibility that they would not see each other again; there was no need to say more. His letter to his mother was one of concern for her and her loss, and the letter to his son, it was... well, just to say: *I loved you and I'm sorry I wasn't there for you.* All the things he wished he'd been able to say to his own father. Death was so final and there was always something more you needed to say but couldn't.

He left the letters for collection and then went to the

canteen, before taking time for some sunbathing. There was nothing much to do until the call came for take-off.

14

They were approaching the enemy submarine base in its Aegean Island fortress under cover of darkness. It had been a hot day and the night air was humid. Tom's men sat hushed and tense in the small boats that had been launched from the British warship, their oars making hardly any sound in the water as they approached. Lights from the shore swept over the sea from time to time, but they were too far away to be spotted by the human eye as yet.

'It looks as if we had the right information,' one of the men whispered to Tom. The sheltered harbour, protected by sheer rocks on either side, was difficult to hit from the air and so they had been sent in to attack it from the sea. Six of their number were trained underwater operatives, and, even as Tom gave the order to halt, those men slipped into the sea and disappeared below the surface.

Their plan was to fix mines to the hulls of the submarines that were resting in their island home base, where they had anchored on the surface, clearly visible as the searchlights swept over them every few minutes. Here they believed themselves untouchable. Meantime, Tom's group was to land slightly away from the harbour and create a diversion, giving the divers a chance to do their work and escape. One boat would remain here, out of reach of the searching lights, to take up the divers and return to the ship waiting to receive them. It was Tom's job to keep the enemy defence concentrating on them rather than the true assault.

They rowed swiftly towards the cove slightly further along the coast; here there were buildings of various shapes and sizes. It was thought they were stores and workshops, also recreational areas for the soldiers guarding the base. Their information was not 100 per cent accurate, but it didn't matter. They just had to cause as much damage as they could in a short time to give their comrades a chance of getting away.

Lights swept across the bay once more, but it was a dark night and everyone's face was blacked. Only a very observant watcher would pick them out as they abandoned their boats, leaving just two men to secure them, the rest of the unit wading through the waves towards the shore, their arms high above their heads as they held their equipment above the water. The security would be tighter in the port where the submarines were stationed, but an observant guard could have alerted the enemy to the attack.

Tom called a halt as the lights swept over them and everyone froze, but they passed on and no siren disturbed the quiet night. Then men climbed onto the rocky shore and looked about them. Tom pointed to various buildings, nodding and directing as they crept stealthily towards them.

A door opened ahead of them and light spilled out, laughter and noise disturbing the peace, and then it was gone. Everyone had stopped, but now they crept forward again. Highly dangerous materials were brought out, fuses fixed to dynamite, clamped to building walls and across doors so that if they were opened, they would set off the explosion.

'All done?' Tom urged his men to hurry, checking his watch. 'Come on, you two...'

He beckoned to Blackwall and Stanley, who were lagging behind the others. As they clamped the last explosive device to a building set some distance from the others, a door was opened and there was a loud bang as the night was suddenly lit up by fire.

'Back to the boats!' Tom hissed, urging them all on as suddenly a siren blared and all hell broke loose. Shots were fired from a lookout post somewhere above them, but the explosions were going off all round them and it was like being in the centre of a volcanic explosion as flames began to shoot into the sky, illuminating the figures as they ran for the shore.

Tom was the rearguard, one of only three equipped with rifles. The other men had carried explosives. He and the others fired back as figures started to run towards them. Seeing Blackwall trip and fall, Tom motioned to one of the men to get him, as the others retreated. He kept firing at the enemy soldiers who were trying to get to them through the flames. It was almost impossible because there was a line of burning buildings all the way across the shoreline. They hadn't known it, but there must have been a fuel store in one of the buildings and the flames has caught fiercely, spreading like wildfire.

'Come on, sir,' Stanley called urgently. 'We're ready to move on.'

'Keep going,' Tom said. He moved slowly backwards, still firing as a few brave men broke through the fire and came towards him, firing their machine guns. He felt a bullet enter his arm, the pain searing and brutal, his rifle falling as his arm hung limply at his side.

'Go on, sir,' Stanley urged. 'Get into the water. I'll hold them back...'

'No— Go.' Tom muttered but turned and staggered back to the shore, where he was caught by eager hands urging him into the sea. Stanley had produced a pistol and was firing as he ran after them, but, as Tom turned to look, he saw him fall to a hail of bullets, his body riddled with them.

He wanted to go back, to grab the fallen man and bring him with them, but he knew it was too late. No man could live through that... and he had no strength, the effort to wade out to the boats almost more than he could manage.

'I can't swim with this arm... go on without me,' he said to Walters, but he was grabbed by two of his men and propelled into the deeper water. Together, they dragged him through the waves until the first boat was reached. He was hauled into it and lay back, pain washing over him as there were suddenly multiple explosions further up in the submarine port and once again the night sky was lit with flames and smoke. They had achieved their aim and most of the submarines were on fire.

'Bloody hell!' one of his men muttered. 'I thought we made a mess, but that beats all.'

Tom looked towards the port and saw the sky lit up. The first aim of their mission had been achieved and they'd given the enemy something to think about; a few submarines would not affect the outcome of the war, but it unsettled minds, and jumpy nerves caused mistakes. He glanced back at the shore they'd just left, seeing that his group had inflicted enough damage to keep the men on duty there busy. It must be pandemonium for them, because they couldn't know whether it was a big attack or just a diversion for something else. He smiled. If he was in command, he would be wondering if the island was to be invaded.

As they rowed silently away, he could still hear more explosions and sirens. The divers had done a good job, but Tom's men had caused a diversion that had helped them to get among the submarines and do their work.

'Are you all right, sir?' Corporal Walters asked. His face looming above Tom.

'Yes, bloody marvellous,' Tom muttered. 'We lost Stanley – anyone else?'

'Two wounded – three including you, sir.'

'Good job then,' Tom said, relieved they'd got away so lightly. He'd wondered if any of the group would get back. 'Keep an eye out, corporal. They may come after us in motorboats.'

'Haven't seen anything,' he replied. 'I reckon you've given them enough to think about tonight, sir.'

'Well done to all of you,' Tom said, gave a gurgle of pain and passed out.

* * *

Tom woke aboard the British cruiser that had kept the tryst for them. His arm hurt like hell, but he was lying in a bed and he'd been patched up by someone.

'You've come back to us then, Captain Gilbert?' A young ensign was leaning over him, grinning.

'Seems like it,' Tom murmured groggily. 'What about the others?'

'A couple of your men had flesh wounds, but they've been treated. Your mission worked well and I've been told there was only one man lost – that is quite remarkable considering what you achieved, sir. Congratulations.'

'Could I have some water?' Tom asked, aware that his mouth tasted of ashes.

'I've been told just a sip.' The sailor lifted him up in his arms, putting a cup to his mouth. The water was tepid, but it eased his dry throat as he lay back.

'I shouldn't have taken him,' Tom mumbled, more to himself than the younger man. 'He wasn't up to it...'

'Sorry, sir. What was that?'

Tom lay back and closed his eyes. He'd allowed sentimentality to cloud his judgement, because Blackwall had shown loyalty, and because of that a life had been lost. It rankled in his mind and he knew it would linger for a long time. The mission had gone well despite his error, but Tom knew he'd made a mistake.

Lying back with his eyes closed, the thought came to him that at least he'd be going home after this. His arm wasn't going to work very well for a while. He could only hope he would recover full use after the wound recovered.

15

It was summer now in England, mid-August, and the sun was beating down outside, the fields of corn and barley beginning to ripen to rich gold in the heat. Life went on its usual rhythm: work, sleep, and more work – there was never much time for play these days. Three months had passed since Arthur's funeral, but the loss of him was still felt sharply at Blackberry Farm.

Pam looked at the small pile of letters that Artie had brought in, having met the postman as he was about to deliver. He was at the sink washing his hands as she picked them up and flicked through them.

'One from John,' she remarked smiling as she saw the familiar scrawl. 'I'll save that for a moment.' She glanced at the others and frowned. Three were just bills that she was expecting, but the fourth had an official look to it. 'I wonder what this is...' She stared at it, feeling coldness at her nape. 'Artie... will you open this for me?' Pam's stomach was clenching and she felt suddenly afraid. 'I can't...'

'What is it?' Artie came to take the envelope from her. 'It's from the War Office.' He ripped it open and read it quickly. 'Bloody hell!' he said in a tone of disbelief and looked at his mother. 'I'm sorry, Mum – but John has been lost—'

'What do you mean *lost*?' she asked, clutching at her chest as all the breath left her.

'He has been recommended for gallantry in action...' Artie said, sounding choked. 'He was on a raid of some kind and they came under fierce attack. The last they heard was that he had taken over control of the plane as the pilot had been killed – and the final glimpse of the crew was two men parachuting out before it went down in the sea... they haven't recovered them and believe they may have been picked up by enemy ships.' He turned the page. 'This happened a while back apparently...'

'Oh my God,' Pam said and sat down hard in Arthur's old chair. 'I suppose they don't know whether John was one of them...'

Artie tutted in disgust. 'As if they couldn't let us know sooner...' He went back to the letter. 'It is believed he did his best to keep the plane airborne for long enough for the two of them to get out...' Artie handed it to her. 'Read it yourself, Mum. I doubt they would be telling us about the medal if they thought he'd survived. This all happened weeks ago...'

Pam took the letter with shaking hands. She tried to read it, but the lines blurred in front of her eyes. 'I can't—' she whispered. 'It's too much, Artie. Just too much... my John... and Jonny. If he loses his dad as well as his mum – and he's only two...'

'I'm so sorry, Mum,' Artie said and came over to her chair. He knelt beside her. 'I know what hell you've been going through with Dad dying and now with this... I'm sorry I reacted the way I did when the will was read. I was just disappointed. I had such plans. I want to do more with my life than just run the farm.'

'I know, Artie,' Pam said. 'It is only right you should...' She sighed, putting aside her distress for a moment to think of him. Although her heart was full of sorrow at what might have happened to John, Artie was also her son and very dear to her, despite his moods. 'This isn't the right time, but I've been meaning to tell you something – I am giving the land the piggery is on to you. Not the pigs. We have to account for them in the farm records – but it's ten acres. You can buy more pigs – keep a couple of sows and breed up again – or you can plough it for crops...'

Artie sat back on his heels, looking at her face. 'Can you do that?' he asked. 'Dad's will—'

'Doesn't cover the piggery. That land was in my name, so I can sell it if I wish, but I want you to have it. I know it doesn't make up for the land you'd expected – but—'

'Are you sure?' Artie asked. He looked wary and still in shock over the contents of the letter they'd just read and yet there was a gleam of excitement beginning to shine in his eyes. 'I could start to build something with that land, Mum – but what about the girls? They only have their trust funds.'

'They will have my house in Chatteris one day—' Pam faltered. 'I was going to try to save a bit extra for John—' She choked back a sob as her grief overwhelmed her. Her eyes were filled with tears that ran silently down her cheeks.

'He could be one of the lucky ones that got out,' Artie said, but his tone wasn't convincing. 'He came back last time, Mum. They thought he was dead then, but he got through somehow...'

'I know.' She took out her hanky and wiped her cheeks. 'I shan't give up hope yet, Artie, but...' She shook her head, did such good luck strike twice? 'Artie, if John—' Pam broke off as the kitchen door opened and Lizzie rushed in. She was clutching a letter in her hand and clearly upset. Pam's heart went cold with fear. Not more bad news!

'It's from Tom,' Lizzie said breathlessly. 'He has been injured, but he's back in England now, in hospital in Portsmouth, and will be home in a week or two for a long leave.'

'Oh, Lizzie—' Pam's voice broke on a sob. 'Thank God he's alive. If he'd been killed as well—' She couldn't go on.

Artie turned to Lizzie as his mother wept. 'We've had news of John. He's missing, presumed lost again… in the sea this time.'

'Oh no! I am so sorry, Mum. That is awful news…' Lizzie went to her immediately, kneeling by her side. Artie had risen at her entry and now moved away, staring out of the kitchen window. 'Is there anything I can do?'

'We ought to let Lucy know,' Pam said. 'Does anyone have her address? John said she was being posted overseas…'

'I don't think any of us have it,' Lizzie replied. 'I could ask Annie if she knows. Jeanie says she hasn't been posted overseas yet.' Annie was a nurse, too, and had already served one foreign posting.

'Yes, Jeanie's sister might know where to send it,' Pam agreed. 'We must tell Lucy. John was intending to marry her…'

'I know—' Lizzie faltered. 'Jonny…?'

'Will stay with me,' Pam replied. 'Of course he will. Lucy couldn't be expected to take him on her own. We will look after him as a family.'

'Yes, we shall.' Lizzie looked thoughtful but said no more. 'Poor Lucy. I think she loves John very much. I'm not sure he loves her as he did Faith, but…'

'Yes, poor girl,' Pam echoed. 'I know how she feels, Lizzie. I lost Tom's father to the first war and I didn't think I would ever love again, but I did.'

'Oh, Mum,' Lizzie said and leaned up to hug her. Pam had

lost weight these past weeks and it showed in her face, as well as the clothes that now hung loosely on her. 'I wish I could help you.'

'There is nothing anyone can do for me,' Pam replied with a bleak look in her eyes. 'You can't bring them back... no one can.'

'We don't know John is dead,' Artie said roughly without turning. 'Don't give up on him. I will try to find out if there's any more news – in a few weeks.' He turned then, the emotion raw in his face. 'I won't believe it – not yet!'

'I think he is this time.' Pam looked from one to the other. She placed a hand over her heart. 'I believe he's gone. I feel it in here.' Pam stood up. 'I'm going upstairs for a while to be alone. Lizzie, if you've got time, could you finish the lunch for me? The pie will come out in twenty minutes and the veg needs to go on now.'

'Yes, of course. Don't worry, Mum. Susan has taken Arthur for a walk in his pram. I can serve lunch.' She looked at Artie. 'Are the land girls coming back for it?'

'Yes, they will be here by twelve. They didn't have much to finish when I left them to count the bullocks on the wash and fill the water trough from the river. We'll be harvesting next week; I shall need them now Jeanie can't do much physical stuff.' Jeanie had gone up to London to visit her parents and buy some bits and pieces for her baby, if she could find what she needed.

'You go up, Mum, and leave it all to me,' Lizzie told her. 'I'm not going into the salon today. I wanted a day off... after Tom's letter.'

'At least he is alive, Lizzie,' Pam said. 'We must be thankful for that – and Tom will get through. He always does.'

'I know. He told me not to worry but—' Lizzie faltered on a sob. 'I wish I could visit, but he says he'll be home soon.'

Pam nodded and went out. Her steps were laboured as she

walked upstairs to her bedroom, her feet as leaden as her heart. Arthur dead and buried; John disappeared, most likely dead, and Tom wounded. It was almost enough to break her.

* * *

Pam lay on the bed, her eyes closed against the tears that threatened. She heard the land girls come in and their laughter, abruptly stilled by something Artie said. She tried to sleep but found she was too restless; then, thinking of John's letter, which had arrived at the same time as she learned of his death, she sat up and opened it.

The letter was long and several lines had been censored; John's attempts to tell them where he was scored out many times, but she guessed their meaning. She thought he might have been somewhere in the Mediterranean. He'd written of his sadness at his father's death – so he'd got her letter – and his love for her and his family, his hopes for his son and he'd included a letter for Jonny, to be given to him one day if John didn't make it. He'd written something about wishing he could be with them and how much he disliked what he was doing, but it was scored through and she could only read a few words.

Pam felt a well of sadness inside her. John had been filled with enthusiasm at the start of the war, eager to do his duty, but he didn't enjoy killing innocent citizens when they'd bombed Germany, and she thought that when he wrote this letter, he'd known of something he had to do that he didn't truly wish to.

'Bugger them all!' Pam muttered as a rush of anger boiled inside her. Her lovely, gentle, kind son had been forced to do things he hated, instead of making a wonderful life for himself. He should have been doing the job he loved as a plasterer, married, looking after his son – watching little Jonny grow up. Now he never would.

Pam thought of Jonny and went along the corridor to his room. He was awake, playing with a rattle on a ribbon above his head, but he smiled and gurgled with pleasure when he saw her, trying to get up on his chubby little legs and falling back. Pam's throat caught and she went to pick him up, holding him close.

'Thank God I have you,' Pam whispered, her cheeks wet again. 'My little John come back to me...'

Jonny burbled with pleasure and squirmed in her arms. Pam carried him back to her room and placed him on her bed, where he rolled and kicked his legs with pleasure. She let him play on the big bed. In future, she would make sure that she had some playtime with him every day, as often as possible.

'You've lost your mummy and your daddy,' Pam told him, his blue eyes on her face in wonder. 'I've lost my husband and my son – but we've got each other. I'll be here for you as long as I can, my darling, and I know Lizzie and Tom will look after you if I'm gone – but until then, we're going to make the most of life.'

Pam smiled as he bounced up and down, crawling rapidly across the bed so that she had to launch herself to catch him and stop him falling. He laughed and she laughed. Pam knew she had to shrug off this mantle of sorrow that had clung to her for months, since she'd been told Arthur didn't have long. Jonny needed her, especially if his father never returned – and somehow Pam's heart was telling her he wouldn't this time. Last time she'd clung to hope but this... this seemed so final. John had given his life trying to save his friends; she was as sure of it as she could be.

16

Everyone had eaten and Lizzie was washing up the dishes when Pam came down. The land girls and Artie had gone to do the usual chores of feeding the animals and cleaning the sheds, before the evening milking.

'You get off home, Lizzie. I can finish this now.'

'It's all right. Susan took Arthur home for me and she wanted to feed him, so I let her.' Lizzie's eyes darkened. 'Artie told the girls and Susan walked in. She was upset, didn't want anything to eat so I asked her to take Arthur home and stay until I got there. She wanted to come up, but I thought you needed a little time alone.'

'Of course she is upset and Angela will be devastated when I tell her. She thought the world of John – and he was always good with her.'

'We mustn't give up hope yet, Pam.'

'It is different this time, Lizzie,' Pam replied. 'I know it – but I shan't let it break me. I have to look after Jonny and my family.'

'Yes, they need you, Pam.' Lizzie nodded, drying her hands as she finished the dishes. 'The girls you've got now are nice, respectful – especially Betty. I like her, Mum. She asked if there was anything she could do to help you, but I said you would ask...'

'Yes, they are nice girls,' Pam replied. 'Frances was a little difficult at times and Nancy was a pain, but it seems we've been lucky this time. Hopefully they won't go off and leave us too soon.'

'They seem to enjoy their work,' Lizzie said. 'Betty was really good with George. He wanted to milk the cows and she said he could help her, so he went off with them. I think he was a bit upset with the news, but he didn't know John well.'

'No. John's visits were few and far between,' Pam admitted. 'I'm glad he's here with us, Lizzie. He can be a big brother for Jonny as he gets older. I'm not sure Artie wants to go on living on the farm forever. He'll do his share of the work but... he wants to do other things. He can't do much for the moment, but in time he'll have his own business – and I don't mean the land he'll inherit when I've gone. He has plans, though he didn't tell me what he hopes for...'

'Jeanie told me he wants to build houses,' Lizzie replied. 'Artie has been talking to her father and he's got the idea that he can make some big money after the war from building homes, if he's willing to work.'

'Artie has always been a worker,' Pam said with a nod. 'Do you think he wants to go away – London, perhaps, when the war is over?'

'He wouldn't – what about the land?'

'It's not his until I die,' Pam said. 'If he can get some money together, he might invest elsewhere. At least I think he might...'

'He wouldn't leave you in the lurch?'

'No, he wouldn't do that,' Pam agreed. 'He will wait until the war is over and Tom is home. Tom is better with the land, we all know that – and after the war, we can employ men to help, with harvests anyway.'

Lizzie met her eyes. 'Are you happy with that, Pam?'

'Arthur wouldn't have liked it if Artie chooses London,' Pam said. She sighed. 'I don't have the right to stop him, Lizzie. He is my son. I love him and I want him to do whatever makes him happy. In a few years, George will leave school and he is mad about joining his cousins at the farm – well, at the moment, he is.' She smiled a little wearily. 'There's little Jonny too. He will inherit the house and money my John should have had.'

'Will he?' Lizzie frowned. 'You should ask the lawyer about that, Pam. Make sure he does...'

'Oh, he will, because John left a handwritten will with me. Everything goes to Jonny if he doesn't return. So he will get what would have been his father's.'

'Good...' Lizzie sighed. 'I don't know if Tom got my letter about Arthur. He is going to take it hard, Pam. Tom thought the world of him.'

'I know. It was felt on both sides, believe me. Artie may have got more land than Tom, but Arthur thought this land here was the best – and this house and yard goes with the home land, so it will be Tom's. I looked at the deeds and it is all part of a parcel of land bought in Arthur's grandfather's time and never separated when the house was built. I asked the lawyer to make sure and he confirmed it.'

'Does Artie know that?'

'Probably not. I suppose Arthur must have. I have no intention of telling Artie. We need things to settle, Lizzie – get back to normal.'

'Yes, we do,' Lizzie agreed. 'I'll go, Mum – unless you need me?'

'I'm all right, love,' Pam told her. 'I have to be. There's Jonny and George to think of – and we need to keep this family together. While Arthur was alive, we were good as a family, but I fear that bond has weakened. I don't want us to split apart, Lizzie. We need to be together to be strong.'

'Tom won't leave you to manage alone,' Lizzie replied. 'Once the conflict is over, he will be here every day – just as always.'

'Yes, I know I can rely on Tom,' Pam said with a sigh. 'Is it asking too much for Artie and Jeanie to stay?'

Lizzie shook her head. 'I don't know, Mum. Jeanie has been talking about her family a lot recently. Artie wasn't keen on her going to London without him, but she went...'

Pam inclined her head but didn't answer. Lizzie shrugged on her jacket, gave Pam a hug and left.

Pam filled the kettle. She had a feeling that Artie and Jeanie hadn't completely made up after the quarrel they'd had when he was so rude after the will was read. Pam hoped there wouldn't be a permanent rift between them over it. Artie had apologised to her, more than once. The first time it had been offhand, but today he'd meant it.

Pam was his mother and she'd forgiven him, because she loved him. She understood him, understood his moods. Artie had always been difficult, but he felt things so deeply and it was the turmoil of emotions inside him that made him angry and sometimes rude; he hadn't yet mastered them. Arthur had been a bit hot-tempered when he was young, but he'd mellowed with time and so would Artie. They both had good hearts.

It must be hard for Artie stuck in the same old job when his brothers were away fighting – she could see how he might want a different life. However, he could not be allowed to split the family. His brothers were risking their lives for King and country and Artie should be proud to be a part of such a family. She had done what she could to help him, but in return he must work hard and keep things together and Pam would see that he did… at least until the war was over and Tom was home.

17

Artie stood in the field, a feeling of satisfaction as he surveyed it, knowing it was his, watching the snorting pigs as they rootled in the ground, searching for food, with a wry humour. He'd resented having to cycle all this way to feed them and fill their water troughs, wondering why the hell his father had chosen to buy this land so far from their home fields. He couldn't wait for the latest brood of piglets to fatten sufficiently so they could sell them off – and he wasn't going to keep the sow his mother had offered and rebuild the herd. No, Artie had other plans for this land; it's closeness to the small town of Chatteris was attractive to him now. Eyeing the landscape, he reckoned he could build a small estate in here – big houses that would have lovely gardens and lawns. The land at the back was farmland and would never be built on, so they would have good views over the fens. It could be a money-spinner.

Of course he'd have to get some money together to build them first – but he thought Jeanie's father might be interested in coming in with him. Jeanie's brother, Terry Salmons, should have been the one to work in partnership with his father, but he'd lost a leg in the early stages of the war and was now unfortunately fit only for light work, mostly in the office.

Artie and Jeanie had popped up to see her family earlier in the year, just for a couple of days. Mr Salmons had taken Artie with him to his current building site and he'd been interested in watching the bricklayers; some of them were so fast, it was incredible, but they were only the older men, those who couldn't fight.

'After the war, we'll have the youngsters eager for jobs – and a big need for housing,' Mr Salmons had told Artie. 'I'm doing all right now, Artie, just ticking over, but I'm hoping to make a fortune once things get going again – when we can get all the bricks and materials we need. We're using recycled bricks for the moment and they have to be cleaned first – slows us down.'

'I reckon there will be a huge need for housing,' Artie had agreed with his father-in-law. 'Those prefabs they are putting up now won't last.'

'People like them – they are modern and don't have creepy-crawlies coming out of the walls, like the old tenements did.' Mr Salmons had laughed. 'I reckon Hitler did us a favour getting rid of some of those slums, boy – but after the war, the men will want decent homes for their families. We'll need to rebuild the country after the devastation, but we'll build it better.' He'd looked at his son, Terry, a glimmer of sadness in his eyes, and then back at Artie. 'I could do with a good man I can trust on the sites – maybe as a partner once you know the trade...' He'd sighed. 'My Terry looks after things in the office, God bless him, but he can't be out working with the men.'

'No. It was rotten luck for him – losing a leg like that. Still, you must be happy he came back – and I'm sure he looks after all the paperwork for you.'

'He does...' Mr Salmons had looked at him. 'I mean it, Artie –

I'll teach you the trade and you'll run some of the sites for me as a junior partner – it will be a three-way thing with Terry. Keep it in the family.'

Artie had laughed and said he had his land to think of, but it had given him pause. There was a busyness about the bricklayers that he liked; every day, their job was different. Bricks were laid, roofs were built with wood and then tiled, then the insides needed all kinds of things. It must be a varied job overseeing such work and to Artie it had a strong appeal. He'd known nothing but the land all his life, but that was no reason he couldn't do more – perhaps he could do both if he could persuade Mr Salmons that they should build on this land.

* * *

Artie's dreams were for the future. The war was still raging. It seemed likely that the threat of an invasion of Britain was over for the moment, but there were no signs yet that it would end any time soon. For a while now, Artie had fretted at being tied to the farm, but his father had been ill and needed him; he'd knuckled down and done all the work without complaint, but he'd expected that the fenland would be his when his father died.

He frowned, torn by regret at the loss of a father he'd loved. Artie had always wanted to impress his father, to make him proud, but it had always been Tom who did that... and that had rankled inside him. He couldn't help it, but he was a bit jealous of Tom, always had been. Now his father was gone and John was lost... his little brother he'd teased unmercifully. That hurt more than he could express and it made him angry. He swore and got cross, because he didn't know what else to do. He was frustrated and helpless, unable to make things right, and that festered inside him. Shaking his head, Artie thought about the future.

He wanted to be rich. He wanted a big house for his wife and children, a nice car, holidays, and the luxury of knowing he could afford these things. His plans were ambitious, but with the start that land would've given him, Artie had seen himself a wealthy man by his early forties. He still wanted those things but knew that it was going to be harder to get his foot on the ladder now.

His plans for this land would need to wait. For the time being, he would have to plough it and sow crops. A smile touched his mouth. At least the pigs had ensured it would be enriched for his first crop, which he decided should be part potatoes and part wheat. It wouldn't bring him a fortune, but once he could save a bit, there might be other opportunities to make some extra cash.

* * *

Jeanie was back from London when he returned home that evening. She smiled at him and Artie's heart lifted. He'd wondered if she would still be angry with him, but he could see he was forgiven. Jeanie had been really upset with him and it had given Artie a shock, because he hadn't known she could hold anger over something the way she had, insisting that he must make amends to his mother for his behaviour.

'After all she's been through,' Jeanie had told him. 'She is your mother, Artie. Of course your father had to look after her – it's because of the war. The farm has been losing money and he's had to keep it going – keep us all going – from his savings.'

Artie had felt awful when he realised that he must have hurt his mother. He'd dwelt on it sullenly, nursing his grievances, and a part of that was down to guilt. The farm profits had gone steadily down since the beginning of the war. Part of that was due to prices, part due to the difficulty of using all the land to the best advantage, and, Artie feared, part due to his lack of experience on the heavy land. And, of course, they'd lost good land to the Air Ministry when it was bought by compulsory purchase for the airfield. However, the crops had been down by nearly a quarter the first year and last harvest had been very poor on the home fields. Artie's father had made excuses about the weather and quality of the seed corn, but Artie had seen speculation in his face and he knew he'd had a word about it with Tom when he was home on leave.

It wasn't Artie's fault he didn't understand the heavy land; that had always been Tom's responsibility. Artie enjoyed the easy-working fenland with its rich black soil; he hated the cloying clay that clung to your boots and made each step a huge effort when it was wet. Normally, the potato crop was good on the home fields, but last year it had been scabby, as well as poor yielding. Artie wished he didn't need to plant it, but his father wouldn't hear of him letting it lie fallow.

Artie sat down at the kitchen table and accepted the tea and cake his mother provided. His eyes moved over Jeanie's face; she looked a bit tired but beautiful.

'How were your parents – and Terry?' he asked her.

'Terry is just the same. He doesn't much like what he does...' Jeanie looked towards Pam. 'I said he could spend his holiday week down here with us... if you wouldn't mind? Later in the year when they're not busy with the building.'

'No, of course not,' Pam replied. She hesitated, then, 'He can have John's room. I'm sure John wouldn't mind...'

Jeanie looked at Artie. 'Thank you, Pam. Terry has fond

memories of his stay and I think he would prefer to live in the country, but Dad wants him there in London.'

'Yes, I expect he does. We like our children to be around...' She glanced at Artie.

'I'm going up to unpack,' Jeanie said, giving Artie a meaningful look. 'I bought something for you...'

He got up obediently and followed her upstairs to their room. When he entered, he saw that Jeanie had already unpacked most of her stuff. She looked at him anxiously.

'Is your mum all right?' she asked as soon as Artie closed the door. 'She's had so much to bear with losing your father – and now John is missing again...'

'She is upset but putting on a brave face,' he said. 'I have made it up with her, Jeanie – and I'm sorry I was such a pig.' He moved towards her, putting his arms around her, and kissing her.

Jeanie lifted her face for his kiss.

'I've missed you,' he said. 'Am I forgiven?'

'Of course. I wasn't angry, just upset. Your mum looks so frail... no, that's not right... She looks sad, as if all the life has gone out of her eyes.'

'It's losing John on top of losing Dad,' Artie replied. 'It knocked the stuffing out of me, too, when we heard. I still can't believe it – he's my little brother...'

'They said he was missing before but he came home. Perhaps he will this time?'

Artie shook his head. 'Mum doesn't think so. His plane crashed into the sea and he'd taken over as pilot after the pilot was killed. Only two crew got out, Jeanie. Sounds pretty final to me.'

'Oh, poor Pam – poor little Jonny. He hardly knew his father.'

'It is rotten luck all round,' Artie said and drew a sighing breath. 'I wouldn't want it to happen to our child, Jeanie.' He looked down into her face. 'You seem a bit tired, love. Are you all right?'

'Yes, a little. The train was late arriving at King's Cross. Apparently, there was some damage to the line that had to be repaired...' Jeanie yawned. 'Then, we had a scare – low-flying planes. We all thought the train was under attack, because we thought they were dive-bombing us, but they turned out to be British.' Jeanie gave a little shudder. 'Someone said they were probably foreign pilots joyriding... it happens near where she lives.'

'Yes, I read about a young Polish pilot who got killed flying under low bridges,' Artie said. 'Daredevils, I suppose – but I hope they didn't give you too much of a fright.' He placed a loving hand over her bump and Jeanie laughed.

'Nothing unsettles him,' she said and turned to the bed, taking a package from her suitcase. 'I brought you a new shirt, Artie – to say sorry for being so stroppy before I went away. Mum said I shouldn't have been cross with you because you were entitled to be disappointed after your father promised you the land and then changed his mind.'

'I was disappointed, but I've accepted it. Mum can't live on thin air...'

'No, she can't, but you had a lot of plans.'

'I did – and do,' Artie said. 'Mum gave me the piggery land. It is just outside Chatteris and I reckon I could turn it into a good housing estate after the war. Your dad might want to be a part of it...'

Jeanie looked thoughtful. 'He was saying he hoped you might think about his offer. He knows you can't leave the land now but... when Tom gets back?'

'I could do both maybe,' Artie said vaguely. 'I haven't thought it all through yet, but...' He looked at Jeanie. 'Tom and me – we don't see eye to eye on a lot of stuff, mainly the land. He has his ways and I have mine. When Dad was around it was fine, but now... and with John gone...' He shook his head at his own thoughts.

'Would you consider moving to London?' Jeanie asked, staring at him in surprise. 'I thought you loved it here?'

'I enjoy the work on the fenland but...' Artie shrugged. 'I'll see how things work out, but I want a better life, Jeanie. Dad gave his life to the land and Mum has done the same. What have they ever done but work?'

'Pam always seemed happy – or she was...'

'It isn't what I want or intend for us. There is a bigger world out there, Jeanie. I've never been further than once to York on a school trip. I couldn't take you anywhere fancy for our honeymoon, but when the war is over – and it has to end – we'll go places: here and abroad perhaps.'

'Go abroad?' Jeanie looked at him in surprise. 'I'm not sure I'd like that, Artie. Perhaps Scotland or Cornwall... but not France or Italy...' She made a wry face. 'Don't fancy it; all ancient monuments in Rome – and they eat frogs' legs in France.'

Artie laughed. 'There are wonderful things to see. I'd love to go on a big liner to America and see something of that country. The land of opportunity...'

'Gangsters and Hollywood,' Jeanie said and wrinkled her nose. 'If you go there, you will go alone, Artie. I'm not coming...'

'Little mouse,' Artie teased. 'Where's the fire, ginger nut?'

'You'll soon see if you call me that,' Jeanie told him, her eyes sparking with amusement and relief that they were on good terms again. 'It's just that I'm happy here. Perhaps one day I'll enjoy a holiday in the sun somewhere, but not yet. I've got a baby to bring up.'

18

Lucy stared dully at the letter. She hadn't recognised the writing when it was given to her with others from home and, on opening it, she'd stared at the words in disbelief. John's mother had written to her, to tell her that he'd been shot down at sea, was missing, believed dead.

'No. No! I don't believe it,' Lucy whispered as the colour drained from her face. Surely it couldn't be true. She would have felt it if John had been killed; she was sure she would.

She read the letter again and gave a little sob. Lucy felt a great stab of pain in her heart. How could he be dead when she felt he was alive? Tears stung her eyes, trickling down her cheeks. She'd had so little time with him. His proposal had come out of the blue and Lucy had known that a part of his reason for asking was his concern for his son.

'Mum loves him and he will be cared for,' he'd told Lucy after they'd left the farm after that last, less than successful, visit. 'But she is a bit too old to have the responsibility of a young child. She won't be able to do the things he needs when he is growing up...'

Lucy thought Pam was still young. Quite a bit younger than her husband, and quite capable of bringing up a child but she hadn't said as much to John. She'd loved him too much to risk losing him. If the reason he'd turned to her, after the death of his first love Faith, was his son, then she would gladly accept it. For a while, she'd thought he might be lost to his grief forever, but he'd fought it and won. Surely he couldn't have survived that personal battle only to die in a crashed plane?

Lucy felt the pain in her heart drive sharper. She couldn't bear the idea that John was gone... she would never see him again. It wasn't true. It couldn't be.

'Hi, Lucy.' The door of the billet she shared with two other nurses opened and Shirley Grant entered. Shirley had travelled out with her on the ship and they'd become good friends. 'I'm beat.' Shirley kicked off her shoes and flopped down on her bed, closing her eyes. For a few moments, she was silent, then, 'Are you coming to the dance on Saturday? The army boys have set it up, but there might be some fly boys there... You never know, you might even see your fiancé – stranger things have happened.'

Lucy tried to strangle the sob that welled up suddenly but couldn't.

Shirley jerked up and looked at her, seeing the tears on her cheeks. 'What's wrong, Lucy?'

'I had some bad news,' Lucy replied. 'John is missing – his plane went down. He might be...' She couldn't finish the sentence.

Shirley was off the bed instantly. She came to sit on the edge of Lucy's and slipped an arm round her shoulders. 'That's rotten luck, love,' she said. 'But you don't know for sure, do you?'

'No...' Lucy hesitated. 'I don't feel he is gone, but his mother says it seems certain that he couldn't have got out in time...'

'She can't know,' Shirley said fiercely. 'Keep your head up, love. A lot of men turn up again. All you can do is pray.'

'I shall,' Lucy assured her. She sniffed hard. 'We were going to be married as soon as we both got leave...'

'Maybe you still will be,' Shirley told her and Lucy nodded, but the more her friend tried to give her hope, the less likely it seemed that John could have escaped almost certain death. 'You shouldn't sit here and mope,' Shirley said. 'Come for a drink this evening – and the dance on Saturday. You don't have to dance with a bloke. It's just for a bit of company.'

'I'll see,' Lucy said, standing up. 'I'm going for a walk. I'm on duty again in a couple of hours so I can't go with you this evening, but... I might come on Saturday, just for the company.'

Lucy left the billet, which was just a temporary hut near the field hospital. They were stationed on a beautiful island, not too far from the sea. Their work didn't change wherever they were, the nursing of the sick and dying never got any easier, but there were moments when they saw a patient feel relief for whatever they had done, and that was when it all became worthwhile. Working in such an idyllic place was a privilege. Lucy had hoped John might be stationed here on Cyprus, one of the most strategic of British outposts, but she hadn't received a letter from him since she'd been out here yet, because any mail he'd sent would go to England for redirection – and perhaps now she never would.

* * *

Lucy couldn't sleep that night. Her thoughts were of John, their plans for the future and his family. Was it her duty to return and take on the responsibility of John's son? Lucy felt it might be what he would wish, but she did not feel able to bring Jonny up alone, and she was sure John's mother would fight to keep him. No, for the time being she was needed here and that was as far ahead as she could think, but her thoughts kept her restless.

She could hear the planes taking off at regular intervals and guessed there must be a raid or something going on for so many planes to be leaving the base at the same time. The drone as they went overhead made her place a pillow over her head, her tears wetting her cheeks. How many of those young airmen would make it back alive?

When she got up the next morning, she was feeling tired, but she washed in cool water and that refreshed her. The sun was shining overhead and she could hear someone singing. It was a man and he sounded joyous.

Leaving her room, she crossed the compound to the hospital, a mixture of wooden buildings and large tents. More permanent buildings were still being constructed but the tents were cool and they served a purpose. She ducked inside the open flap and went in, her eyes moving over the lines of beds, all of which were presently occupied, though not all with wounded men. Some patients had simple things like a case of tonsilitis and another an emergency appendectomy.

'Ah, there you are, Nurse Lucy,' Sister Jane said, smiling at her. 'I am going to need you today. We have to squeeze another four beds in... Yes, I know we are already full, but it has to be done. We have had some badly wounded men brought in.'

'I suppose we could put two at the other end, sister,' Lucy replied, her practical mind taking over. 'And we might put one where your table is... and... on the end there. If we move those two beds closer together, it could just fit.'

'Yes, I think that might do it,' sister said. 'I'll have my table moved outside. I will just have to bring the paperwork in if it rains... which, thankfully, it doesn't often.' She beamed at Lucy. 'Clever girl. I knew you would help me settle it.'

Lucy blushed. Sister Jane was so pleasant to work for, much nicer than the senior nurse at her old hospital. She was happy that she'd made the transfer and enjoyed her work.

Pushing her personal fears and grief to a small corner of her heart, Lucy began her first round of the morning, offering water and medicines to the men. She knew them all well, because most had been here a few days, some longer. From here, they would eventually transfer on to a hospital ship heading home, apart from the appendicitis and tonsilitis cases, who would return to duty after a rest.

* * *

It was halfway through the morning when the new cases were brought in. Three were army men, one with a broken leg, two with wounds to their heads, both unconscious, and another with thick bandages covering his head and face. He had been in a plane that caught fire and was badly burned, though lucky to be alive, so the doctors said.

Sister listened to the doctors' instructions and then called her nurses to her, assigning two new patients to each of her two nurses. 'Nurse Ruth, I want you to take the two beds at the end with the head wounds. Nurse Lucy, you have the broken leg and the burns case. Corporal West won't trouble you much with that leg for a while – but the other... we will have to watch him carefully. The doctors said he was fished out of the sea more dead than alive and is in a bad way.'

Lucy nodded, her heart catching at the wounded man's plight. 'Do we know their names, sister?'

'Yes, the officer with the broken leg is Lieutenant Ken West and Flight Captain Jack Rossiter is our burns case. You know the general rule. We address them by their rank, unless they ask to be called by their first names.'

'Yes, sister...' The nurses nodded obediently, though most of the patients soon begged to be called by their names.

'And I am going to cancel your leave this weekend, Nurse Lucy. I am very sorry, but I want Captain Rossiter to have the same nurse constantly. You will, of course, have time to sleep, but I am going to ask for your dedication, nurse. He must have constant reassurance once he awakes and that means he needs the same voices around him – at least until those bandages come off and we know if he will regain his sight.'

'Were his eyes badly burned?' Lucy asked in concern.

'Yes, I believe so,' Sister Jane said sadly. 'I always feel it is one of the most frightening injuries to receive. He will need a lot of comforting and understanding.'

Lucy nodded her assent. For a young man who had been strong and confident enough to fly a plane in combat, the terror of losing his sight would be so encompassing and bewildering, his whole life turned upside down. She'd seen men crying for the loss of a limb, or, when very ill, for their mother, but only one other patient who had lost his sight. He had been close to despair when he was sent home to a life he did not wish to contemplate.

'I wish they'd just let me die, nurse,' he'd told Lucy before he left. 'It would be better for everyone if I'd died.'

She had felt so sorry for him. Now she had another patient who might potentially be in the same trouble. All she could do was be patient and kind and pray that the sight would gradually return to him...

* * *

Lucy sank into her bed that night, too exhausted to think of anything other than her own weariness. Two extra patients had kept her busy the whole day and it wasn't until she was finally between the sheets that she had time to think of John.

'Please let him be alive...' she whispered, but her eyelids were heavy and she was asleep within seconds.

19

'Tom...' Lizzie let out a shriek of relief and delight as she saw her husband getting out of a car near their house. It was early September now, but still pleasantly mild. She had been about to walk home from the farm to her house at the end of the lane, but she ran towards him, her heart beating wildly with the happiness of seeing him. As he stood and looked at her, she stopped, feeling a rush of concern as she saw his arm was in a sling and there were signs of fatigue in his face. 'Tom, my love – are you in dreadful pain?'

'It isn't as bad now, Lizzie,' Tom said and smiled. 'Trouble is, my arm doesn't work that well yet. I'm told I should get the use of it back if I exercise and do as I'm told...' He grimaced. 'At least I'm home for a long leave. I was due one anyway, but now it may be a bit longer.'

'Good,' Lizzie said and smiled up at him. 'It's time you had a rest, Tom.' She nodded to the young soldier who had brought him home; he grinned and took Tom's kitbag from the car, depositing it by the door of their home. 'Thank you.'

'Thanks, corporal,' Tom said. 'Enjoy your leave, soldier. You've earned it.'

'Thanks to you,' the young soldier said and saluted, before getting into the car and driving away.

'One of your men?' Lizzie asked, going on ahead to unlock the door and lift Tom's heavy bag into the kitchen. She was filling the kettle when he came up behind her, putting his left arm about her and nuzzling her neck. Turning, she put both arms around him, lifting her face for his kiss; it was long and sweet and ended with a sigh from Tom. 'Tired, love?'

'Bloody knackered,' Tom said. 'Sorry, Lizzie. Everything is exhausting at the moment. I want to sweep you up and make love to you, but I can't...'

'You'll get better,' Lizzie promised, stroking his cheek with one finger. 'Don't worry about anything, Tom...' She drew a deep breath as he sat down in the rocking chair by the range. 'There is one thing – I know your mum wrote about John, but I am not sure you got the letter?'

'Is John hurt?' Tom asked, looking concerned. 'I know about Dad but haven't had any letters for a while...' He saw Lizzie's face and flinched. 'Confirmed?'

'They say his plane was hit during a mission and went down,' Lizzie said. 'Two men got out, but they don't think John did, because he'd taken over as the pilot and he flew the plane out of sight. But they don't know; he wasn't seen to eject...'

'If he got out, he might have been picked up by an enemy ship,' Tom said. 'If he was, he'll be a prisoner of war and we won't know for a long time...'

'Your mum is convinced he is dead,' Lizzie told him.

Tom nodded, sighing wearily. 'Where is Arthur?'

'Susan took him out in his pushchair. She is getting ready for college and says that looking after Arthur helps her relax.

She will be back soon, because she has a date this evening. One of the officers from the base is taking her to Ely to the pictures.'

Tom arched his eyebrows. 'And Mum allows that?'

'Susan is eighteen, Tom. Some of her friends are married – and one has a baby. I think that is why Susan is so good with Arthur. She likes playing at being a mother but can give him back when he starts grizzling.'

'Does he do that a lot?' Tom asked, watching contentedly as Lizzie moved about the kitchen. She brought a tray of tea to the table and they sat down together to enjoy it. 'I miss this a lot when I'm away, Lizzie.'

'I made these this morning...' Lizzie offered him a tray of almond and honey cakes. 'I managed to buy some honey from the market in March – and I've still got a couple of bottles of almond flavouring, because I know it is your favourite.' She smiled as he took one and ate it, clearly enjoying the flavour. 'Arthur is still teething, so yes, he does cry a bit... a lot sometimes, but, bless him, I expect it hurts.'

'Bound to,' Tom said. 'Poor little chap. Still, I can help with him sometimes now I am home.' He frowned as he eased his right arm from its sling and clenched his fist. 'There aren't many jobs I can do on the farm just yet. Might drive the tractor, but nothing strenuous, I'm afraid – and I wouldn't be much good at milking...'

'Don't even think about it, Tom. Not yet. You need a rest first.'

'Yes, I know,' Tom said and smiled at her. 'I can't do much else and it took it out of me this time.'

'I won't ask how you got it, but I believed you were training new recruits rather than fighting, Tom?'

'I was asked to replace someone at the last minute,' Tom replied, frowning. 'It made sense. I'd trained the men and there really wasn't any reason why I shouldn't go with them – but I was unlucky and this arm is the result.'

'I'm just glad to have you home,' Lizzie said and passed him the plate of cakes. 'I know you all have to do your duty, Tom.'

'Not for a couple of months, or maybe a bit more,' he returned with a laugh. 'I think that may be the longest time we've had together since we married.'

'Yes...' She laughed, happiness at seeing him bubbling over. 'You were off soon after our wedding and you've been back and forwards ever since.' She reached for his left hand and held it, but whatever she intended to say was lost as the door opened and Susan came in, manoeuvring the pushchair over the doorstep. She was too busy for a minute to realise her brother was there.

'He has been really good, Lizzie. Mrs Fawks was— Tom!' Susan gave a cry of delight and rushed towards him, then stopped as she saw his arm hanging limply. 'How are you? When did you get back?'

'I'm getting better – and about half an hour or so,' Tom said with a grin. 'You look well, Susan. Thank you for helping Lizzie with Arthur.'

'I enjoy it,' Susan said and laughed. 'If I don't get on well at college, I can always marry and have a baby...'

'Mum would have something to say about that – and you have to find a husband first,' Tom said, teasing her.

'Oh, I've had offers,' Susan said airily and giggled as Tom's brows went up. 'Don't worry, Tom. I have every intention of becoming a teacher. Marriage and babies can wait until I'm as ancient as you...'

'If this arm was in working condition, I'd give you a spanking,' Tom said and she laughed in delight.

'No, you wouldn't, because you're my big brother and you

protect me,' Susan said. 'I'm going home to get ready now, Lizzie. Are you coming to see Mum, Tom?'

Lizzie had lifted her son from the pushchair and was sitting with him on her knee. She gave him a sip of tea and he wanted more, gurgling, and laughing up at her.

'I'll come in a few minutes,' Tom said. He watched her leave and smiled at Lizzie. 'Are you going to feed him? Can I help?'

'Yes. He can feed himself but is apt to throw it on the floor if I don't stay with him. Sit in the rocking chair and I'll bring his food. I've got some rice pudding with softened dried apricots. Just little squashy bits I've mashed with a fork. He loves his fruit and the rice.'

'Is he completely weaned now?' Tom asked, marvelling at the size of his son, who seemed to have grown such a lot. He was now a few days away from his second birthday and could walk well and run too, though he sat down suddenly sometimes.

'Yes, has been for a while, though he likes a cup of milk, and weak tea as well.' Lizzie smiled and watched as Tom settled himself. She carried Arthur's high chair over and adjusted it to the right height, then she fetched the food she'd prepared earlier, stirring it round with a spoon.

'Mum mum...' Arthur burbled. 'Dada...' He made a grab for the spoon and promptly emptied it over himself. So Tom went back to helping him, despite his noisy protests.

Lizzie smiled as she watched. It was always a messy job feeding a small child, but Tom was enjoying it, and if rather a lot of dribbling and dropped food was going on, what did it matter?

She turned away, leaving them to enjoy themselves while she started to prepare the evening meal. She had bought some stewing lamb, which had a lot of fat on it, but would be tasty when cooked. She chopped her precious onion, which she'd been lucky to get, some carrots, and a turnip, then browned her meat, before adding it to a saucepan and topping up with the vegetables and water with a crumbled Oxo cube. She placed it on the range to bring to the boil and then simmer. When it was nearly cooked, she would add potatoes to the mix and it would be delicious – one of Tom's favourites. She'd bought it specially when he'd rung to let her know he was being released from hospital. It should have celery in it too, but there was none to be had yet.

At certain times of the year, fresh vegetables were plentiful locally, but at others, Lizzie liked to visit a market once a week, either in March or in Ely. Some things were almost impossible to buy these days, like bananas, which had to be imported and were rarely seen. However, it was possible that something nice might get through and always worth a trip to see what was about. This week, Lizzie had bought two large tins of red salmon, which had come from Canada – a real treat, which she'd shared with Pam.

'Well, I'm not sure whether he ate more than he dribbled down his bib,' Tom's voice brought Lizzie's head round. 'But it has all gone.'

'That's lovely,' Lizzie said, smiling as she saw Tom wiping the mess away from Arthur's chin. 'He's done well – he must like his daddy feeding him. Sometimes, I find more goes on the floor than in his mouth...' She went to pick Arthur up and discovered his nappy needed changing. Mostly he asked for the potty, but there were still accidents. 'I'll just take him upstairs, Tom. Why don't you pop up to your mum's now? She's been feeling so sad and unhappy with the news about John. Supper won't be ready for a couple of hours.'

'If you're sure?'

Lizzie nodded and he watched as they went out of the room. Lizzie heard him leave as she reached Arthur's bedroom and lay him down to change him. A feeling of happiness spread through her. Tom was home and for her everything was just as it should be, the war and all the sadness it brought forgotten for the moment.

* * *

'Tom love.' Pam stood up as her eldest son walked in and opened her arms. She hugged him, careful not to press on his right arm. 'I'm so glad you're back, love.' She gave a little strangled cry of pleasure and pain. 'I've needed you...'

'Mum.' Tom drew back and looked into her face, seeing the new lines and the sadness in her face. 'I am so sorry I wasn't here when Dad went – and you've had worrying news about John, too.'

Tears trickled down Pam's face, but she scuffed them away. 'Your dad went peacefully, love – in his sleep. I miss him terribly, but I feel he is still with me in this house. Sometimes I turn to talk to him and I'm surprised when he isn't there.' She gave a little sob. 'But John has gone. We've lost him, Tom.' She placed a hand on her heart. 'I feel it in here.'

Tom wanted to comfort her, but he knew as he looked into her face that it would be useless to try to persuade her that his brother might still be alive. He said the only thing that came to his mind, 'John will never be gone while Jonny lives, Mum.'

She stared at him, her eyes opening wide, and then burst into tears. 'Oh, Tom,' she said. 'I've been hurting so bad, but I know you're right. We're so lucky to have him. I thank God for him every day...'

'We're lucky to have him and Arthur,' Tom said. 'They are the new generation, Mum. I just hope we can get this war over so that we can make it a life worth having again.'

'It must end soon,' she said. 'If you read the newspapers, it seems there is some good news for the Allies.' Pam looked at her son. 'We shan't lose it now, shall we?'

'No, Mum. We're winning, on all sides, believe me. It might not seem like it and I know the news reports can be dire – ships sunk and losses; but this year has been good; we triumphed in Sicily, and Mussolini has been deposed... There are a lot of small victories that never get into the papers, and they aren't having it all their own way. No matter what some doomsters would like you to believe.'

'You'd know about that, Tom,' Pam said, looking meaningfully at his limp arm. 'What do the doctors say – will it mend?'

'Yes, in time, though perhaps not quite as it was, but I'll exercise it and find ways to manage.'

'This rotten war...' Pam sighed. 'It has taken too much, Tom. Not just from us but from lots of other local families, too. Jimmy Faux was killed last month and Keith Roberts has been taken prisoner by the Japanese. I suppose he should be safe...'

Tom knew both men well, had gone to school with them. 'I'd hardly call it safe as a Japanese prisoner of war,' Tom said. 'Poor devils have a rotten time of it, from what I've heard.'

'Artie said John might be a prisoner of the Germans...' Pam looked at Tom. 'Would they look after him if they took him injured from the sea?'

'Yes. There are rules about the treatment of prisoners – but I don't think the Japanese follow those rules. I believe the Germans might, though not the Gestapo... I doubt John would come up against them, though – not where he must have been...'

'Do you know where he was?' Pam looked at him, suddenly alert.

'Not for certain, but I think he might have been somewhere near the Greek islands, Mum. I'm guessing he was based in

Cyprus; he thought it his likely posting – well, hoped it might be really, and I know our people attacked a German convoy earlier this year...'

Pam frowned. 'John can swim... might he have reached one of those islands? Is it possible, Tom?' For a moment, hope flared in her eyes.

'I don't know, Mum,' Tom said. 'Some of them are uninhabited and others have very small populations – he might be on one of them, but... we can only hope.'

She shook her head. 'No, he's gone. I shouldn't deceive myself.'

Tom would have said more, but before he could think of an answer, Susan entered the kitchen. She had changed into a light tweed skirt with a white blouse and a blue cardigan and done her hair up in a French pleat at the back.

'You look nice, love,' Pam said and smiled at her. 'Where are you off to now?'

'We're going to the pictures in Ely,' Susan said as she heard a knock at the door. 'That will be Pete, Mum. I'll be home straight after the film ends so don't worry.'

'I know...' Pam smiled as Susan went out. She turned to Tom as the door closed behind her. 'She is so grown up now. I'd be worried, except that it is a different boyfriend every other week. She is just enjoying herself...'

'Susan is a sensible girl,' Tom said. 'I always thought she might...' He shook his head, because the friendship between Susan and Terry Salmons had come to nothing, though he'd suspected his sister had feelings for the injured soldier. 'Where is everyone?'

'Artie is working down the fens. The land girls and George are milking – and Angela is at a friend's house. They do their homework together, one day here, one day there, and we feed them. It works well enough and I can't refuse, Tom. Angela is going to miss Susan when she goes away – she needs friends.'

'Yes, of course she does,' Tom said as they heard a wail from upstairs. 'That must be Jonny. I fed Arthur his tea; I could try to feed Jonny, if you fetch him down. Not sure I could manage the stairs and him...'

'You sit down and get comfortable, and I'll get him,' Pam said. 'He likes a nap in the afternoons and it gives me time to get on a bit.' She smiled at him. 'You can have a go at feeding him if you like. I've got a nice egg for his tea.'

20

After Tom had gone home, Pam spent half an hour or so playing with her grandson. The vegetables were gently simmering on the range and she enjoyed this time with Jonny before the others came in.

Jeanie was the first to arrive. She'd walked to Sutton to the local butcher and her cheeks were pink from the mixture of autumn sunshine and a gentle breeze.

'You must be exhausted walking all that way and back,' Pam said, taking her heavy basket from her. 'Why didn't you let someone take you in the car?'

'Because it was a lovely afternoon, and I went to see a friend and had a cup of tea with her,' Jeanie said, smiling. 'Mr Goodman had some pork chops for us, Pam, and I got some streaky bacon and a nice big slice of ox liver.'

'Gosh, you did well,' Pam said, looking in the basket. 'What is in this box?'

'A fresh cream sponge,' Jeanie said and laughed as she saw Pam's disbelieving face. 'Mr Thornton said it was a special order, but the person who asked for it didn't collect it, so he let me have it. I thought it would be a little treat for us.'

'Thorntons always had lots of delicious cakes before the war,' Pam told her. 'They used to come round with them in a basket and I sometimes bought one to save making them, but they don't do it now.'

'They can't get enough petrol to do their delivery round,' Jeanie said. 'Blooming rationing! Still, I suppose if the government didn't ration stuff, there wouldn't be enough to go round. Mr Goodman said they might be easing the rationing soon, now that more merchant ships are getting through.'

'Well, that cake will make a nice change,' Pam said. 'All I've been able to bake recently is fatless sponges and jam tarts. It is impossible to get almond or vanilla essence at the moment, and I don't know when I last saw any dried fruit, though Lizzie got some apricots.'

'I managed to get some carraway seeds from the co-op,' Jeanie said. 'I love your seed cake, Mum.'

'Oh, that's good. I can make one this weekend.' Pam smiled at her. 'You are a good girl, Jeanie. Sit down and have a cup of tea; the others will be in soon.'

'Yes, I know,' Jeanie smiled. 'Artie hasn't come back yet?'

'Not yet, love. You know what he's like when he's working down the fens on his own; he forgets the time and just keeps going until he's finished whatever he is doing.'

'I think he is hoeing his early potatoes,' Jeanie said. 'At least that was the plan – though he also wanted to start cutting the barley.'

'Is that ready yet?' Pam asked as she checked the rabbit pie she had cooking in the oven. The smell that wafted towards them was delicious. 'A bit early?'

'He thought that five-acre bit might be ready; it went in early and he was going to test it and see...'

Jeanie accepted her cup of tea and Pam hesitated, then, 'Shall we taste the cake – just a tiny slice each?'

'Why not?' Jeanie smiled. 'Just to see if it is as good as it looks...'

* * *

Everyone arrived back together. Artie came in, smiling as he saw Jeanie on her knees playing with Jonny, who had a smear of jam and cream on his mouth and cheek. He went to wash his hands at the sink and was just drying them when they heard laughter and George burst in, followed by the two land girls, all chattering away.

'Tom is home,' Pam told Artie as she took the pie from the oven and started to serve. George gave a shout of joy, but Artie just nodded. Jeanie removed the potatoes from the hob, drained them and started to mash them with margarine, a pinch of salt, pepper and a drop of milk. She whisked them with a fork, beating them until they were lovely and creamy and then ladled them onto the plates Pam was loading with slices of her pie.

The kitchen was filled with delicious smells of food as the plates, filled with pastry melting in rich gravy, tender chunks of meat, potatoes, peas and baby carrots, were served up.

'Oh, this is delicious, Pam,' Betty said, rolling her eyes. 'I didn't get food like this at my last posting. I don't know how you manage it.'

'Artie is good at shooting game of all kinds in season,' Pam told her. 'We are very lucky. The fields near the river are teeming with rabbits in spring and summer. Of course, we're not the only ones after them these days, but Artie is up early in the morning and that's the best time to get them.'

'Poor rabbits,' Olive murmured, but it didn't stop her eating her portion of the tasty pie.

Betty was a strong, outgoing young woman with brassy blonde hair – out of a bottle! – as she always informed folk. Olive was dark and thin but wiry with a narrow face and serious expression. Both of them were proving to be good workers.

'Did you cut the winter barley?' Pam asked Artie when she was sitting down, having served everyone else first.

'No. It needs a couple of days longer. We had a bit of rain in the night, so I shall leave it to dry. They say no more rain for a week, so I want to start cutting as soon as I can.' He ate a mouthful of pie. 'Maybe Tom can give me a hand with the harvest now he's back.'

'He won't be able to do much,' Pam said. 'His arm is worse than I expected. Ask him though, because he says he's going to find ways to do things.'

'I'll walk down after this,' Artie replied, swallowing some mashed potato. 'Do you want to come, Jeanie – have a chat with Lizzie? We might walk down to the pub. They were out of beer again yesterday, but Don said he might get a delivery today.'

'A pub with no beer.' Betty gave a burst of hearty laughter. 'I hope they got their delivery. I'm meeting someone this evening and we intended going for a pint.'

'What about you, Olive?' Pam asked the other land girl. 'Any plans for the evening?'

'No. I'll just read a book or something...'

'You can keep me company if you like,' Pam suggested. 'I've got some material I'm using to make curtains for my bedrooms – you can help if you fancy it?'

'I'd like that,' Olive said. 'I used to help my gran make her curtains.' She took a sip of water from the glass at her side. 'I'd like to make a new dress for myself, but I'm not good at cutting it out...'

'I'll help you with that,' Pam offered. 'Have you got the material?'

'Not yet. I'm going to buy it on my half-day off.'

'You should go into Ely on Thursday, if you can be spared, Olive. You might get a bargain from the market. I often buy from the man with the remnants. He has some good-quality stuff, but not always enough for what you need – though it's usually sufficient for a dress.'

'I don't need that much. I want a sheath dress and they only take a couple of yards or so.'

'Sleeveless?' Pam asked and Olive confirmed. 'You will probably need less if there is a good width, but two is enough. You're not as big as me...'

'If I've got any over, I'll make a bolero to match.'

'Yes, that would be nice,' Pam agreed. 'I've got a lot of bits and pieces left over. Sometimes you can use them to make inserts or bindings.'

Olive nodded her agreement.

Artie and Jeanie had finished their meal. Jeanie carried the used dishes to the sink, but Pam told her to leave them.

'I'll see to them, Jeanie. You get off with Artie if you like.'

'I'm just going to freshen up,' Artie said and the pair of them went off upstairs.

'I'll help with the dishes, Pam,' Betty said. 'I've got time before I meet my fella.'

Pam accepted her help. Olive picked up some dishes and brought them to the sink and then sat down to read a women's magazine as Pam washed and Betty wiped. When the dishes were dried and placed on the long table, Olive got up and carried them to the tall oak dresser, setting the china out on the shelves. Pam was drying her hands. Then she went through to the front room and came back with a parcel done up in brown paper. She opened it on the kitchen table, revealing several lengths of a blue floral pattern with a nice silky feel.

'That's pretty,' Olive said, coming to look. 'Yes, that will make lovely curtains, Pam.'

Pam smiled at her and got her tape measure out. 'If you help me tack the hems, then I'll get the sewing machine out and we'll have them done in no time... but you needn't help unless you like?'

'Oh, I'd like to,' Olive said and took up a length of the material. 'Now how long do you want them and how wide do you want your hem?'

The door opened then and Angela entered. She threw down her school satchel and her jacket and looked at her mother. 'Is there anything to eat, Mum?' she asked in a plaintive voice. 'Jill's mum gave us bread and dripping for tea and it made me feel sick so I didn't eat it.'

'Oh dear,' Pam said and laughed. 'Not everyone is as lucky as us, love. Never mind, you can have a piece of the cake that Jeanie bought. It's in the larder – but only a small piece. If you want anything else, I will make you a slice of toast when I've got these curtains tacked.'

Angela went off to cut herself a slice of cake.

Pam looked at Olive. 'She is feeling a bit left out of things, I think. Susan has started courting and going out with her friends. They used to spend a lot of time together – and she misses that.' She smiled at Olive. 'Do you have a sister? You've never said...'

'I'm an only child, as far as I know,' Olive told her. 'I don't have a family, Pam – just an elderly grandmother. Last year, she had to give up her home and go into an old folks' place; it used to be the workhouse, but they call it the infirmary now. She is still alive but doesn't really know me.'

Pam stared at her in dismay. It was the first time she'd really been on her own with Olive and hadn't been aware that she had no family to speak of. 'I'm sorry for that, love,' she said. 'So where do you live when you're not working on a farm?'

'I had a room in a lodging house after Gran went in the nursing home,' Olive told her. 'My landlady didn't want to keep it for me when I got my first posting, so I had to put all my stuff in store. Not that I own much... just some clothes and a few bits Gran gave me.'

'That's unfortunate,' Pam said, feeling sympathetic. 'Why didn't you tell us?'

'There wasn't time. When we arrived, you'd had bad news – and since then we've all been working hard.' Olive looked at her wistfully. 'You've got a lovely family, Pam. I was really sorry when you had that awful news about your son.'

'Thank you...' Pam sighed and touched her hand. 'I've been so lucky, Olive. I had a wonderful husband and five beautiful children. My life has been comfortable and blessed. Some folk never have that.' She smiled as Angela reappeared with her cake, sitting on the mat to munch it. A cat appeared from some secret corner and snuggled up to her. 'Now, then, Olive. I want to hear more about you and what you did before you came here.'

* * *

Pam lay in bed that evening, unable to sleep as she thought about what Olive had told her. Orphaned at a very young age, she had no real memory of her parents. She'd lived with her grandparents, who had been kind enough to her in their way, though they would never speak of Olive's mother.

'Mum wasn't married,' Olive had told Pam as they sewed hems together. 'Grandfather called me *her shame*, but Gran was kinder. She said I was a little mistake. They looked after me; I had food and clothes, at least until Grandfather died suddenly. After that, Gran didn't have much. She did her best to cope and I did odd jobs for people, but it was hardly enough to manage on. So I left school as soon as I could and I worked in a factory. I was only the errand girl for a time so my wage barely paid for our food... then I came home one night and found Gran on the floor.'

'Oh, you poor child,' Pam said. 'That was awful for you.'

'I ran next door and the neighbours were kind. Gran was taken away, to hospital and then the home. Her cottage belonged to Grandfather's employer and he took it back once he knew – and so I got a room. Then the war happened and I volunteered for land work. I like it better than being in a factory. I shall probably find similar work after it ends.'

'I am sure there will be similar work,' Pam had told her. 'Before the war, the gang masters picked up women in their vans and took them to where the jobs were. It might be hoeing one week, picking up potatoes or picking fruit – or there's the jam factory. It's a factory, yes, but you could live in the country – or you might marry a farmer.'

Olive's face had lit up. 'I'd love to do that, Pam, but I doubt I'll be that lucky. I'm not pretty like your Susan or Lizzie or Jeanie...' she'd sighed.

'You could make yourself look more attractive if you tried,' Pam had suggested. 'I'll get Lizzie to do your hair one night; it could make all the difference... Not that I want you to get married and leave us! But I'd like to see you happy, Olive.'

Turning on her side, Pam thought about Olive and about others whose lives she knew nothing of, but was aware of – the homeless and the childless and those who had lost everything, because of this war. Her heart would always hurt for those she had lost; Arthur and now John. There was an empty space inside her that would never stop hurting, but she still had so much. It was her duty to carry on for the sake of all those she loved, and she would.

On that thought, Pam closed her eyes and slipped quietly into a peaceful sleep.

21

Artie looked at his brother Tom as they stood together in the top field, surveying what was admittedly a poor crop of wheat. Tom had taken off his sling, but his arm hung limp by his side and it cost him a great deal of effort to lift it even a few inches.

'I know I went on the land while it was still too wet,' Artie said, his expression grim. 'I can't manage the heavy land the way you did, Tom. There's no point in my pretending otherwise. If you were here to tell me... but you think they will want you back?'

'I imagine I will be recalled after my arm heals enough,' Tom said. 'It is healing gradually. I couldn't move it at all for a start – and I can still train men, even the way I am.'

'Then what do I do?' Artie asked him. 'This crop is hardly worth the cutting. We can't continue like this...'

'Put it down to grass for the rest of the war,' Tom suggested, surprising him. 'Run bullocks on it for fattening – or get some more cows. Milking is constant work, so you might as well build the herd up – and it is better than what you've got now. The land will be all the more fertile when we plough it up once I'm home for good.'

'I thought of it, but I was sure you wouldn't like it...' Artie said reflectively. 'It would certainly make things easier for me. The land girls are all right – but they need watching. I can leave them to the milking, but for most things they need supervising. Not bad workers, though.'

'I haven't seen much of them,' Tom said. 'The blonde girl seems cheerful...?'

'Betty is a bit on the loud side; Olive is completely the other way,' Artie said with a grin. 'I have to watch and make sure they know what they're doing, apart from with the cows. They seem fine with them...'

'That is your answer then. Cut down on the arable and increase the milking herd. With the extra grass, you'll be able to raise more calves for beef – can't see anything to complain about in that...'

Artie nodded, then looked at Tom. 'What do you think about the change to Dad's will?'

'I imagine he had no choice,' Tom replied. 'I expect you're disappointed, Artie. You're like Dad, and I dare say you've got plans for the future...' Tom shrugged. 'I never expected to get any land, so when I do it is a bonus. I've saved a bit, not much – and I'll find a way to use it when my time in the army is over. Not sure what I want to do yet.' He took his right arm with his left hand and eased it up and down. 'Depends on this to an extent. I'd hoped to combine land work with something else – perhaps I might build a house and sell it...'

'I'm thinking of building myself, a few big houses that will sell for good money.'

Tom looked at him with interest. 'Got anywhere in mind?'

'Yes. On the piggery,' Artie replied. 'I'll farm it for a while and then apply for building when the war is over.'

'The piggery?' Tom's brows rose in surprise. 'Have you spoken to Mum about it? I know Dad put it in her name...'

'He did, as well as a house in Chatteris. She gave the piggery to me – not the stock. I'll be selling the last brood off for her in the autumn, and then I'll plough that land and crop it.'

'What kind of land is it?' Tom asked. 'I'm not sure you'll get good corn crops on that, Artie.'

'Potatoes when I can – maybe sugar beet. I've heard that's a good crop, though we've never tried it.'

'You'll need a permit for sugar beet,' Tom told him. 'It would do well on this heavy land, I imagine. Mum might want to try it after the war. I think you might do better with a market garden on the piggery land, Artie.' He was silent for a moment. 'Dad got that land cheap. There has to be a reason... He thought the soil might be a bit sandy, not great for potatoes, but perfect for the pigs. You might do better to keep the pigs there until you get permission to build.'

'You always think you know best,' Artie snapped, irritated. 'I've seen other crops nearby and I know how to work fenland.'

'It is fenland but not the same as you're used to.' Tom shrugged. 'Do as you think best, Artie. It's yours now.'

'Yes, I bloody will...' Artie glared at Tom and strode off. Tom didn't attempt to follow.

Artie was aware that he was reacting foolishly, but Tom always did things so effortlessly. The heavy land had yielded wonderful crops when he was in charge of it and it rankled that Artie had failed. Tom was so good at everything – and he wasn't even a damned Talbot. Artie knew that in his heart he'd always secretly resented his elder brother. Arthur had often held him up as an example to Artie and it had smarted like a thorn in his foot.

It was stupid. Artie knew that. His father had given him the lion's share of the land in his will, even though his ownership was delayed. He had no reason to feel that Tom had been Arthur's favourite, but he couldn't help it – and he knew that Pam looked to her eldest son for comfort and reassurance.

He was a damned fool to let Tom get under his skin, but he did. Tom didn't try to be superior; he just was – and now he was a bloody war hero to boot. Artie would never be more than his younger brother; the one who had stayed at home and done the donkey work, while Tom and John went swanning off to become bloody heroes…

The thought of John cooled Artie's heated thoughts. He cared deeply about his younger brother and didn't want to lose him. If one of them had to die, why the hell couldn't it be bloody Tom? It was a flash of evil in his mind and Artie banished it. Of course he didn't want Tom dead! Tom was his brother and he did care about him; he was just fed up with him being right all the time…

Artie swore. He was being a bloody fool! There was no need to feel jealous of Tom. Artie had a decent life on the farm, a beautiful wife and would soon have a child of his own. He knew deep down he was lucky and told himself that he would banish the flicker of jealousy that lingered in his head; it was childish and he was a man now.

* * *

Tom walked up the hill towards the airfield. He knew Artie resented what he'd told him about that land, but it was true. Arthur had discussed it with him when he'd bought that ten acres. Tom knew that his father had had plans for that land after the war; he'd thought there might be sand and gravel if you went down far enough and that could be worth a lot of money once building started again.

Perhaps he should have told Artie that, but his brother's attitude angered Tom at times. He'd been told of Artie's reaction when the will was read and it made Tom want to give him a good shaking. What did he mean by upsetting their mother when she was suffering terrible grief? He should be ashamed of himself! Tom could understand his disappointment. It was unfortunate his father had promised him the fenland, but the war had changed things dramatically. The farm had gone from being very profitable to barely breaking even and it had to be kept together until things settled down after the war and they perhaps were able to have their old land back from the air ministry. No doubt that would require loads of work to get it back to what it had been before the compulsory purchase.

Tom wasn't sure what he wanted to do when it was all over. Sometimes, he wondered if they could ever get back to where they had been before the war had started. His mother would need him around, just to keep an eye on things for her. However, it wasn't going to be plain sailing in future, because there would be many more clashes like the one just now. Was it even possible for the two of them to work the farm together now that Arthur wasn't around to keep the peace?

Reaching the far end of the top field, Tom stopped. He could go no further now that the airfield stretched over so much of what had once been their land. Good land that yielded decent crops. He stood looking towards the planes parked outside their hangars. It looked as if they were preparing to go into action any moment as men were pouring out onto the field – pilots and ground crew.

'This is private property, soldier!' a strident voice addressed Tom and a large, fierce-looking dog started barking. 'What are you doing?'

'Looking at my crop,' Tom replied. 'I'm Captain Gilbert – my family own this farmland.'

'Oh, well, you'd best move on. We have to clear these planes – enemy bombers spotted coming this way.'

'Right. I'll get back,' Tom said and turned to return across the three fields to the farmhouse and yard. Behind him, he could hear the roar of engines as planes were started and then the take-off began, a whole series of planes, one after the other, flying low enough that Tom felt he ought to duck. He smiled grimly to himself. They'd been lucky the farm hadn't been attacked all this time, so close as it was to the airfield, but the fighters taking off behind him would intercept the enemy and engage them in the air. It was better to have all planes in the air rather than on the ground, where they were sitting ducks for any enemy bomber that managed to get through.

Tom ran the last few yards to the house. His mother, Jeanie and Lizzie were in the kitchen with the young children, playing on the tiled floor.

'What's going on, Tom?' Pam asked, looking at him. 'It's unusual for so many planes to take off at this hour and all at once.'

'An enemy bomber force is headed this way so they've scrambled all their planes – and the fighters will intercept.'

'Some might get through…' Pam said, looking worried. 'What should we do, Tom?'

'If we hear them coming, it might be better to take the children out into the dyke,' Tom replied thoughtfully. 'It is still dry and you'd be as safe there as anywhere.'

Pam nodded. 'Yes, that's what your father said we should do, but we've been lucky, Tom. I don't think there's been an actual raid on the airfield. There were a couple of dog fights over the fields last winter but no bombers got through.'

'Get a few things together in case,' Tom advised them. 'I'm going outside to watch and listen. If I think there's a chance of an attack, I'll come for you.'

'Where is Artie?' Pam asked. She looked at Jeanie, brows arched.

'After his walk with Tom, I think he went to feed the pigs,' Jeanie replied. 'He was in a bit of a mood, because he had to cycle – no fuel for the car and he needs what he has for the tractors.'

'It is a bit of a way for him,' Pam said. 'It might be a good thing when he sells the herd and puts the land down to some other crop – although the pigs have been bringing in more money than the crops recently.'

'Surely the fenland is producing as well as ever?' Tom asked, frowning.

'Artie says the yields are poor with the potatoes. The first earlies were down by nearly half this year.'

'That's a bit odd...' Tom said but to himself as he left the house and went out into the fields.

* * *

Tom stood brooding, gazing out over fields that should have been heavy with golden goodness but had produced a poor crop. It would do better to put them down to grass, at least while Tom was stuck in the army. When he came home, he would plough it up... A little groan left him as he felt the twinge of pain in his arm. He gritted his teeth and gripped it with his left hand, forcing it up... up... up until it was high above his head. It hurt like hell but he did it again and again. He had to push through the pain and get that arm working, because one day he would be back home and he needed to make this farm show a profit again. That might be difficult, but he would keep an eye on the land – all the land, whether Artie appreciated his efforts or not.

Hearing the loud crack of guns firing, Tom looked up and saw two planes attacking each other. They were away to his right – over the washes and the river, if he judged right. He saw them swirl and dip as they chased each other, saw flashes of light as they fired their guns, and then one of them scored a direct hit and the other plane stuttered, faltered and then fell like a stone. Tom saw the flames shoot into the sky as it crashed into the ground. Looking up, he watched the second plane do a victory roll, caught a flash of the colours of the RAF and smiled as it flew off into the distance. Black smoke was curling into the sky, somewhere along the Chatteris road... It was mostly fields that way, hardly any habitation once you left the village of Mepal until you reached the small town of Chatteris.

Tom frowned, wondering if Artie had seen the dog fight. He hoped his brother wasn't anywhere near the crashed plane. Artie might be a bit of a sod at times, but Tom didn't want anything to happen to him, for his mother's and Jeanie's sake. The family had had enough grief recently.

* * *

Nearly half an hour had passed since Tom had spoken to his mother. He thought the likelihood of an attack on the airfield was over now; the fighter pilots had done their job, turning the planes elsewhere or downing them. Nodding, he went back into the farm kitchen, where his mother was nursing Jonny and feeding him rice pudding with strawberry jam.

'All right?' she said a little anxiously. 'We heard something, but you didn't come?'

'It was a dog fight. The British plane won – and the other plane crashed somewhere over Chatteris way...'

Jeanie looked at him anxiously.

'I am sure Artie will be all right...' Tom said.

As if to prove him right, they heard voices outside and then Artie came in, followed by the two land girls. They'd had a morning off to go into Ely together, because the harvest would start soon and then they wouldn't get a chance until it was all gathered in.

'Bloody close...' Artie said as he came in, followed by the girls, who carried several parcels wrapped in brown paper. He looked at Tom. 'Did you see the dog fight? I was cycling home and they went right over my head. They crashed in a field – but not our side of the river. Nowhere near the piggery...'

'Well, that is good,' Pam said. 'Did the pilot get out? Did you notice, Artie?'

'No, not that I saw,' Artie said. 'Bloody good job – I'd kill the lot of the buggers...'

'You pulled a German pilot out of the plane that crashed in our field,' Pam reminded.

'That was before...' Artie growled. 'Sorry, Mum. I know it hurts to think of John – but I hope that bugger roasts.'

Pam's face went white.

'Artie!' Jeanie admonished and Artie swore.

'You know what I mean, Mum.'

'Yes, Artie, I know,' she said. 'It's just that it makes me wonder what happened to John. Did he get out...?'

She handed Jonny to Jeanie and left the room. They heard her hurry upstairs.

Artie swore.

Tom gave him a look fit to kill and went after his mother.

He found her sitting on the edge of her bed, her arms crossed over her body, the tears trickling down her cheeks. Tom sat beside her, his arm about her shoulders.

'It wouldn't have been like that for John,' he said, trying to clear her mind of the fearful pictures. 'If he went in the sea, no fire, Mum. If he didn't get out, he was probably unconscious on impact – but it is possible he did manage to get free of the wreckage. Don't give up hope entirely – and don't torture yourself about how he died. It won't change anything.' It was possible that fire had been raging in the cabin before the plane ditched, but Tom wanted to ease her grief.

'I know, Tom,' Pam sniffed. 'I'm trying really hard, love, but sometimes I get pictures of him suffering in my head and… I can't bear it. He was my youngest son. Well, you know what he was like. You two were close.'

'Yes. I love him, Mum. I'm not going to give up. I know a few people. I'll try to find out a bit more – if he was picked up by the Germans, he might be in a camp.'

'On those islands?'

'Maybe there for a while, but I expect he would be taken to Germany. I think there are several prisoner of war camps in Germany – and they treat the officers reasonably well, so I've heard.'

'How would you know that?'

'Because someone escaped from a camp and got home,' Tom said. 'I met him briefly. He said it was OK – but depended who was in charge. Their high-ranking army and air force officers have their own code, but the Gestapo are different.'

Pam looked at him. 'You've seen and learned so much since you left home, Tom. You're not the same lad as you were – but it suits you. You've grown up, my son.'

'The army does that to you, Mum.' Tom grinned at her.

'How will you settle down on the farm when it is all over?' Pam looked anxious. 'You and Artie together...' She sighed and shook her head.

'We'll manage,' Tom said and smiled at her, dismissing his own fears. 'Did Dad ever tell you about that ten acres where we kept the pigs... about his plans for it after the war?'

Pam shook her head. 'No. I didn't know he had any, except as a place where he could increase the pig herd.'

'He thought there might be sand and gravel under the top layers – and he was going to investigate and then sell it to whoever would pay him the most. He expected to make rather a lot of money once building starts up again. Rich deposits of aggregate can be worth a fortune.'

'Yes, I suppose it would be worth quite a bit,' Pam agreed, looking at him oddly. 'Arthur was a shrewd and enterprising man. I had no idea. I knew he didn't think it would be good arable land. Does Artie know?'

'I haven't told him, but I shall,' Tom said. 'He could be sitting on a small fortune, Mum.'

'Oh dear. That wasn't my intention... It isn't fair to the girls, or you, and John, Tom.' She faltered, then, 'John's share of everything will go to Jonny if—'

'Yes, of course it will.' Tom squeezed her hand. 'I'm not bothered how much the piggery is worth, other than it should have been for you. If you're content, then I am. I'll find my own way, Mum – but that money ought to have been yours. It's what Dad intended. Had he been able to sell, he wouldn't have needed to change his will. I know he'd hoped the war would be over by now.'

'It doesn't look like ending any time soon...' Pam sighed. 'Well, I've given it to Artie now and I've got all I need here on the farm. Perhaps it will make him happier to know what he has, Tom. Will you tell him?'

'Yes, I will. I'll tell him everything Dad told me. It may not come to anything – depends how big the deposits are, but there are some good deposits along that road, and if Dad's turns out to be as good, Artie could end up with several thousand pounds to build whatever he wants...'

'Well, I'm glad for him,' Pam said. 'I don't need much, Tom. I'm happy here in my kitchen and I know that the land will be profitable again when you get back...' She looked at him sadly and touched his limp arm. 'Does it hurt a lot, Tom?'

'Only when I make it do things it doesn't want to,' he said. 'But that's a small price to pay, Mum. I can clench my fist again. Look...' He gritted his teeth and clenched his fist, the veins standing out at his temples in the effort.

'You'll do it, Tom,' Pam said and smiled. 'You'll do it for yourself, for your family and me. Go down now and I'll come in a minute. I'm all right – thank you.'

Tom nodded and went down to the kitchen. Artie had gone.

Lizzie was serving up food to the land girls. 'Artie went to the cowsheds. One of them is due to deliver a calf any time now,' she said.

'Thanks. I'll go and find him,' Tom said. 'Then I'm going home for a while.'

'I'll be there soon...' Lizzie smiled and continued to dish up the delicious-smelling shepherd's pie.

22

Artie was stroking the cow's back when Tom found him. The animal's lowing told of its distress, but Artie was talking to it and his voice had a soothing effect.

'First calf?' Tom asked, because it was a young heifer and obviously distressed by something it did not yet understand. 'She'll settle once it starts for real; it's instinctive with them. Daisy was just the same with her first...'

'Yes, I expect so,' Artie replied. 'Dad was so good with the animals. We miss him – he didn't have to do anything when they calved. Just to be there was enough.'

'Yes, I know. We all miss him, Artie. It is a big responsibility for you, having the land and the animals to look after, but Mum is relying on you. I'll help while I'm here – as much as I can with this...' Tom indicated his limp arm. 'I can probably drive a tractor, but not much else.'

Artie nodded, giving Tom an odd look. 'I know I have to look after Mum and the girls, at least until the war is over – but I don't want to be a farm labourer all my life. I want more than that, Tom.'

'Yes, of course, and I'm sure you will do it somehow...' Tom hesitated, then, 'The land the piggery is on may be worth more than you expect. Dad believed there might be considerable deposits of sand and gravel underneath the topsoil. You know there are large deposits along that road and they will bring a fortune to whoever exploits them – not yet, but when the war is over and people want sand and gravel for building again.'

'You mean quarry them?' Artie stared at him. 'You're kidding?'

'No. Dad couldn't be sure, but after he purchased the land, he had a preliminary test done and he was told it was likely to be a big deposit.' Tom saw the dawning realisation in his brother's eyes, because sand and gravel were valuable commodities. 'You couldn't build on it – at least, not until you exhausted the reserves. By then, you'd have a large pit. Not sure what it would cost to fill that in with earth. You might be stuck with a small lake and no building land – but the sand and gravel would bring in a substantial amount of money. You'd have to decide whether to extract it yourself or sell the rights to someone else – either way, it could set you up in whatever business you fancy. You just have to be patient for a while, Artie.'

Artie looked at him for a long moment, the faint hostility in his face fading. 'Yes, I know. I'm lucky Mum gave it to me – or did she know what it was worth?'

'I've no idea,' Tom lied. 'You could ask her, but she wanted you to have it, Artie. You are Arthur's eldest and it is right you should have something in return for everything you do. I know farming can seem nothing but slog when things don't go well – and you're not your own boss. The Ministry of Food will be round asking what's wrong if your yields drop too much or too suddenly—'

A bellow of pain from the heifer brought their conversation

to a halt. Nostrils flaring, eyes wide, the beast's sides heaved as she struggled to push the calf from her.

Tom moved to look. He grinned at his brother as he saw the hind legs appearing from its mother's rear quarters. 'Good girl, Maisie,' he said in a gentle, caressing tone and caught the body of the calf on his chest as it slid out in a sudden rush, causing the heifer to bellow once more. Letting it slip gently down on the clean straw, Tom wiped some of the mucus from the calf's head and nose and down the long body with a handful of straw in his left hand. Maisie looked round and down, her lowing softer now as she started to nose at her calf. 'That's right, girl. You know what to do now, I reckon...'

Maisie was pushing at her calf, encouraging it to try to get up, and after a few minutes of licking and gentle persuasion, it did so and soon found the source of comfort, sucking lustily at its mother's full teats.

'I'll leave you to it,' Tom said to Artie. 'Going home for a rest. I'm not properly fit yet.'

'I know...' Artie hesitated, then, 'I'm sorry I'm a bit of a sod sometimes, Tom.'

'Don't worry. I can be, too, if I feel like it.' Tom grinned at him as for a moment they were united by the miracle of birth.

Tom walked off without looking back, though he knew his brother watched him until he was out of the yard. He hoped the realisation that the piggery was likely to be worth more than he'd expected one day would help Artie to feel more satisfied with his lot.

Reaching his own house, Tom took off his jacket and boots and padded to the sink in his socks. He filled the kettle, intending to take a mug of tea up to bed, but just as it boiled, Lizzie arrived with their son. Arthur was wide awake and cried out as soon as he saw his father. 'Dadda... Dadda...' He waved his chubby fists in the air, clamouring for his father to take him.

'Sit in the rocking chair and I'll put him on the rug at your feet,' Lizzie said. 'I'll make us a cup of tea. Are you hungry, Tom?'

'Not at the moment,' Tom replied, looking down at his son, who pulled himself up to stand holding his father's knee. He was chattering away in his own way, laughing as Tom steadied him with his injured arm and gave him his left-hand fingers to grab. 'I think he is getting stronger, Lizzie. He has quite a grip.'

'Yes, I know. Everyone says he's going to be big and strong like his father,' Lizzie said. 'I'm going to toast some bread – and I've got marmalade or honey, if you fancy a piece?'

'No, you go ahead. I'll drink this.' Tom smiled as she placed a cup of tea on a small chest next to the range. 'Then I think I will take a nap, Lizzie. Sorry, but this arm aches so damned much and I feel weary.'

'Yes, go up and have some sleep,' Lizzie said, looking at him anxiously. 'You haven't quarrelled with Artie?'

'No, though I came close to it a couple of times,' Tom admitted. 'We have to keep the peace for Mum's sake. I wish John was home. It won't seem the same if he has gone for good.'

'John was always the one you got on best with.' Lizzie nodded her understanding. 'I think Artie resents you, Tom. I'm not sure why – but Jeanie says he has been sulking since Arthur died.'

'He expected to get the fenland,' Tom said. 'Dad changed his will in Mum's favour at the last minute. Things have gone downhill since the war started. The Air Ministry forced us to sell a lot of our best land to them for next to nothing, and then the Food Ministry controlled everything, paying far less than we got before the war. Dad was hampered in every direction by their regulations – and then he was ill. So the farm suffered and the profits dropped – and all his other assets dropped in value, because who wants to buy a house in wartime? Dad's cash reserves were eroded, so he had to look after Mum.'

'It is the same for you and John,' Lizzie pointed out. 'It didn't make any difference to the girls, because their trust funds remain in place until they are twenty – but the boys all have to wait. Why Artie resents that I don't know. He's always had that two acres of council land he crops and his wage. He doesn't do that badly.'

'Yes, he was lucky to get two acres. A lot of farming sons get an acre of council land, but he got two somehow.'

'You don't have any allotment land?'

'I never applied for it,' Tom replied. 'I had some plans, but I shelved them when the war started.' He smiled wearily as Lizzie's brows lifted. 'Mum's second cousin, Bernie, owns a small industrial buildings firm. They use asbestos roofs on easily constructed sheds – for industrial use, agricultural machinery, drying wheat, and suchlike. He offered me a partnership just before the war. I've got a bit saved and he asked if I wanted to invest it in the business…'

'I didn't know that…' Lizzie looked at him. 'Is it something you want to do, Tom?'

'As an investment, perhaps,' Tom replied thoughtfully. 'Bernie told me to think about it. No hurry, because not much building's going on now – but it is one idea. I thought I might build a house in my spare time. I could buy a plot cheaply and do it a bit at a time. I'd need to pay a builder to do the groundwork and the bricklaying. I could do a lot of jobs myself, and a mate of mine would give me a good price for the roof. I could manage a lot of the inside work – or I could have.' He grimaced. 'If I could build and make a profit, it would give me a nice capital sum.'

Lizzie nodded. 'Jeanie says Artie wants to build on the piggery one day.'

'Maybe. He might have other plans for it now,' Tom said and finished his tea. He got up, smiled, and reached out to squeeze her hand. 'We'll talk later, love. I'm bushed...'

* * *

Lizzie nodded, watching as he went out. She'd been considering an idea of her own for expanding her business but hadn't wanted to worry Tom while he was still unwell. Another little shop had come vacant in Chatteris and Lizzie thought it could be used for a dress shop. It would cost a couple of hundred to set up and could bring them in a small income. Lizzie's hairdressing salon was doing well and she'd recently taken on an apprentice, making the girl she'd had an improver on a higher wage, because you were only allowed one apprentice per qualified hairdresser. Even though she only worked part-time, Lizzie showed a healthy profit each week and had saved nearly seventy pounds, besides the money she put by for running costs. That would be enough to set up the dress shop and she had already found a young woman who would run it for her – but she would be left with very little in the bank for emergencies.

Perhaps Tom would like to invest some of his savings. For the moment, he had no chance of improving his finances, because the army gave him little time for anything but his duty. She would talk to him when he was feeling less tired...

Lizzie smiled to herself as she picked up her son, who was now yawning. When she'd opened her salon, she'd planned it only as a small thing where she would earn little more than a wage, but her business had grown and she now had customers who came in from many villages – some of them from as far away as March.

'You should open another salon in March,' some ladies had told her recently. 'I am sure you would be busy.'

Lizzie didn't doubt it, but she'd worked it out and at the moment couldn't think how to do it. She would have to split her time between the two salons and, with a small son to care for, that was too time-consuming. One day perhaps – but experience had taught Lizzie that she would do better to train up good staff and keep one salon really busy, at least until Arthur was at senior school.

Laughing at her own dreams, Lizzie decided that Arthur needed a nappy change. A new business was appealing, but she would talk it over with Tom before she did anything. She sighed. This rotten war had cast a shadow over everyone's life and she knew there were far more important things going on right now than whether she should risk her savings or not. People were dying of their wounds, others missing, presumed lost...

Lizzie's eyes filled with tears as she thought of Tom's brother and the girl he'd asked to marry him. Where was Lucy? Did she know that John was missing – and how was she coping with her grief? Lizzie felt sorry for her. She really hadn't had a chance to get to know any of them, so it wasn't easy to reach out to her, though perhaps Lizzie would write to her one day and invite her to visit...

23

'Nurse... Nurse, please, could you help me?'

There was a hint of desperation in the soldier's voice, making Lucy turn towards his bed, even though she was about to change a dressing on the patient at the end of the ward. It was her burns case calling out, and he was due to have his bandages off when the doctors found time to do their rounds later that day.

'Yes, Captain Rossiter – what can I do for you?' she asked, reaching out to touch his hand.

'I need to pee, nurse,' he said, sounding apologetic now. 'I'm sorry to be a bloody nuisance again.'

'You aren't,' Lucy assured him. She took the china bottle that was used as a urinary flask by bedridden patients, pushing it into his hands. 'That is what I'm here for. I'll adjust the screen so you have privacy, Captain.'

'Thank you...' he muttered.

Lucy moved the screen so that his bed was closed off from others nearby. She heard the sounds as he relieved himself and went back as he called out to her.

'You'd best take the damned thing. I'll knock if over if I try to put it on the cabinet beside my bed.'

'Perhaps things will improve after Doctor's rounds,' Lucy said, taking the receptacle from him with secure hands.

'Pigs might fly,' he muttered. 'Don't humour me, nurse. You know I'll be blind.'

Lucy put down the china bottle and reached for his hand, giving it a firm squeeze. 'Neither of us knows either way,' she told him. 'I've seen a case similar to yours where the patient could see. Not well at first, but shapes and faces. It will take time.'

'And if my eyes were so badly damaged that I'll never see again?' he grunted bitterly.

'Then you will learn to see with your hands and your senses,' Lucy said gently. 'Again, it will take time and patience, Captain Rossiter.'

'Call me Jack. You call other men by their names. I know, because I've heard you.'

'I will call you Jack, if you wish,' Lucy replied, letting go of his hand. 'I have to dress a wound now, but I'll be back soon.'

'Will you be here when they take the bandages off?' he asked suddenly. 'Please. Please, nurse. I'll need you then...'

She hesitated, because she was due to go off duty soon, after a long night. 'If I am still here when they come,' she said at last. 'I will try, I promise.'

He let her go then and she walked quickly to the bed of her next patient, knowing that sister's eye was on her. They were not encouraged to become close to any one particular patient, because it was too painful if a man had a sudden reversal and died, and it happened. Men they thought were getting better and almost ready to be sent home on the hospital ships became worse without cause or reason and went quickly downhill. It was normally an infection, of which there were many, despite the disinfectants constantly in use. For a young nurse, half in love with a brave and desperately wounded young soldier that could be devastating, and it happened all too often.

It was easy to give too much of yourself to these men, Lucy thought as she dressed a suppurating wound and exchanged a few cheerful words with her patient. He was young and handsome, his smile charming as he flirted with her in a gentle manner. They all flirted with the nurses, even Sister Jane, and she allowed it.

'These boys give their everything for us,' she'd told her nurses. 'They take their lives in their hands every time they fly on a mission – and many of them end up here. So we smile and we accept that they may be a little naughty at times – but we keep our hearts to ourselves.'

'If we have a heart to give...' Lucy had murmured, causing sister to look at her hard, but she hadn't enquired further and Lucy hadn't given her any cause to suspect that she was suffering from a broken heart.

For Lucy, the time she was at work, caring for desperately injured men, was her solace. She had found the will to smile and carry on, because she knew she had to. Nurses were needed desperately, here and at home, while the war raged on around the world.

At night, Lucy slept badly. For the first few weeks after she'd read the letter telling her John was missing, she'd cried every night, but now her tears had dried and there was just a painful ache in her chest that never left her – and anger, too. It was just so unfair that she had lost the only man she'd ever loved! Sometimes, when she was alone, it would become so bad, she thought she wouldn't get her breath, but she always did. Her heart might have become stone, but her will to live would not let her give in. Sometimes she wished she could just lay down and die she hurt so much, but she never did.

Lucy knew that she could get leave if she told sister of her loss, but what was the point? She would just sit at home and cry and her mother would fuss over her and look sad. At least here, there was a reason for her to go on.

She saw the doctors had arrived as she left her patient and took the used bandages to the waste disposal bin outside the tent. When she returned, she noticed they were by Captain Rossiter's bed and walked quickly to join them and sister.

'Well, Rossiter – shall we see how the land lies?' one of the doctors asked with practised cheerfulness. 'Nurse – take the bandages off for us, please.'

'Yes, doctor,' Lucy said and went to stand by his head. She carefully unwound the thick bandages, revealing the worst of the scarring, which had been hidden until now. She could see that Captain Rossiter's eyes were shut, the skin still red and puckered on his eyelids and across both cheeks, though it had begun to heal. He had no eyelashes; they had not grown back yet, though it was likely they would. 'Should I bathe his eyes?' Lucy asked, her gaze flicking to the doctor. She thought it might make it easier for him to open them, but the doctor shook his head at her impatiently.

'Open your eyes, Captain,' he commanded in a strong tone. 'Let's discover what you can see.'

For a moment, Captain Rossiter did not respond, then he did, but there was not a flicker of anything that Lucy could notice. 'I can't see you...' he said and his head was turned towards her. 'Just a blur...'

'Can you see light? Can you see a shape?' the doctor asked, a hint of excitement in his voice.

'I... Yes, there is light. I can see a shape but not a face...'

'That is good,' the doctor was suddenly smiling, relieved. 'I know you're disappointed that you can't immediately see – but the fact that you see light and shapes gives us hope.' He leaned in, shining his torch into Captain Rossiter's left eye and then his right. 'Close your left eye and now look at my hand...' He held it up close to Captain Rossiter's face. 'How many fingers?'

There was hesitation, then, 'Two... I think it's two.'

'Right. Now try the other eye.'

The procedure was repeated, but Captain Rossiter shook his head. 'I can only see light now.'

'Yes, that fits with what I thought. I believe you will recover your sight in your right eye, but the left may not be much more than you have now.' The doctor looked at Lucy. 'I want a fresh bandage on every day – and half an hour morning and night with it off...' He nodded. 'We will give it a little more time to rest and recover – and maybe some drops to moisten the eye.' The doctor glanced at sister. 'Who is next?'

Lucy rebandaged Captain Rossiter's head, then she felt his hand on her arm. 'Why is he saying that when I can't see your face?'

'Because your eyes were badly burned by the fire and it needs time for them to recover. Had you lost your sight for good you would not have seen anything.'

'Do I have to wear this bloody thing?' He touched the bandage as he spoke. 'Surely it would be better to have it off and let me see what I can?'

'He is a good doctor,' Lucy told him. 'Try to be patient a while longer, Jack. In time, you may see my face – but you might need spectacles.'

'I think they would suit me – dark ones,' he said. 'It looks a mess, doesn't it, Lucy? That is your name, isn't it?'

'Yes, that's my name,' Lucy said with a smile, because when a patient began to ask such questions, he was getting better. 'At the moment, your skin is still pretty red and inflamed,' she admitted. 'In time, it will get better – and I think they can help a bit with skin grafts. It is a specialised thing and only a few doctors can do it, but you look all right. You will do. You just have to be—'

'Patient. I bloody know,' he muttered. 'Maybe it's as well if I can't see myself.'

'Don't sulk, Jack,' Lucy said, suddenly angry. 'It doesn't suit you. If my John came back with injuries like yours, I wouldn't care. He was an airman, lost at sea. I'd thank God he was alive whatever his wounds...'

'Lost someone, have you,' he grunted, then, 'I'm sorry, Lucy, I didn't know. Wouldn't hurt you for the world.'

'Not your fault,' she said but caught back a sob. 'Tell you what, when you're well and you can see, you can take me dancing to make up for it.' Lucy said the words in a mood of bravado.

'You're on,' he said and laughed. 'I'll wine you and dine you, and make *your* eyes shine again, Lucy—'

'Nurse Lucy – can you assist...?'

'Yes, sister,' Lucy said. 'Have a rest now, Jack. Keep positive. It will get better.'

'You too,' he responded and she gave a little nod as she walked quickly to the other end of the ward.

* * *

'Oh, Nurse Lucy,' sister called to her as she was about to leave after doctors' rounds. 'Can you spare me a moment, please?'

'Yes, sister.' Lucy smothered a yawn. She really needed her bed.

'I know you're tired and need your rest...' sister gave her an understanding look. 'I've just learned that you were engaged to an airman who went missing...'

Lucy was silent. She wasn't sure how sister knew that, because very few of the nursing staff did, and her friends had all sworn to keep her secret.

'Sister, I... How do you know?'

'You were overheard speaking to Captain Rossiter. I am truly sorry for your loss. I won't try to console you, because I know it doesn't help. Don't look like that, nurse. You aren't in trouble, but you ought to have told me. You must know I would've released you, sent you home on compassionate leave?'

'I don't want that, sister. I'm better here.'

'I did notice you looked pale and very tired sometimes. If you feel that you can't carry on, you must tell me. Tired nurses make mistakes and I can't risk that with seriously ill patients, nurse.'

'Have I done something wrong?' Lucy asked, keeping her eyes down.

'No. You are one of my best nurses and I do not wish to lose you – but nor do I want you to become exhausted and ill yourself. Please, tell me now – do you need to go home for a while, until you feel better?'

'No, sister. Please don't send me home.'

Sister looked at her in silence for a moment. 'Very well – but I am giving you five days off. Sleep, go to the beach and swim, lie in the sun – but when you come back, I expect you to be looking refreshed. If not, I will send you home on the next available ship.'

'Yes, sister,' Lucy said. 'Thank you.'

She left quickly at sister's nod. It was true she had been

burning her candle low and a few days' rest could do no harm, but she couldn't face going home. Her mother would cry and worry about her and then she'd say she must visit John's family – and Lucy couldn't face that yet. She just couldn't...

24

Despite her initial reluctance, the rest did Lucy good. She did as sister had ordered and went to the nearest available beach to swim and lie in the sun for hours at a time. It was completely empty, just her and some sea birds swirling overhead. Gradually, the peace and beauty of the coastline, here and there interspersed with lush greenery, and the deep blue of the sea, seeped into her soul. Just for a while, she could forget the war and all the pain and suffering that she witnessed daily.

On the second day, she fell asleep, her towel spread out on golden sand and woke up, stiff and a little sore, but feeling much better. Cyprus really was a little bit of paradise. For some reason or other, the enemy had not made as many full-on attacks on this British outpost as they had on Malta, which had suffered intense bombing raids from the air and the sea.

After the strain and grief of the past weeks, Lucy's nerves had reached breaking point without her realising and on the third day she had a good cry, but then the tears stopped and she lay back, feeling the healing warmth of the sun on her face. Lucy felt as if a heavy weight had lifted from her shoulders as she let go. She would never forget John, she knew that deep inside her, but she had to learn to live without him. A part of her deeply regretted that they had never been married, never made love, but another part of her accepted that it might have been even worse had she known the happiness their future had promised. She wasn't the only young woman who had lost the man she loved, and to go on punishing herself day in and day out wouldn't bring him back.

Lucy went back to her room that night feeling more like herself. She didn't think there were many tears left inside her. They had all been cried out and she'd exhausted herself. The next day she stayed in bed the whole day, sleeping and only getting up to make herself a drink or eat some biscuits she'd found in her cupboard. By the fifth day, Lucy was ready to return to work, but she didn't. Instead she went shopping in the nearby town, then went to eat at a local restaurant, enjoying a salad with freshly caught seafood and a glass of locally made white wine.

The wait staff were young girls and they asked her if she was a nurse. When she said yes, they wanted to know all about the patients and what it was like to nurse them. They giggled a lot until their father came out and ordered them to stop annoying her, but Lucy told him that she was enjoying their company and he sat down at their table, sent his daughters to fetch coffee and the whole family sat and talked to her for the next hour. When Lucy asked for her bill, she was told that for her it was free, because the café owner's son had been nursed at the British base when he was wounded and they were grateful. Names were exchanged, money was refused twice, and Lucy was invited to visit whenever she had the chance and to bring a friend.

Lucy's eyes were moist as the owner – Luigi – hugged her and told her she was wonderful, before letting her go to catch her bus. She sat smiling to herself on the way back to the field hospital. Some people were so friendly and generous and their kindness had made her realise that there was something to live for still. The world hadn't stopped because John had died and Lucy's life could be whatever she made of it.

* * *

'Ah, that's better,' sister said when Lucy presented herself for duty the next morning. 'I see you took my advice, nurse. You look very much better – and that is good, because Captain Rossiter is being a pain in the rear. He does nothing but ask for you, and except for you he won't let anyone but me change his bandage.'

'Would you like me to start with him?' Lucy asked and sister nodded.

'Yes. I am certain his sight is improving, but he won't admit it to me.' She sighed. 'He insists he wants you, Nurse Lucy.'

Lucy smiled and went away to fetch her trolley with the bandages and instruments she needed for her work.

As she approached Captain Rossiter's bed, his head turned towards her eagerly. 'You are back,' he said. 'Why didn't you tell me you would be away all that time?'

'It was five days,' Lucy replied calmly. 'Sister forced me to take leave and I am certain you were well looked after while I was away.'

'Humph!' he muttered. 'Are you feeling better now? She told me you were exhausted – were you?'

'I hadn't been sleeping,' Lucy said as she began to unravel his bandage. 'I've been to the beach. It was warm and lovely and I fell asleep in the sun. My skin was a bit red, but I'm turning a nice light tan now.'

'Yes, you are,' he said and Lucy started as she realised that he was looking at her. 'It suits you. Your hair is lighter than I imagined. I thought you would be dark-haired – it's more chestnut when the light touches it.'

'That's the effect of the sun,' Lucy told him, looking into his face. 'How long have you been able to see faces?'

'I saw indistinctly the day after the bandages first came off – but this is the first day I've seen your face. You are perfect, just as I thought you would be.'

'I don't think I'm perfect,' Lucy said with a laugh. 'My nose has freckles. I thought it might peel but it hasn't – but it doesn't matter about me, Jack. It's wonderful news that you can see. Is it with both eyes or just the one?'

'I can see better like this…' Jack put his hand over his left eye. 'The left is blurry and it affects what I see – but my right eye is almost as good as it used to be.' He grinned at her. 'I won't be a walking liability after all, Lucy.'

'You wouldn't be anyway,' she replied and smiled. 'I'm so pleased for you, Jack. It is marvellous.' She leaned close to him, looking at the scarring across his face. 'The redness is beginning to fade. I think you would be better to leave the bandages off now, but I'll speak to sister and make sure.'

Jack reached out and caught her by the wrist as she was moving away. 'Thank you,' he said. 'You've looked after me all this time – when I was close to despair and wished I'd died. You pulled me through this, Lucy. I couldn't have done it without you.'

'That is what we're here for,' Lucy said. 'I did what I could, but anyone would have done the same…'

'No. It was you, your voice I listened for,' he insisted. 'I want to thank you properly, Lucy. When they let me out of here – and that will surely be soon – will you let me take you for a meal or to a dance, when they have one up at the base?'

Lucy hesitated, then remembered what she had decided. 'Yes, if you wish,' she said. 'Now, I must get on.'

'I know what you've lost,' he said as she turned from him. 'I won't make demands, Lucy. I just want to give back some of your kindness...'

Lucy blinked away her tears and she left his bedside. She approached sister and told her that Jack could now see faces and one eye was recovering well, the other still blurry.

'Does he need to keep the bandages on now?' she asked.

Sister looked at her consideringly. 'I think so, yes, just until doctors' rounds. We'll let them decide – but perhaps you could just cover the left eye.' She nodded. 'Yes, put a patch over the left eye and leave his right open to the air. I'm sure it can't harm him now.'

Lucy went back to her patient and did as she'd been instructed. Jack grumbled a bit until he realised that he was being allowed to see with the recovered eye. Then he smiled up at her.

'That sister of yours is a dragon, but she knows a thing or two – and she's been through a lot. Did you know she was married? Her husband died in 1940, at sea. He was in the navy... She returned to nursing immediately and hasn't been back to Britain since.'

'No, I didn't know any of that,' Lucy said and glanced at sister, who was bending over a patient who was in a lot of pain, trying to make him more comfortable.

* * *

Lucy went off to change some bandages, tidy beds and make patients as comfortable as possible. They'd all had their early medication and no more would be issued until after doctors' rounds, because the doses might be changed, according to the pain levels. Fortunately, they had plenty of opiates at the hospital, which was not always the case at field hospitals when supplies were late in coming through.

Cyprus had so far not suffered a successful invasion attack from the enemy, which was fortunate since it was an important base for the British and their Allies. Malta, another strategic outpost, had suffered terribly from air raids and food shortages at the beginning of the war, but the allied forces had successfully defended it, and the people stubbornly refused to surrender. The reconquest of Egypt after the second battle of El Alamein and Operation Torch in the Mediterranean meant the island had been saved. For some reason, the Germans had paid less attention to Cyprus and Lucy thanked God for it as she went about her work.

It was truly a miracle that Captain Jack Rossiter had regained at least partial sight after the severity of his wounds. He was obviously scarred for life, but as yet he hadn't asked to look at himself, so perhaps he realised that he'd been lucky and a loss of the undoubtedly handsome looks he'd once had was of less importance.

Lucy was used to seeing men with terrible scars all over their bodies and knew that if they lived it was something they had to take in their stride. It was possible to save lives, but you couldn't replace a lost limb – at least not with one of flesh and blood. Prosthetics were not always easy to use and they often rubbed tender flesh, making it painful to wear them, and a lot of the men hated it that they had to rely on false limbs. Some could accept it easily, glad to be alive, others lay and cursed, tempers frayed and moods sullen. All she could do as a nurse was change bandages, treat wounds, and administer painkilling medicine.

When someone thanked her as Captain Rossiter had, it gave her a warm feeling inside.

'Time for you to take your break, Nurse Lucy,' sister's words cut into her thoughts. 'We have a new influx of patients coming in this evening – so be prepared to stay late. Get yourself some food and something to keep you going.'

Lucy nodded and smiled. Sister was showing her approval. She'd passed the test and would not be sent home for a rest just yet.

* * *

Lucy returned after her break to see that some of the beds were empty, including Captain Rossiter's. She didn't need sister to tell her that those patients feeling well enough had been moved to the recovery unit to await transport home. The hospital ship that would bring them more badly wounded patients would be continuing its journey home with those men considered well enough to complete the long voyage back to Britain.

'Captain Rossiter left a note for you,' sister said when Lucy went to her for instructions. 'The doctors decided he would benefit from some sea air, so he was taken with others by ambulance to the port. He asked me to give you this and to say goodbye for him.'

Lucy nodded, slipping the note into her pocket. She wished she'd been able to say goodbye to him, but it was right and proper that he should go home to his family. He would soon forget her once he was with friends again and feeling better.

'Right, it looks as if we have our new arrivals,' sister said and glanced at her notes. 'We have two cases with burns, three amputees – and one man in a coma. I'd like you to take on the patients with burns, Nurse Lucy. You did well with the last one, so I shall make that your job.'

'Yes, sister. Do we have their names?'

'All but the one in a coma,' sister said. 'He was found in the sea, no identification – the sea takes everything, clothes, whatever you had...' She nodded cheerfully. 'No doubt we shall discover once he wakes up.'

If he wakes, Lucy thought but didn't say. Sister's cheerful attitude was the right one. She carried hopes for all their patients, no matter how dire their injuries, until the last.

'I'll get on with my routine then, sister,' she said. 'Until they are settled.'

'Good girl,' Sister told her. 'Captain Rossiter will do very nicely now. Let's see if we can do the same for our new patients.'

Lucy smiled and went away to change a bandage. She thought sister might be imagining that Lucy had fallen for Captain Rossiter. Lucy liked him, but for the moment no one was in her heart but John. She decided as she worked that she would write to John's mother. Until this point, she hadn't felt able to acknowledge Pam's letter, but she felt able to now. She would tell Pam Talbot how sorry she was and ask her to keep in touch without saying any more because until the end of the war she really couldn't make plans.

25

'Are you feeling all right, love?' Pam looked at Jeanie anxiously. She was now well into her seventh month of pregnancy and beginning to feel ungainly and uncomfortable. Artie refused to let her do anything but the small jobs, like feeding the hens and looking for eggs, and Jeanie wanted to help with the milking and mucking out. She complained that Artie treated her as though she was made of fine porcelain.

'Just a bit of backache,' Jeanie said and sighed. 'I'm bored sitting around half the time. I'm sure there are jobs I could and should be doing...'

'There are jobs you could probably still do on the farm,' Pam admitted with a smile. 'Artie is just taking care of you, love. I've got ironing and window cleaning to do – you can choose which you prefer, if you want a job.'

'I'll clean the downstairs windows,' Jeanie said, instantly looking more cheerful. It was a lovely fresh October day and the mild sunshine was enticing her outside. 'I'll do some of the ironing later – but I can't go up ladders or Artie will have me locked up in my room.'

They laughed and Jeanie went off in search of a bucket of warm water and the wash leathers.

Pam nodded to herself as she rolled pastry for their meal. She was making minced-chicken pasties with diced carrot and potato fillings and fresh onions from her garden. Once baked, they could be eaten warm or cold and were easy to pack when the workers were off in the fields and wouldn't be back for lunch. The farm girls loved them and couldn't get enough of them. Artie preferred a sit-down meal with lashings of gravy and vegetables, but for the moment he was having to take a packed docky with him.

The grain harvest was gathered safely, and even though the yields were down, Tom had told her that there should be sufficient funds to resow their fields for the following year. The money she could count on to keep the home running would come from the potato harvest and that, she was told, was good; it seemed the yields were better than Artie had thought they might be. Of course, there was the money from the pigs, which was useful as a little nest egg for the future. Artie had decided that he would build up another herd for himself.

'I'm not sure the land would support potatoes,' he'd told her when informing her of his decision to keep two of the breeding sows. 'I've had a word with someone and he says he remembers potatoes being grown there and they were always scabby. Tom doesn't think it would give good wheat yields either. So I think I'll stick to pigs for now, Mum – and we'll share whatever we get from them.'

'That's a nice thought, Artie,' Pam had thanked him but refused his offer. 'I can manage without that money, Artie. It is yours to help you get started with whatever you want to do. Besides, we're putting the home fields down to grass and increasing the number of bullocks that we rear. That should more than compensate for the income from the pigs.'

Pam was pleased that he'd made the offer. If it was worth a lot more for sand and gravel than she'd realised, Pam didn't regret it. Artie worked hard and he deserved something extra. It might not be quite fair to his sisters and brothers – but if John didn't return... But Tom had told her she mustn't think that way. She had to be positive and keep believing.

Pam had just put her pasties in the oven when someone knocked at her front door. She went to open it and discovered the postman, Jock, talking to Jeanie as she washed a window.

'Letters and a parcel for you,' Jock said, handing them over. 'The parcel is for Miss Susan Talbot...'

'Oh... so it is,' Pam said, looking at it in surprise. 'I wonder who sent that? She hasn't ordered anything that I know of...'

'London postmark,' Jock said helpfully. 'Probably from those friends of yours. You've got one from Cyprus, Mrs Talbot. It isn't easy to see because they blur the postmarks on purpose – but I've seen them before... military hospital...'

Pam's heart raced as she grabbed the letters and tore open the one that was different from all the others. Could it possibly be news of John? She could hardly breathe as she scanned the few lines written on the very thin paper, but then the bubble of hope burst. 'It is from Lucy...' she said to Jeanie and saw her nod.

Pam went back inside the house. She laid the letter down on the dresser and sat in Arthur's chair as the tears started. Just for a moment she'd hoped it was from John to tell her he was in hospital and recovering.

Pam wiped her cheeks on her apron and went to the sink, where she washed up the utensils she'd used for making her pasties. Drying her hands, she picked up the letter from Lucy and read it properly. It was a pleasant little letter and kind.

'Jonny wants his granny...' The kitchen door opened and Tom came in, holding the toddler by his hand, though he was perfectly able to walk unaided now, but tended to run off if left to his own devices. 'He has been to see the new calf feeding, but now he wants a drink and a cuddle.'

'I'll make a cup of tea,' Pam offered, smiling at him. Jonny came running to her and she bent down to give him a kiss and half a biscuit, which he started to suck immediately. Most of it would end up on the floor. 'Where are Lizzie and Arthur?'

'She went into work this morning,' Tom said. 'She took Arthur with her, even though Dot Goodman offered to have him, because she is going to pop over to see her mother in March. They will be home around four this afternoon – unless she has someone asking for a rush appointment.'

'Oh yes, Lizzie visits her mum once a month as a rule. She can always leave Arthur with us. I could look after him, though I know Dot enjoys having him sometimes.' Pam nodded and smiled. 'She bikes over and takes him visiting when Lizzie lets her have him for a few hours.'

'I suggested he stay home with one of us, but Lizzie says her customers and her mum like to see him. It is surprising really, because Maud wasn't a bit interested in Arthur at first, but now he's toddling and talking, apparently, she loves him.'

'Lizzie's mum is a strange one,' Pam replied. 'Lizzie never knows what sort of mood she will be in. It isn't easy for her, because she can't get enough petrol to take the car all the time so she has to catch the bus.'

Tom nodded and bent down to lift Jonny into his high chair. He winced slightly but was able to hold the little boy securely with both hands.

'Your arm is much better, Tom,' Pam observed. 'Does it still hurt to lift things?'

'It hurts a bit, Mum, but I've made myself do it. Exercise will make my arm strong again, but I have to put up with the discomfort.'

'I must admit I wondered whether you would ever use it properly again,' Pam told him. 'Well done to you for sticking with the regime you set yourself.'

'It isn't as good as it was by a long shot,' Tom told her with a grimace. 'I haven't got the same instant reflex I had, but I can do most things – it's just more deliberately thought out.'

'I can understand that. Pain slows you down, Tom. It might make a difference to your skill at playing darts and other sports, but you can use a knife and fork again and lift a child. I think that's a good start.'

'I doubt I could throw a three-darter at the moment,' Tom said, his expression slightly rueful. 'And I don't think I'd be able to deliver a knock-out punch, but I can drive a tractor and that is more important for the future.'

Pam nodded. 'I'm just glad you are getting better, love. I hope you'll be able to do all the things you once loved.'

'I had my time in the sun when I was a lad, playing football for the county and winning championships with our darts team. When I get home for good, I shall be looking to make a good life for my family, Mum. It's more important that I can drive than throw a dart.'

'Yes, I know. You were always the practical one; I think you get that from me, Tom. Your blood-father was far more likely to throw his hat over the windmill.'

'Do you still think about him, Mum?'

'Now and then,' she admitted. 'We were so young, Tom, and we thought our love was everything. We believed it would protect us, but it didn't.' She sighed. 'He wasn't even as old as you are…'

'Do you wonder what your life would've been like if he hadn't been killed?'

'Not really. I think Tom wanted his own business one day – a carpenter he'd planned to be – but he might have settled for working for a builder and a steady wage. Who knows?' She smiled at her son. 'I've had a good life and I've no grumbles, none at all.'

'Arthur was good to you and me,' Tom said. 'I can't be like my father. I've no desire to be a carpenter – I prefer the land. I might build a house and sell it to get some capital behind me – after the war – but then I'll probably buy more land. It's what I enjoy. The more of the world I see, the more I like my own little piece of it.'

'If I didn't know for sure, I'd think you were Arthur's son,' Pam replied with a little laugh. 'I used to watch you two discussing the land and your plans for it – and you got on so well.'

'Possibly because we weren't father and son,' Tom said. 'Artie rubbed him up the wrong way. Dad probably loved him more than the rest of us, but Artie never saw it. He didn't understand that Dad's nagging was because he wanted him to do well.'

'You've got a wise head on you,' Pam said. 'Be careful you don't get old before your time, Tom. You've had a lot to put up with, my son, but you should make time for fun in your life, too. Why don't you take Lizzie somewhere nice? Now the main crop is in, you could go to the sea for a few days – or just take a day or two off and go out with her. Buy her some clothes or a present or take her dancing. Have some together time. I can look after Arthur and Jeanie would help...'

'I'll wait until the potato harvest is in and then we'll go to the sea for a few days, if Lizzie wants to – she'll have to clear a space in her appointments. I know she doesn't work every day, but she has a lot of regular clients who want her to do their hair every week. I think on the days she goes in, she is very busy.'

'Yes, I know. I tell her she works too hard.'

'Lizzie is ambitious for us, Mum. She wants to open another shop – to sell ladies' clothes. She needed a little bit of extra money, so I gave it to her. I think she will be busy getting that ready for a while.'

'That is all very well, but you both need time to have fun,' Pam said. 'Before the war, Arthur was doing well, putting money by and he wanted to take me on a grand trip. His plan was to take a long holiday one day, when you children were all grown up. We talked about going on a luxury liner to America and a bit of a tour round there...' She sighed. 'Arthur kept saying one day, but then the war came and our time ran out.'

'Perhaps you could go – take one of the girls with you – when this insane war is finally over.'

'It's the last thing I want to do,' Pam said firmly. 'That was your dad's dream – I'm just reminding you that it's good to enjoy yourself.'

'What is your dream?' Tom asked and she shook her head.

'I don't know... I'd have liked to go to Scotland one day. I think it would suit me better than going on a ship, but... Maybe I will when things settled down again.'

'Lizzie and I will take you,' Tom said, 'and that's a promise, Mum. As soon as we get a chance, we'll all go on a trip round the Highlands. We can take the train part of the way and then hire a car in Scotland. Both Lizzie and I can drive and we'll stop along the way, take our time, make it a proper holiday. Goodness knows, we've all worked hard enough and I think it's time we had a bit more fun, all of us. Explore and go fishing.'

'Yes. You used to like a bit of fishing, didn't you?'

'Still do when I get the chance – but salmon or trout would be good. We could eat those...'

Pam laughed. 'And that's the smell of those pasties making you hungry. I'd best get them out before they burn.'

26

Artie finished filling the water troughs for the latest litter of pigs to be fattened, glancing round as he heard an engine stop. A car had drawn up next to the gate and a man got out and walked towards him.

'Good afternoon, sir,' the man said, taking off his smart trilby hat. 'Are you the owner of this?' He nodded towards the collection of huts the pigs were housed in. 'Mr Arthur Talbot?'

'Arthur Talbot was my father. He passed away a few months ago and, yes, I own this piece of land. This herd belongs to my mother – but it is going to market next week.' Artie nodded as he looked round. There were thirty pigs ready for market, leaving him two sows and a boar to rebuild his own herd.

'Ah, then perhaps I've come at a good time.' The man offered his hand and Artie wiped his on his trousers and then shook it. 'I was hoping you might sell me this small piece of land – what is it, ten acres?'

'Why would you want to buy it?' Artie asked cautiously. 'It isn't much good as arable land. That is why we have the pigs on it...'

'I want to build a garage on it,' the man replied. 'Bernard Stanfield; I should have introduced myself. I am hoping to set up a service and repair station – and I'd like to build myself a house at the back. It isn't too far from Chatteris and there is plenty of room for what I want to do...'

'Nice idea,' Artie said appreciatively. 'Good luck with finding yourself the right location, but this land isn't for sale – not yet, anyway. I've got plans for it myself.'

'Really? What are you thinking of?' Bernard Stanfield looked at him with interest.

'Maybe building, maybe something else,' Artie said. 'Anyway, I don't want to sell at the moment.'

'Up to you, of course – but I would offer a fair price.' He took a small printed card from his suit pocket and handed it to Artie. It was a local address, one of the big houses on London Road in Chatteris.

'What would you consider a fair price?' Artie asked.

'I was thinking of a thousand pounds...'

It was double what Arthur had paid, Artie knew that much, but he thought that if Tom was right, the deposits of sand and gravel might be worth many times that figure.

'No, I wouldn't consider that,' Artie replied with a nod of dismissal. 'It's worth a lot more to me.'

'I should've thought you could move your piggery nearer your home farm, save yourself a lot of time and energy, cycling all the way here and back?'

'Does me good,' Artie said, grinning now, because he suspected the stranger had been trying to pull a fast one. 'I'm not an idiot, mate, even if I look as if I don't know black from white.'

'Ah, I see...' Bernard Stanfield laughed, amused rather than annoyed that he'd been sussed. 'So you are aware of what is under here then?'

'I might be,' Artie said. 'Whatever it is, it's stopping there until the war is finished, and then I'll consider offers. And they won't be for a thousand pounds.'

'Well, you can't blame me for trying,' Stanfield said, trying to make light of it. 'If the deposits are there, it is worth a lot more – but we don't know for sure yet.'

'My father believed there were rich deposits here,' Archie said and Stanfield nodded.

'I'd need to do tests, to make sure the deposits are good enough – but if they're as deep as some of the other sites along this road, then of course I'd be willing to pay more.'

'Why should I sell to you, when I can dig it out myself and sell it direct to whoever is paying the best price?' Artie asked.

Bernard Stanfield's oily smile slipped a bit. 'We might talk about a partnership – if we could agree terms. You'd be paid a guaranteed amount per tonne and—'

'Thanks for the offer,' Artie put in sharply. He wouldn't deal with this man if he could help it. 'But I prefer to keep my options open. I haven't explored the possibilities yet, but I shall in my own time – and if I want a partnership, I have a brother.'

'Suit yourself, but you won't find it as easy to deal on the open market as you think,' Stanfield said. 'I'll give you a few weeks to think it over – but if I were you, I'd take my final offer, and that's five thousand pounds for the land. No work, no bother, no trying to find customers once you've dug it up – and there's all the problem of getting permission, don't forget that, Mr Talbot.'

'What do you mean? It's my land. I don't have to ask anyone.'

'Well, I think you will discover that you do need a licence to remove sand and gravel from the earth, Mr Talbot. I'll leave you to think about it. You have my card.'

Artie frowned as the other man walked off. He'd thought

when Tom said what his father was planning it was all straightforward. Bugger it! Artie knew he wouldn't have the patience or the knowledge to apply for licences and all the red tape that went with such things. It was bad enough trying to follow all the rules the Ministry of Food had in place for farmers at the moment.

Artie scowled as the posh car drove away. He'd been feeling pleased with the world, but now he was irritated. Why couldn't anything ever be simple? But that was why some folk were rich; they took advantage of others who didn't know how to go about getting the various permits, buying the land cheap and making a fortune from it. Well, Mr Stanfield wasn't going to do that to him if he could help it! He would speak to Tom about it that evening and ask for his help. Tom was good with things like that.

* * *

'Yes, I expect you would need permission from the County Council if you wanted to dig it out and sell yourself,' Tom said, looking thoughtful. 'Dad hadn't gone into it thoroughly. I think he knew someone who owns a lot of similar land and he was going to speak to him, when he was ready. I think everything like that is controlled, Artie. For one thing, there would be a lot of extra traffic going in and out – also, you have to agree on what happens to the land once the sand and gravel has been extracted, what impact it might have on neighbouring land…'

'A lot of bloody rigmarole then,' Artie said. 'I suppose it means a hundred and one forms to fill out…'

'Some, I expect, but we'll help you. Lizzie is good with stuff like that – but if you could get a decent price for the land, why not just sell? You might make a lot out of the sand and gravel, but it would be a big business and take over your life for possibly years to come.'

'Stanfield started at a thousand, when he thought I was some country bumpkin who didn't know A from B,' Artie muttered with a scowl. 'Then he flung the figure of five thousand at me when he left...'

'Five thousand pounds and no bother is a considerable offer,' Tom said, looking at Artie gravely. 'It could buy you a farm in the fens and enough land to make you comfortable for life, Artie.'

'Yes, but the aggregate could be worth many times that,' Artie said. 'Maybe ten times as much... even more.'

'If the deposits are rich, yes, perhaps, in time,' Tom reasoned. 'I know it sounds like a huge amount, Artie, but you couldn't manage it all alone – you'd be working all hours of the day and night. What about your farming land? With five thousand, you could own more than you'll eventually inherit, but immediately.'

'You would sell then?' Artie frowned. 'He said he'd need to do some tests...' A long sigh escaped him. 'Five thousand is a lot of money, Tom. I don't know what to do.'

'Try asking for ten thousand,' Tom suggested. 'He will scoff at you and walk off, but he'll be back with an offer. If you get six or above, I would grab it. You could do so much with that money...'

'I thought I could sit on it, extract a bit when I felt like it and sell a few loads...' Artie looked sulky. 'I didn't realise there would be licences and controls.'

'And site visits,' Tom said. 'No one can just take the minerals as and when they feel like it, Artie. They are considered too valuable – and extraction can cause problems in neighbouring land. So the council will be visiting and badgering you to get it right.'

'Might as well bloody sell then,' Artie grumbled. 'Don't like going back to him – didn't like him. Didn't trust him. Taking me for a bloody fool!'

'Would you like me to make enquiries for you?' Tom asked. 'I do know who Dad was going to speak to. I could ask him what he thinks it is worth, if you like – and I don't mind going to this other chap for you. I'll get the last penny out of him...'

Artie stared at him for a long moment, then he inclined his head. 'If I say I've changed my mind, he'll drop the price...'

'I'll get another price first,' Tom promised. 'Cheer up, Artie. You'll be a rich man come Christmas.'

Artie gave a snort of laughter. 'I was a mug. I thought it would be easy. Dig a few tonnes up and sell...'

'Don't think it is quite like potatoes,' Tom said with a grin. 'You can't nip round the local chip shop and sell him a couple of bags on the quiet. It either has to be a business you're prepared to commit to, Artie – or sell, use the money to make more and forget it.'

'You make it all sound so simple,' Artie said, a hint of resentment in his look. 'Dad made things look easy. I find everything a struggle... I can do the donkey work but give me a pen and paper and I'm lost.'

'You're a good farmer, Artie. Once you have some spare cash – after buying your farm, and there's cheap land to grab at the moment – then you could build a couple of houses. That's what I intend to do when I can.'

'Jeanie's father offered me a working partnership with him...'

'You wouldn't go to London?' Tom stared at him, shock and anxiety mingled. 'Mum couldn't manage the farm without you.'

'No – not until after the war. I had considered it, but Jeanie likes it here best – and if I could buy a hundred acres of good farmland, I wouldn't bother. I might go into a partnership with a bit of building this way...'

'We could do it together, help each other,' Tom suggested. 'Let me see if I can get you six thousand or above for that land, Artie. It would give you a really good boost.'

'Yeah, we could. I'll be grateful if you could sort it, Tom.'

'I promise I'll get you the best price I can.' Tom grinned at him. 'I like a bit of a haggle.'

'Don't you feel a bit aggrieved because Mum gave me that land?' Artie asked him suddenly. 'It wasn't fair on you or John...'

'It was Mum's to do with as she wished,' Tom replied with a shrug. 'Doesn't bother me. All I care about is that she doesn't go short. When the war is over, I can get this home land producing again. Mind you, beef and milk will probably bring in as much as the arable crops. You can't be sure of your yields from year to year.'

'Can't be sure of milk prices or yields either,' Artie said. 'I'm going for arable if I can get that money, Tom. Once your crop is in the ground, that's it until harvest, bar a bit of spraying and harrowing.'

Tom nodded. 'I prefer arable myself, too, the cows are a tie. Someone has to feed them and milk them, even at holiday times. We still have to work on Christmas Day, and get someone to stand in if we do manage a bit of a holiday – though I've promised Mum a trip after the war and I'll make sure she has the time of her life. By the way, are you taking Jeanie away for a few days once the potatoes are lifted?'

'I asked her if she'd like a week at the sea, but she says no. She would rather stay home until the baby is born.'

Tom nodded. 'She must be feeling it now, Artie. She is always so active, it must be hard to sit down and do nothing.'

'Well, if we get our own farm, she won't have much time to spare, so she should make the most of it now,' Artie said with a grin. 'Thanks, Tom. I appreciate your help. I think I made a mess of things with that bloke... too cocky...'

'He wouldn't have offered you the five thousand if he wasn't keen,' Tom replied, smiling. 'Besides, why should you give your land away? Don't worry. We'll make him pay or deal with Dad's contact.'

Artie nodded. He was grateful for his brother's help, because he'd known he was out of his depth. Artie had been brought up to understand farming, but he knew he wasn't capable of running the kind of business Tom seemed to think necessary with its licences and the amount of labour it would take to extract the deposits.

'Yeah, we'll make him pay,' he agreed. 'I've promised to take Jeanie to the pictures this evening. She wants to see *Gone With the Wind*; it is on again at the Rex in Ely. I'd better get going...'

'Lizzie has seen it,' Tom replied with a smile. 'I offered to take her but she said no.'

'Jeanie wants to see it again...' Artie rolled his eyes. 'Rubbish if you ask me, but if it is what she wants...'

He walked out just as Lizzie entered with Arthur in her arms. Tom got up to take the boy. 'You look tired, love...' Artie heard him say as he walked away.

* * *

Artie's mind was busy with sums. He knew of some fenland going for less than it was worth – there were three lots: a thirty-acre, a forty-acre and a twenty-five-acre bit. The farmer was retiring and it was good land. Artie felt the excitement build inside him. He'd had dreams of a fortune from the sand and gravel and someone would undoubtedly make a lot of money from it, but in his heart, he knew Tom was right. He should haggle for as much as he could get and then buy what he truly understood. With ninety-five acres of his own land to farm, he had a chance of becoming wealthy. In fact, by most men's standards, he was already rich – that piece of land the piggery stood on would make all the difference. If Tom got him somewhere in the region of six thousand for it...

Artie chuckled to himself. His father had done him a favour by changing his will, because otherwise the piggery land would never have been given to Artie. It wasn't fair on his brothers and sisters, but the girls would have their trust funds one day and Tom didn't seem bothered. John would lose out, because both he and Tom had their own homes... *if* John ever came home. As for the girls. Well, Artie could give them a nice wedding present if he'd made his fortune by then – and he would; he'd make certain his mother didn't go without, too.

His shoulders straightened. How long would it be until he got his money? He hoped that land down the fen hadn't been sold. There was other land, but the land he fancied was near Talbot land and it was good – cheap too at forty pounds an acre...

27

Lizzie picked up the letter from the doormat and looked at it. She knew at once what it must be. Tom had told her that he was likely to be called back for a medical soon. He'd had almost two months of sick leave and that time had flown, summer fading to autumn more quickly than ever before, because it was so good to have her husband home. It was the longest time they'd had together and it had been glorious. Tom had asked if she wanted to go away for a while, but Lizzie was content to be at home with him. He did what he could on the farm and helped to take care of the children. Lizzie cooked, cleaned, went into work three days a week, and simply enjoyed the simplicity of her life. It was how life should be for a young married couple, but it was, she knew, an oasis of peace that couldn't last.

She went into the kitchen, the letter in her hand. 'It is for you, Tom. I think it must be your medical...'

'Damn,' Tom swore softly. 'Sorry, love. I was hoping they might have forgotten me.'

'Me too,' she said and watched as he opened the letter. He read it quickly and nodded. 'How soon?'

'Next week, Tuesday,' he said. 'That means we have a long weekend to spend together. We'll go to the sea for a day, Lizzie. Pack a picnic – and have a nice tea somewhere on the way back...'

'Yes, all right, let's do that,' she said. 'This weather is glorious – a real Indian summer. I hope it lasts. When shall we go?'

'Are you working tomorrow?'

'No.' She smiled at him, catching his mood. 'Yes, let's go tomorrow. I have to go in for a couple of hours today. When I get back, I'll make some sausage rolls to take with us and I'll bring some stuff for sandwiches. It will be fun, Tom. Arthur has never seen the sea...' She hesitated. 'I know it is our day – but do you think your mum would like to come and bring Jonny?'

'Would you mind? I mean... we could have the day just for us.'

'Ask Pam and see,' Lizzie replied with a smile. 'I love being alone with you, Tom, but I have that here. It would be nice for your mum. She hardly ever goes out. She could leave a cold lunch for the girls – and Jeanie can hold the fort for one day.'

'All right, I'll ask,' Tom said. 'I am sure the two little ones would enjoy a paddle together.'

'Yes, they would,' Lizzie said and went to him as he stood up. He put his arms around her and kissed her. 'I love you, Tom.'

'Love you more,' he teased. 'I'm going up to Sutton to see someone later this morning. Do you need anything from the butcher or the baker?'

'Yes, if they have some ham at Mr Goddard's; I like his ham better than Goodman's, even though he's always got extra for us. I'll have whatever he can spare for us – and a large loaf, please.' She smiled. 'If you're going, I don't have to. I'm going to get ready for work, but I'll be back by half past one at the latest.'

'Right. I'll ask Mum and see if she fancies a trip to the sea,'

Tom said. He grinned. 'I've got another customer for Artie's land. He's a Haddenham man with local connections and already owns a lot of the land on the Chatteris road, and he knows there is a rich deposit on Artie's piggery. He was going to talk to his partners, who live in Sutton, and come up with an offer...'

'Let's hope it is a good one. Artie has been in a mellow mood this past week. I don't want to see the frowns back, for Jeanie's sake. She doesn't complain, but your brother can be a bit on the sulky side, Tom.'

'Yes, I know. I sort of understand him, Lizzie, but John wasn't – *isn't* – like that and Susan certainly isn't. I think Angela can be a bit moody at times.' Tom was still refusing to accept that John was dead, still holding hope that somehow, he'd survived.

'She is an awkward age,' Lizzie excused. 'She'll grow out of it – but Artie. Oh well, if he gets what he wants, they will be living in Sutton and we shan't see as much of them.'

'You will miss Jeanie if they move?'

'Yes, but I think your mum will miss her more.'

'She has Jonny and Arthur and you, and me when I'm home,' Tom said. 'Susan comes home from college at weekends sometimes – and Artie will be in and out of the yard, Jeanie too, once she's had the baby. Not as much, of course, but Mum will still see them.'

'I know.' Lizzie left it there. Tom was a man with a busy life. He wouldn't understand that once the working day was done, Pam would be bound to feel lonely. Yes, she had children in the house, but no husband to talk over the day with.

It was the same for all widows, of course, and the war had made many more of them.

* * *

'Are you certain you have all you need, Susan?' Pam asked, looking at her daughter as she entered the kitchen carrying a pile of books. Susan had passed her exams with flying colours and gained a place at the college of her choice. Based in Cambridge, she was able to come home for weekends sometimes and at half-term. She packed her books into a big case that Pam had had brought down from the attic. 'That is going to be so heavy. Artie can put it on the train for you, but how you're going to get it to the college, I don't know...'

'The station porter has them sent to the lodge and then the college porter has them brought up to the students' rooms. I'm lucky I've got accommodation on campus, Mum. Otherwise, I'd be in a crumby lodging house and then I would have difficulty getting my stuff...' Susan laughed. 'Don't look so anxious, Mum. I'm loving college.'

'Good.' Pam laughed. 'You're all grown up all of a sudden, Susan. I don't know what happened...' She shook her head. 'Don't listen to me. I'm daft. As I said, do you have all you need?' Pam looked at her. 'That parcel Jock delivered. Was it another book? You seem to need so many.'

'I do and I'll need more,' Susan replied. 'Not yet, though. I have enough money for my books. Dad gave it to me when he was ill. Just to be sure I had it – and no, the parcel wasn't a book.' Susan smiled and went out of the room. A few minutes later, she returned with a package wrapped in silver tissue paper. 'This is what Jock delivered – and it is for you, Mum. I asked Vera to buy it for me and she did...'

'For me?' Pam looked at her. 'No, that's silly. It isn't my birthday – you should spend your money on you, love.'

'I do and I have and I shall,' Susan said, laughing. 'This is for the very best mum in the world with all my love. If it hadn't been for you, I would never have kept up my studies – and I'm so glad I did. It is my chance to become a teacher and have a good life.'

'Oh, Susan...' Pam took the gift and stared at her. Then she undid the paper to reveal a cashmere cardigan in her favourite shade of cornflower blue. 'Oh, this is beautiful – but it must have been so expensive. However did Vera find anything this nice these days?'

'She says it's knowing where to look – and that came from Harvey Nichols in London. She saw them there and told Jeanie she thought you would love them. So I asked her to buy one in blue...'

'Oh, thank you, my love,' Pam's eyes teared up as she looked at her eldest girl. 'It is beautiful and I love it. I shall wear it on Sunday when I go to church.'

'Good. You should go out and meet your friends sometimes, Mum,' Susan told her. She went to her and hugged her. 'I love you lots and I know I've been a pain in the bum sometimes, but I always loved you – and I always shall.'

'I shall miss you, love,' Pam said and hugged her back. 'I'm glad you're happy at college. Your dad would be so proud. I know he's sitting up there in the sky somewhere watching and he will be puffing his pipe and cheering you on. You make sure you have a good time. Study hard but have fun, too, Susan.'

'I shall, Mum, I promise you,' Susan said. 'I'll need to fetch another two loads and then I've done. I'll be home in a couple of weeks with a load more washing for you...' She laughed and Pam laughed too. They were still laughing when Tom entered.

'Well, that's nice to hear,' he said. 'I like to see you happy. Are you all right for money, Susan?' He took a little bundle of one-pound notes from his pocket and gave her two. 'It's not much, but we soldiers don't get paid much – have a few drinks with your friends on me, love.'

'Thanks, Tom. I've got money, but I won't refuse,' Susan said and gave him a hug. 'What are you doing today?'

'That's a secret,' Tom said and grinned. 'At the moment, I'm on an errand. Mum, Lizzie and I are going to the sea somewhere tomorrow – Hunstanton or Heacham – we'd like you to come and bring Jonny...'

'Come to the sea with you?' Pam looked at him. 'But you and Lizzie should spend time alone together...'

'We do at home all the time – and Lizzie wants you to come. She says the two boys would love to be together for their first visit to the sea.'

'You should go, Mum,' Susan said. 'This weather is glorious, make the most of it. I'm not going anywhere. I'll help Jeanie get the meals for once.'

'Well...' Pam looked from one to the other. 'Yes, I will come, Tom. We can take a picnic and the boys will have a lovely time paddling.'

'I am going to Sutton now – is there anything you need from the shop?'

'Two large sandwich loaves,' Pam said. 'I shan't be baking bread tomorrow. And if you can get a big pork pie from the butcher or a pound of sausages, if they are available. If not, some ham or... anything easy really. I just need to feed the girls. We'll give them an easy lunch tomorrow for a change...'

'Right, I'll see what I can get,' Tom said. 'If I don't see you before you leave tomorrow evening, have a good time at college, Susan.'

'Thank you, big brother.' Susan grinned at him as he went out.

'Wonder what Tom is up to,' Pam remarked as he closed the door. 'He looked very pleased with himself, didn't you think so?'

'Yes, he did,' Susan said. 'Shall I ask Lizzie?'

'No. Tom will tell us when he is ready,' Pam said. 'Now, what can I make today that I can leave for you all to have cold tomorrow?'

'What about blackberry and apple turnovers?' Susan said. 'There are loads on the bushes and we've got cooking apples. I'll go and pick a big basket for you, Mum.'

'Yes, that would be nice and filling. If Tom gets a pork pie or sausages, that will do. I can put some big potatoes in the range and let them cook slowly and I think there are a couple of tomatoes left in the green house. I might do some hard-boiled eggs.'

'I will go and collect all I can,' Susan said. 'Would you iron my best silk blouse, Mum? I'd like to wear it this evening. Mark is taking me to a dance in Haddenham.'

'Mark? Who is Mark?' Pam asked. 'Have I met this one?'

'No, I don't think you have,' Susan said with a little giggle. 'I only met him yesterday when I was doing your shopping in Ely. He is a New Zealander and he has just been sent to the airfield… He seems nice, but just a friend…'

Pam shook her head at her as her daughter took a light jacket from the door, picked up a basket and went out. 'You girls these days…'

At least there was no need to worry over Susan. Her daughter liked lots of men friends, but she wasn't serious about any of them. She was just having a good time and her heart was set on becoming a teacher. It was what Arthur would have wanted for his daughter. Pam did, too, as long as she was happy.

28

Mark had been drinking steadily all evening. Susan hadn't expected him to take her to a pub and then down pint after pint of beer with a whisky chaser every other round, and she'd become more uneasy as the evening went on. All the other young men she'd dated had been talkative, friendly, just pleased to be out with a pretty young girl; most had taken her to the pictures or a dance and she'd had fun, but she wasn't having fun now. She wasn't at all sure whether Mark was in a fit condition to drive home. Fortunately, they were only in Witcham and Susan could manage to walk home if she had to. She glanced at the wristwatch that had been one of the last gifts her father had given her; it had just gone nine. Early to call a halt to a date, but she'd had enough. Mark hadn't said much for the past half an hour, seeming to be brooding on some dark thoughts of his own.

'I think I need to get home,' she said as he reached for his empty glass, clearly intending to buy another drink.

'It isn't late,' Mark said. 'I'm having another. Come on loosen up, Susie. You've been drinking lemonade, have a proper drink.' He winked. 'Put you in the mood for later?'

'What do you mean?' Susan asked, feeling a hot flush creep up her neck, because she couldn't truly miss what he was hinting at. 'I don't think so. We hardly know each other and I only came out with you as a friend – I told you that when you asked—'

'Like you don't give it to all the others. They all know what you are... little Miss No Knickers.'

Susan didn't reply. She was shocked and horrified. None of the other men she'd been out with had spoken to her like that; they'd all been like her, happy just to enjoy themselves together and be friends. A little goodnight kiss and that was it – but there was something about Mark. A brooding look that she'd thought attractive until he started drinking so heavily.

He went off to the bar to fetch more drinks. Susan didn't hesitate. Picking up her bag, she walked quickly out of the pub. It was dark, because there were no street lights, but, after her eyes became accustomed to the change, she discovered that there was just enough light in the sky, whether from stars or the sliver of moon that peeped from behind purple clouds, for her to see. She walked quickly past the houses of the village, all of them curtained with thick black drapes so that no lights should show. The blackout was enforced by wardens who checked regularly, because of the remote chance of a stray bomber being attracted by the light from a window. In towns, it was far more likely, but even here in the country it could happen; they'd had enemy planes overhead in the past weeks, though no bombs had been dropped. Just recently, a plane had crashed into a home in Sutton, but that wasn't an enemy plane, instead, a British one that had been badly damaged and didn't quite make it to the airport. Fortunately, no one was injured.

Susan walked at a good pace. It was chilly, because she only had a cotton dress and a light jacket on; she hadn't expected to be walking home and she felt angry and humiliated by what Mark had said to her. Although she knew it was lies, she couldn't help wondering if people thought bad things of her because she went out with all the young men who asked her. Most of them had been to tea with her family and knew she was a decent girl, because Pam had extended an open invitation to the airmen. Susan had thought it was fine, being friendly with them all, and she'd told everyone that she was concentrating on her college exams and just wanted friendship, but had it been seen in another light by others?

Her feelings were smarting a bit, because she hated that someone thought her cheap or fast; she wasn't. One reason Susan didn't want a steady relationship was because of her college plans, but there was another. She'd given her heart to a man already. He didn't know it, of course, and she'd always known it was foolish. Terry Salmons had been married and was grieving for his wife, who had died after a gas explosion in London. He had a little daughter named Tina, and Susan had been fond of her, too. Tina had stayed at the farm while her father was recovering from his war wounds, and it was bonding with her and watching him gradually find his daughter again, after the grief that had nearly killed him, that had made Susan lose her heart to Terry.

No one knew. Susan had only been sixteen at the time and Terry was learning to live with only one leg and still weak from the time he'd spent close to death in hospital. Susan couldn't let him see her feelings and, being a sensible girl, she'd thought the ache in her heart might go away if she just let it. She was young and perhaps it was just the infatuation of a young girl for a war hero. So she'd gone out with lots of young men, mostly from the airbase in Mepal, but in her heart she knew that her feelings for Terry were real. She'd kept them inside for two years, while she studied and took her exams, but although she didn't cry at night now, she knew they hadn't gone away. However, Terry had never shown more than friendship towards her and it would be stupid to imagine that he felt the same way. It was her secret and must stay that way.

Susan's thoughts had drifted to the time when Terry was staying at the farm, the warmth and happiness of that time, easing the humiliation she'd felt when Mark had spoken to her as if she were some kind of loose woman. She'd walked fast, leaving the village behind, and was now following a long, winding road that passed fields shadowed in darkness, high bushes to either side with deep ditches, still empty after the months of summer, but in winter they would fill with water draining from the surrounding fields.

A flicker of light behind her told Susan that a car was coming up. She stepped onto the verge. Although the car's lights were shaded, they were still brighter than they should be and she wondered who was breaking the regulations, before there was a flicker of recognition as the driver pulled up beside her, winding the window down and calling to her.

'What the hell do you think you're doing?' Mark's voice asked and Susan turned to look at him. His face looked white in the dim light, his eyes dark and yet holding a glitter as the moon sailed out from behind the clouds. He looked furious.

'You didn't want to leave, so I decided to go home,' Susan told him. She kept her distance. There was no way she was going to get in that car with him. She didn't trust him one inch. 'I should have said thank you for the drink, but I didn't like the way you spoke to me. That was insulting – and it was a lie. I don't know who told you that I was easy, but it isn't true. I go out with a lot of people, but they all know it is just as friends. I thought you did too... Now, I'm going home alone. Goodnight.'

Susan started to walk again. She didn't look round, but she heard him get out of his car and then his feet hitting the road as he ran after her. He caught her arm and swung her round to face him. He was scowling, a murderous expression in his eyes.

'No bitch walks out on me...' he said and grabbed her, pulling her in hard as he pushed his face close to hers and then forced his mouth over hers. Susan closed her mouth tight, jerking her head back and trying to avoid the hateful kiss. The smell of his breath was strong with beer and cigarettes. She brought her knee up sharply, but, unfortunately, he was wise to the move and jumped back, swearing, and calling her a bitch and filthy names she'd never heard from anyone before. He grappled with her as she fought him. He wrestled her back against a hedge and she could feel the branches sticking into her back, her heels slipping on the edge of one of the dykes as they both fell back into it.

Susan screamed as she felt the weight of him on top of her, felt his hands clawing at her skirt, pulling it up. She wrenched one of her hands free and struck his face, screaming at him to stop, but he was too strong for her. He was fiddling with the front of his trousers, unbuttoning, as she squirmed and fought, trying to push him off her. Yet she knew it was impossible to stop him and fear made her scream again and again. Then she heard a shout and the next minute someone dragged Mark off her. She heard sounds of a struggle, shouting and yelling as two men fought.

Susan crawled out of the ditch, scratching her bare legs further. There had been some water in the dyke and the back of her skirt and jacket felt wet. She stood on the road at last and watched as the two men fought in the road, and then realised that the man who had come to her rescue was her brother Artie.

They were punching each other in the face, swearing and

jostling, tearing at each other's clothes. It was a dreadful fight, vicious and dangerous. Susan was frightened, breathing hard, wondering what to do. Should she run for help? She wasn't sure that Artie was winning.

Artie turned his head towards her, grunting, 'Get out of here...!'

Susan hesitated and then started running. She ran as fast as she could. The fight was still going on behind her. What ought she to do? She was nearly at the farm when she saw a man walking towards her. In her panic, she didn't know him, until he called her name, 'Susan – what's wrong?'

Tom. It was Tom! Thank God. Her breath came in gasps as she tried to tell him. 'Artie... saved me... he's in a fight... needs help...'

'Calm down, Susan,' Tom said and took hold of her shaking hands. 'Is it that bloke you went out with this evening? Did he try to harm you?'

Susan nodded, her breath easing but her chest felt sore.

'Artie stopped him and they're fighting? Where?' Tom said, making her concentrate.

'Back there...' Susan pointed.

'Go in and don't say anything to anyone,' he instructed. 'You hear me, Susan. Say nothing.'

Susan inclined her head, watching as Tom set off at a run.

For a few seconds, she stood where she was, breathing softly to get herself straight and then she thought about what she would tell her mother. Tom had warned her not to speak of what had happened. She felt the back of herself. It was mostly her jacket that was slightly wet. Susan took it off and held it behind her. No one would notice the patch on the back of her skirt. She would say she had work to do in her room if her mum asked her any questions.

Fortune was with her. Pam wasn't in the kitchen when Susan entered. She thought she could hear her in the scullery, so she went quickly through and out into the hall, on up the stairs to her own room. She threw the jacket onto a chair and sat down on the bed, her legs shaky as she realised what had almost happened to her. If Artie hadn't come at that moment...

Susan felt sick. The realisation that she might have been raped shocked her. Not once had she ever felt frightened before when out with a man, but she'd been terrified when Mark grabbed her and she'd felt herself falling back into that ditch. It was horrible. She felt dirty and cheap, even though she hadn't done anything to deserve it. Did people really think she was some kind of a whore, just because she went out with a lot of young men? What was wrong in having a little fun? They'd all seemed perfectly happy. One or two had tried it on, but laughed and given up when Susan said no. It hadn't occurred to her that a man might get the wrong idea.

Giving herself a little shake, Susan decided she wouldn't let herself be made to feel like this because of one man's opinion. He'd been drunk and he must have his own problems. She would just forget it and get on with her life. She was going back to college and would put it out of her head... Except that she knew the humiliation would always be there at the back of her mind.

* * *

Tom saw the struggle going on as he got near the two men. It was obvious to him that Artie was getting the worst of it. Whoever this man was, he was strong and knew how to fight. Once upon a time, Tom could have floored him with a punch, but not with his right arm as it was now. There were other ways of disabling the man if he could just get near enough but... Even as Tom hesitated, Artie got lucky and pushed his opponent in the chest. He was on the edge of the dyke and fell heavily backwards. Tom heard his shrill cry as he reached his brother.

Artie was peering down into the ditch. Tom knelt down and looked and then back up at Artie. 'I think he's dead...' The words sounded unreal even to a man who had killed without hesitation on the field of battle. 'There's something sharp in that ditch and he hit his head on it...'

'It's an old plough shear,' Artie said in a strangled voice. 'It came off Jack Gregson's plough last winter and he never bothered to fetch it – said it was rusted through...' He sank to his knees beside Tom, his face white in the thin sliver of moonlight that escaped from a bank of cloud. 'Bloody hell, Tom. I never meant to kill him. I caught him attacking our Susan...'

'Yes, I gathered that much,' Tom said. He was thinking fast. It had been an accident – but it looked bad. It might mean Artie going to prison for manslaughter and it would ruin Susan's life and her reputation if it all came out in court. In a small village, it only took a few mean words for a girl to be labelled – and what would his mother do without Artie? She couldn't run the farm alone. Besides, she'd suffered enough grief. 'He was scum, Artie. Only bastards attack girls. Forget him. Get home, Artie, and don't say a word. I told Susan to keep quiet – do the same. You slipped on cow dung and fell on your face if anyone asks about your bruises.'

Artie hesitated uncertainly. 'But surely we should tell the police how it happened?'

'Do you want to be tried for murder – manslaughter at the least? What about Mum and Susan?'

'My God... it was an accident. I never meant...'

'Who would believe that?' Tom asked. 'You even knew the

plough shear was there...' He thought for a moment and climbed down into the ditch, taking a closer look, but there was no mistake. The rusted metal had gone right into the back of the man's head, killing him almost instantly. 'He had been drinking a lot. I can smell it...' Climbing back to the verge, he looked at his brother. 'I'm going to drive his car into the dyke – and leave the driver's door open. With any luck, it will look as if he drove it in himself and fell on that thing as he got out...' He looked at Artie. 'Go on, get out of here. Make sure you look normal. Don't run – and don't ever tell anyone what I'm going to do...'

Artie stared at him in silence, then inclined his head and walked off down the road. Tom watched until he'd gone, then he looked all around him. No one about. He walked across to the car, which had been left running, got in, reversed it and then drove it towards the ditch, letting the front wheels slide over the edge so that it was tipped front down, boot up in the air. He forced the door back and wriggled out on his back. Then he crawled down into the ditch and crouch-walked all the way to the end of the road that led towards the airfield, almost a mile from the scene of the accident he'd created. Here, he raised his head and looked about him until he was certain there was no one standing around in the dark. He got to his feet, walking calmly back down the hill to the farm, passing it and on down the lane to his own home.

* * *

Tom stood in his back garden and lit a cigarette, drawing deeply. He was used to difficult situations in his work, but for all the missions he'd undertaken, all the enemy he'd killed, he'd never felt this way before – a mixture of guilt and disgust. He had committed a criminal act and he could go to prison for a long time; he could even hang if the crime was proven to be murder. It would look as if he and his brother were in a conspiracy to cover a murder if it ever came out – but it mustn't.

That few seconds that had led up to what Artie had accidentally done could have ruined Tom's family's life. If he hadn't been there, Artie would have probably gone to the police – or maybe he would have just run. Tom knew that it was he who had taken charge, made it look like an accident. He could only pray that the military police were satisfied it was an accident, because it would be them who investigated, not a local bobby.

All he and Artie had to do was to hold their nerve when the law came calling. Tom could do it – but could Artie? Susan was distressed by the attack but wouldn't know what had happened afterwards. She would be back at college and hopefully would hear nothing of the fatal accident. By the time she did, it should all have blown over. They just had to pray that luck was with them and no one had seen what had happened. Tom was pretty sure there hadn't been anyone around; he was used to working in the dark and lives were lost if an enemy went unseen.

Now all he could do was wait for developments, but if the worst happened and the military cops got too close, Tom had one alternative. It would be he who went to prison, not Artie. He would take the blame on himself. The man who had died wasn't much of a man in Tom's opinion, and he'd deserved a beating; it was just bad luck that it had ended his life.

29

Susan spent a restless night, unable to sleep. She cried a bit and felt miserable but pushed the incident from her mind and eventually fell into a fitful sleep. It was still dark when she woke. The house was silent, no one was stirring as she pulled on some clothes and went downstairs, leaving the house by the kitchen door. She walked across the field to the house where Lizzie and Tom lived, shivering and feeling tormented by the events of the previous night.

Lizzie had told her she could talk to her if she was worried about anything and she really needed that – but it was so early. She was about to turn away when the kitchen light snapped on. Susan hesitated and then walked quickly to the door and knocked.

Lizzie opened it, looking startled as she ushered her in. 'Is something wrong, Susan? Is it Jeanie – or Pam?'

'No – nothing wrong. It's just...' Susan hesitated. 'You said I could tell you if anything was worrying me...'

'Of course you can, love,' Lizzie motioned to her to sit down and Susan saw that Arthur was sitting in his high chair. 'I just came down to make a cup of tea. Arthur was awake and I brought him down to change him and give him a drink of warm milk. It sometimes gets him back to sleep – and we're going out later.'

'I know – that's why I wanted to talk to you, because I'll be gone before you get home.'

Lizzie was pouring water into the pot. 'Go on, love. I know it is important or you wouldn't be here at this hour.'

'Last night I went out with a man I didn't know very well...' Susan hesitated. 'Tom didn't say anything?'

'No – should he have?'

'I just wondered...' Susan looked at her, tears in her eyes. 'His name was Mark and – he was drinking a lot, so I left him to it and walked home from Witcham...' Her voice caught. 'He came after me and attacked me...'

'Did he harm you?' Lizzie looked at her in alarm. 'He didn't...'

'No. He tried, but Artie came and stopped him. They were fighting. Artie told me to run home. I did and I met Tom. He went running off to help Artie...'

'Then I dare say he got what he deserved,' Lizzie said, smiling at her. 'As long as you're all right, Susan. I know you must have been shocked and upset.'

'He said all the men thought I was cheap – called me a tart, or the same thing...'

'Horrible man!' Lizzie said and rushed over to hug her. 'Everyone knows that isn't true, love. You're just a young girl having fun. You must put it out of your mind and forget it. Some men are nasty – just be careful who you go out with in future.'

'It made me feel so dirty—' Susan gave a little sob. 'I'm not like that, Lizzie.'

'Of course you aren't, my love. It happened to me once – you knew that?'

Susan nodded.

'I was so ashamed and it took me months to get over – but I did. You weren't physically abused so you have no need to feel dirty. Just be angry because he was such a bastard...'

'Susan – is Mum all right?' Tom asked, entering the kitchen at that moment, wearing a robe over his pyjamas.

'Susan was telling me about last night,' Lizzie said, turning to look at him. 'Some horrid man attacked her. You didn't tell me, Tom?'

Tom had gone to the sink, his back towards them as he ran a glass of cold water for himself. 'It wasn't important,' he lied without turning round. 'Artie was crowing he'd scared the bugger off – and he'd gone haring off in his car. Drunk, by all accounts.' He turned, a smile on his face. 'You're all right, Susan? Artie was in time to stop that scum hurting you?'

'Yes, I'm all right – now.' Susan looked gratefully at Lizzie. 'Thank you, Lizzie. You've made me feel so much better.'

'Good. Just put it out of your mind,' Tom said. 'I told you last night, Susan. Keep what happened to yourself. There's no need for anyone else to know. Artie might get into trouble for physical assault – so best not say anything. It never happened.'

Susan looked at him. There was something about Tom at that moment that told her what he was saying was important. 'Yes, all right. I shan't tell Mum or anyone else. It's just that Lizzie understands me.'

'Get off home and back to bed,' Tom said. 'I'm going up. You coming, Lizzie?'

'In a few minutes...' Lizzie smiled as he left the room. 'He's right, Susan. Just put it right out of your mind.'

'I shall.' Susan hugged and kissed her. 'Have a lovely day out. I'll see you next time I'm home.'

* * *

Tom was back in bed but not asleep when Lizzie entered, having put Arthur in his bed. She got in beside him and snapped out the light, then, 'So what aren't you telling me, Tom?'

'What do you mean?' Tom asked, a wary note in his voice.

'What really happened when you found Artie?' Lizzie said. 'I know when you're lying, Tom. Please tell me the truth.'

'It's best you don't know,' Tom replied. 'I would have preferred that Susan hadn't told you but she did...' He grunted, sat up and leaned over to switch on the table lamp beside him, looking into her eyes. 'Will you please just trust me, Lizzie? I haven't done anything wicked – just what I had to. Can you leave it there?'

Lizzie met his eyes for a moment in silence and then nodded. 'You're my husband, Tom. I love you and I trust you. I know you're a good man.' She snuggled up to him. 'We'd best get some sleep. It's our day out today and it will be starting soon...'

30

'What happened last night?' Jeanie asked as she saw Artie wince while dressing the next morning. 'How did you hurt yourself?'

'I told you. I slipped on some cow dung and fell flat on my face, only there was a pile of rubble and it hurt.' He touched a bruise on his cheek and pulled a face. 'Stupid of me.'

'I don't know why you were out wandering about in the dark,' Jeanie said, puzzled. 'Is something wrong, Artie? You seem strange... not like you. Have I done anything to upset you? I mean, I know I nagged you a bit over the way you behaved after your dad's funeral, but I thought we were over all that?'

'I don't mind how much you nag, as long as you never stop loving me,' Artie said and sat beside her. She was still in bed, her hair tousled, and she looked beautiful. Her pregnancy suited her and she glowed. 'I adore you, Jeanie. You must know that?' He held her hand. 'Sometimes I do and say things that hurt, but you won't stop loving me – whatever?'

'Of course I won't,' she said and looked at him in distress. 'Artie – you haven't... There isn't another girl?'

'Good grief, no!' Artie shouted. 'Surely you know better than that, Jeanie? I know I played around before we married, but I wouldn't cheat on you.'

'Then what is it?' she asked. 'I know something is eating at you. Can't you tell me, please?' She saw some redness on his right hand and caught his wrist. 'How did that happen?'

'It's nothing...' Artie turned away. He was haunted by what he'd done. Tom said it was best to keep his mouth shut, and Artie knew he was right, but it was hard, especially with Jeanie. His guilt at causing a man's death burned inside him, but he had to keep silent. 'Nothing that you can help with, Jeanie. I do have something on my mind, but I'll get over it.'

'Well, tell me when you're ready,' Jeanie said and put her legs over the bed. 'I might as well get up.'

'You don't need to,' Artie said. 'You don't have to milk the cows, Jeanie. The girls will do most of it and I'll be down the fen most of the day. I want to plough that small bit of land near the river. I'm going to try to get some cabbages and sprouts on it.'

'Isn't it a bit late for that?' Jeanie asked.

'Maybe. It's only a couple of acres. I can plough it in and plant something else if it fails. It will be an extra crop if it works – and there's a late variety I've been told about.'

Jeanie nodded and Artie went down to the kitchen. His mother was frying eggs and mashed potatoes and mushrooms for the girls' breakfasts. She offered him the same, but he shook his head.

'Maybe later. I'll have a slice of that toast for now.' He took a piece and went out eating it. Crossing the yard, he entered the cowsheds and picked up a milk churn. It needed a wash and was something he could do to keep out of the way for a while. He'd thought up an excuse to take himself off for the day, because he didn't want to have to speak to Susan. If she asked him what had happened, he might betray himself.

It was all such a mess. He'd acted instinctively when he saw what that bugger was trying to do to his sister, his only thought to save her. Artie had gone for a walk last night because he needed to think things through; his life seemed all over the place lately, even though Tom had given him good news about the piggery. He had a second customer who was willing to pay him another thousand above what he'd been offered, if the deposits were there as expected. The new buyer was experienced and thought it was a done deal, but Artie had been on thorns over it and couldn't rest, so he'd gone out to help himself think about what he would do if he got all that money – and if he didn't.

He almost wished he'd stayed home now. If he had, he wouldn't be feeling racked with guilt, as if he were a cold-blooded murderer. Yet he was glad he'd stopped Susan suffering the rape that would undoubtedly have happened. Tom had come because Susan had told him. So Artie had to be glad that he'd been there – and yet he was haunted by what he'd done. He'd killed someone. Yes, it was a tragic accident, but he still felt guilt and remorse.

Artie was torn inside. A part of him knew why Tom had acted so swiftly. The prospect of a trial for manslaughter and almost certain imprisonment made Artie shudder. His brother was right. The police would have suspected murder. Artie had attacked that devil, for good reason, but he'd expected a short, sharp fist fight. Unfortunately, the bugger wouldn't give in; he'd kept coming back for more, pushing Artie, taunting him, never leaving it. Artie would have let him walk off after the first few punches, but he'd come back at him again and again; let's face it, he'd been losing until Tom arrived in the nick of time. Artie thought his opponent had hesitated, perhaps he'd noticed Tom running towards them, and it was in that moment Artie had taken the chance to push him into the dyke. He'd just thought that might finish it – but not in the way it had. Of course, he'd known the plough shear was there somewhere, but in the dark and at that precise place where he'd given the bugger a huge shove? No, no way had he even thought of it – but others might not believe that...

The military police were sure to make enquiries and would learn that Susan had been in the pub with him earlier, but she'd left him there and walked home alone. She would be off to college soon and... Besides, Tom had made it look as if the car had driven off the road. Artie told himself to stop fretting over it. Tom had thought swiftly. Hopefully, the police would accept it was an accident.

Artie took his angst out on scrubbing the milk churns. He needed tough physical work to stop the torment in his mind and was hard at it when someone walked into the cowshed. Artie looked up and frowned as he saw his brother.

'Tom. What's wrong?'

'Thought I might find you here.' Artie set the last milk churn down as his brother spoke. 'I wanted to tell you not to worry. It was an accident – but if it all goes pear-shaped, you weren't there. I did it all—'

'Bloody hell! Do you think I'd let you carry the can for—' Artie broke off and glared at him in shock and horror. 'I'm not that much of a cad.'

Tom reached out and grabbed him by the shoulders. He shook him, staring hard into his face. 'It was my idea, my blame. You weren't there, understand? You are needed here, for Mum and the others. She can't manage without you. You have to be here for her and the family. Besides, I can take it better. It isn't going to happen – but you know nothing. Don't let a guilty conscience ruin your life, Artie.'

Artie stared at him, disbelieving. 'You'd do that for me?'

'For Mum and the family, if I have to,' Tom replied, his eyes meeting Artie's without a blink. 'Susan isn't to know anything. I've told her not to tell anyone that he attacked her. As far as she is concerned, it didn't happen. We don't want her blaming herself.'

'What about Lizzie and your son?'

'Lizzie understands me. If it happens, I'll tell her and she'll get through.'

Artie took a deep breath, then, 'You're a brave man – braver than me – but I shouldn't let you do it. I caused his death.'

'Don't torture yourself, Artie. He had it coming. I doubt Susan was the first to suffer from him. Men like that don't deserve a second thought. Besides, if we hold our nerve and just act dumb, it won't happen.' He turned to leave.

'Where are you going?' Artie asked, marvelling at his coolness.

'I'm taking Mum, Lizzie and the boys to the sea for a day – had you forgotten?'

'You're still going?' Artie stared at him in disbelief.

'Of course. See you later. Don't worry. It will take them a while before they get round to questioning the locals. He's bound to have enemies in camp, a bloke like that. Just remember – keep your mouth shut.'

Tom inclined his head and walked off towards the farm kitchen just as the land girls came out. They stopped to talk to him and, in another moment, were all laughing at something.

Artie felt a shiver down his spine. He hadn't truly known Tom before this; he was certainly a cool one – even cold, it seemed to Artie then. He didn't think he'd been that way before the war. Artie was suddenly glad he hadn't had to go to the Front. For a long time he'd resented it, but now he knew what it was like to kill and it wasn't for him. He didn't have whatever it took to do what Tom did. Even if they got away with what had happened, Artie would never be able to forget the moment that he'd looked down at that bugger's face and realised he was dead. It would haunt him for the rest of his life.

How could Tom do what he did and carry on as if nothing had happened?

Artie had a sick feeling in his stomach as he went off to start up the tractor. He needed to be off on his own for a while, clear his head, because at the moment his thoughts wouldn't give him any peace.

31

'This was a wonderful idea, Tom,' Lizzie said as they sat on a blanket on the beach and watched Pam playing with the boys at the water's edge. They were all splashing in the shallow waves and having a wonderful time. 'I haven't seen Pam this happy in weeks – no months.'

'Not since she learned Dad hadn't got long,' Tom agreed and smiled. It was a lovely day, better than some they'd had back in full summer, warm with a pleasant breeze from the sea, and so peaceful. The beach they'd come to was miles from anywhere. There were no houses near it, just a pub and a little café where you could get a cup of tea, and the huge stretch of gold sand was as clean as anyone could wish, the water clear. 'I'd never heard of this place before, but it is lovely. How did you know of it, Lizzie?'

'Sea Paling?' Lizzie asked and smiled. 'One of my customers told me... You might not remember Tilly? She is an actress and likes the way I do her hair. She's been all over, entertaining the troops and someone brought her here. She told me and I thought it might be nice.'

'Yes, it is,' Tom said and stretched out. There was hardly anyone else on the beach, just an old man collecting driftwood further up and one couple strolling hand in hand right at the far end. 'It's the kind of memory we'll always treasure, Lizzie. When we're old and grey – or if something happened to me. You will be able to think of this...' He turned to look at her as she bent down to kiss him. 'We haven't had as many good times together as I'd like, Lizzie. I hope one day I can give you all the fun and laughter we've missed out on because of this war.'

'I've told you before, I don't need glamour or excitement to be happy. This is a perfect day for me. I love Pam and it is wonderful to see her having fun. I can't ever remember seeing her like this – except perhaps at Christmas before the war. When we had presents after lunch and I'd come round for tea. Pam liked playing games and hiding prizes for the younger ones...' She sighed. 'Since then it seems there's been one thing after another, Tom. We never have time just to be happy.'

'I know, love. I wish it was different...' Tom smiled at her, touching her cheek with one finger. 'You make me happy. When there are things I have to do – things I've done that I don't like – I think about you and how lucky I've been.'

'You do what you have to do, Tom.' Lizzie frowned slightly as she leaned over, studying his face. 'Does it bother you – some of it?' she asked. 'Because you mustn't let it, Tom. I know you, my love. You're a good person, and if you have to do bad things, well, it is because it has to be done. I'll never judge you for it, Tom.'

'I know,' he said and caught her hand, pressing it to his cheek. 'If ever what I've done comes back to haunt us, I know you will forgive me, Lizzie.'

'Yes, I will.' She traced the line of his mouth with her forefinger. 'I don't know what is bothering you, Tom, but whatever it is, I won't stop loving you.'

Tom smiled and kissed her. 'Go and paddle in the sea with Mum and the boys,' he said and she nodded and got to her feet, walking over the soft sand towards the water. Tom watched them for a while and then lay back and closed his eyes. A few more days and he would present at his medical. His long leave was probably over. Well, he couldn't grumble. He just hoped nothing came of his actions the previous night. Tom needed to be around to protect his brother and his family, but he doubted he would be for long.

He went over his actions in his head. Had he left clues for a sharp investigator to find? The ditch was mostly dry, though there might be some footprints leading away if someone was bothered to look. Fingerprints? No, he'd been careful to smudge but not wipe clean where he'd touched. There was no proof, providing no one had seen either him or Artie at the scene – and as long as his brother could hold his nerve if questioned.

Tom allowed himself to enjoy the warmth of the sun on his face. He was guilty of concealing a crime, but that crime had been an accident; he wouldn't allow a man's accidental death to play on his mind. He'd acted in the way he'd trained his men, because stealth was needed to protect those he loved. Why should a drunken fool bent on rape be allowed to ruin all their lives?

It was over and done. Just another job completed and Tom would forget it, as he'd trained himself to do.

* * *

Nothing of the accident had been heard when they got back from their day at the sea. Artie had just taken Susan to the station in Sutton to catch her train back to college. The land girls were enjoying themselves, eating the pastries and cakes Pam had made for them, before going out for the evening.

Pam set about getting Jonny to bed and Angela and George looked for the treats they had been promised and were given a stick of rock each that Pam had bought at a shop on the way back from the beach. They went away to compare homework and eat their treat, envious of the two small boys for a day at the sea when they'd both been at boring old school.

Pam was sitting down with a cup of tea when Artie entered the kitchen. Jeanie had gone upstairs to wash her hair and he went straight up after her. Pam noticed the look of strain in his face but didn't mention it. Artie wouldn't confide in her, so there was no point in asking.

The land girls had their own key to the back door so she decided to go to bed early. It had been a lovely day out but tiring. She laughed to herself. She must be getting old.

As she went up to bed, she had a feeling of sadness. Would this ache in her heart, this feeling of loneliness because Arthur wasn't here ever go away? She'd forgotten it for a day, but it was back now. Her loss of him – and her worry for John. Was Tom right to say he could still be alive? Surely if he were a prisoner of war they would have been told by now?

* * *

Tom was the first one to be told of the dreadful accident that had happened just along the Witcham Road. Jack Peacock came to the farm on Monday morning to ask if they knew anything and met Tom as he was stripping down their tractor and cleaning it.

'Did you hear about that New Zealand chappie killed in the dyke along the road?' he asked Tom. 'They say he was drunk when he left the pub – weaving all over the road as he took off after some girl. She'd walked out on him – sensible lady.'

'No – where was this?' Tom enquired. He took out a packet of Players cigarettes and offered it to the older man. 'How did he die?'

'Half a mile or so down the Witcham Road. Crashed his car in the dyke and fell out of it backwards onto a plough shear of all things. They reckon it killed him instantly. Nasty thing to happen. It's been there for ages, rusting away... But who would have thought something like that could happen?'

'Sounds a bit odd,' Tom said as he lit both cigarettes with one match. His hand was perfectly steady. 'How could he just fall on it like that?'

'Well, Bob Sykes was the one to find him. He says he thinks the poor bugger was drunk and the shock of ending up in the ditch probably made him dizzy – or he might have been thrown out of the car as it ditched. Not much water in the dykes at the moment or he'd have drowned, but bad luck that thing was there, sticking up like a blooming shark's fin. Went right into the back of his head they say.' Bob Sykes was a local police officer and much liked by the villagers, because he was easy-going and didn't interfere in folks' lives unless he had to.

'That sounds horrific,' Tom murmured. 'Poor man. So, are the police investigating?'

'Nah. Bob Sykes says it is a clear accident – mind you, them military police might think different. They're a suspicious lot. I was in the Pike and Eel the other week and they came looking for one of their crowd – he'd been pilfering, so they said, and they gave him a right bashing when he tried to resist arrest.'

'Yes, the white hats can be like that,' Tom replied with a grin. 'How's your missus then, Jack? Has she got over that tummy trouble she had last year?'

'Fancy you remembering that,' Jack said with a draw of his cigarette. 'She's all right, mate, just likes a grumble. It's her bunions that are getting her down these days...'

'Women,' Tom said and they laughed. 'Are you still on the darts team, Jack? I wish I could play, but at the moment I can't throw for toffee.' He demonstrated his weak arm.

'That's rotten for you, Tom,' Jack sympathised and climbed back on his bike. 'I've got to go and see a man about a dog...' He laughed. 'No, really. The missus says she wants one – and I've heard about some puppies. See you around.'

Tom watched as the farmer cycled off. Now Jack had the news, it would soon be all over the villages. Good thing. The more it was accepted as a nasty accident, which it had been, the better. He hoped the police came investigating before he went for his medical. It would be better if it was all done and dusted before Tom had to report back to his base, because he would probably be passed as fit enough to work, even if not for active duty – and he would rather it was him that had to face any questions from the Military Police, not his brother.

Artie had had a fright and Tom was afraid it was going to take him a while to come to terms with the fact that he'd killed a man – accidentally, but still a first kill. Tom had never forgotten the first time he'd killed an enemy. Even though it was his job, and he'd had to do it to save others, it was something that lived at the back of your mind. If you were a fighting man, you got on with it – but for Artie it was different. He would suffer pangs of guilt, but there was no going back. Tom had done what his instincts had told him needed to be done – and if there were consequences because of that, it must be him that took the blame...

* * *

When Lizzie came home from work that following Saturday evening, she'd been told of the gruesome accident just down the road from their home. 'One of my customers was full of it,' she told Tom. 'Apparently, the MPs don't think it was an accident – they believe his car had been tampered with, probably while he was in the pub. The brake fluid was leaking and they think that is why he swerved into the ditch. I heard they believe they've got the man who did it – another airman who had fallen out with the one who was killed. They were both from New Zealand and hated each other. There had been a terrible fight between them earlier that day.'

'Really?' Tom was cautious as he answered. 'So they think the brakes had been tampered with then? He was meant to have the accident that night?'

'That is what my customer was saying.' Lizzie made a pot of tea and looked at him. 'You sound dubious, Tom. My customer's fiancé is Military Police so she ought to know – but I doubt if she was supposed to tell me.'

'I am certain she wasn't,' Tom replied, sighing with relief because Lizzie hadn't put two and two together. 'That sort of thing is top secret, Lizzie. They wouldn't want it commonly known.'

'Well, he shouldn't have told Jilly then, because she was laughing about it, said they'd got him banged up and he was in for it.'

'So they've got their culprit,' Tom said. 'Seems by no means cut and dried to me – not sure that would stand up in court. Just because they'd had a quarrel...'

Lizzie shrugged. 'It hardly matters to us, does it, Tom?' Was there a hint of hesitation in her voice?

'No, not our business,' he agreed.

'When do you go for your medical?' Lizzie asked as she poured tea into two cups, although she already knew.

'Day after tomorrow,' Tom said and took the cup. He was thoughtful as he sipped the hot tea. If the MPs believed they had a man in custody guilty of trying to kill one of their officers, they wouldn't come questioning local folk. They would be busy investigating these allegations of brakes being tampered with for a while. By the time they'd done that, it should all have blown over and Artie would be more able to cope with any questions.

'Do you need your best uniform pressing?' Lizzie asked. 'Tom, are you listening?' Tom looked at her and smiled apologetically. 'Do you want your best uniform pressed?'

'Yes, thanks. I should wear my best uniform,' Tom replied. 'The one I am wearing needs cleaning.'

'I'll take it to the cleaners on Monday and ask the to do a same day service,' Lizzie said. 'You've got a few stains on the trousers. I noticed it yesterday.'

'You're a good wife, Lizzie,' Tom said and smiled at her. Inside his head, his thoughts were churning. There was relief because it looked as if they would not be a part of the official investigation, but also a shadow of guilt that an innocent man might be found guilty of causing a man's death.

Tom could do nothing about that, because his family came first. He had to protect them at all costs. He wondered what Arthur would have done, but then he nodded to himself. His father would approve of what Tom had done – because in a case like this, only the family mattered.

32

Lizzie had fetched Tom's second-best uniform from the cleaners on Monday evening. She'd paid extra to have it done quickly. Glancing at her watch, she saw that it was just gone five in the evening. Tom should be home by seven and then she would know if he must return to duty. Her mind told her that he would have been asked to report back quite soon, even though her heart hoped for a different outcome. Why couldn't he just be allowed to leave the army with an honourable discharge? Surely, he'd done all that any man could for his country?

'That will be five shillings please, Mrs Gilbert. I am sorry we couldn't get out that small stain on the left leg of the trousers. I have been told it is blood not mud, and it won't shift.'

'Oh, well, it isn't very big,' Lizzie said. 'If it isn't good enough, they will have to issue him with a new one.'

'Yes, well, he's done his bit, hasn't he? It's a pity they don't let him come home, Mrs Gilbert. In all honesty, we want all our boys home, don't we?'

'Yes, we do,' she said and thanked him as she left the small shop.

On the bus travelling home, Lizzie thought about the stain on Tom's trousers. Had he cut himself? She hadn't noticed any plasters and he certainly hadn't mentioned a cut on his leg. They didn't butcher pigs on the farm these days, so she had no idea where it might have come from.

* * *

Tom arrived home at just after seven on Tuesday evening. One look at his face told her all she needed to know. She lifted her face for his kiss, her question simple, 'When?'

'Next Monday at ten I have to report on base, so I'll need to leave on Sunday and travel down overnight.' He saw her expression and nodded. 'I know. I'd hoped too, but they need me for a big training session. They are recruiting men now – a certain type of man.'

'What do you mean?' Lizzie asked.

'They are scouring the prisons again for hard men. We have some particularly nasty ops coming up apparently – and the officer who briefed me today said they need to be expendable. Anyone with a death sentence or a long stretch of imprisonment will be given a chance to die for their country.'

'And if they live?' Lizzie asked, arching her brow.

'Then they get off whatever they were charged with and are free to live their own lives.'

'So they either die a hero or go back to doing whatever they did before?'

'Unless they prefer to remain with the team, and it's surprising how many of them do.'

'So you've worked with that kind of man before this?' Lizzie looked shocked and Tom laughed.

'Don't worry, my darling. They know better than to mess

with me – or any other training officer. If they tried it, they could be shot on sight and no questions asked.'

Lizzie shivered. 'That all sounds horrid. It's bad enough that you have to fight the enemy – but to be at risk from men you're actually training...'

Tom shrugged. 'I'm still here, Lizzie. This isn't my first dirty squad and I doubt it will be my last. It seems that they can't do without me. I shan't be sent on another mission, because of my arm, but I'm still the best trainer they have and... well, apparently, there are a couple of medals coming my way. Daft stuff, but there we are...'

'Oh, Tom, that's not daft stuff,' Lizzie said. 'I don't know much about what you do, but I know you all deserve medals.' She looked at him thoughtfully. 'So where do you get your volunteers then?'

'I've been told I can hand pick them myself this time – and I have the authority to visit all the army and air force base prisons I wish to choose my squad, civilian prisons too, of course...' Tom grinned at her. 'I've never done that before. It will be an eye-opener, I believe...'

'I should imagine it would,' Lizzie said and shivered again. 'I don't know why you're looking so satisfied, Tom. I was hoping you would be given an honourable discharge.'

'It was on the cards, but when they saw how well I could use my arm, they said I was needed and it was my duty to continue, if I felt I could...' He shrugged. 'What else could I do, Lizzie?'

'Pretend you couldn't use your arm?' she suggested and then sighed. 'I know you wouldn't do that, Tom – but I just wish you had...'

* * *

Tom went for a last walk round late at night. He liked to get some fresh air before he retired for the night and his mind was buzzing. A promotion had been offered as well as the chance to pick his next dirty squad – and it was that which had swayed him.

He knew who his first man would be. He would drive up to Sutton in the morning and present his credentials, ask to look in the cooler at the airbase. If the man they had accused of murdering Susan's attacker was there, he would give him the chance to serve this country. It was up to him if he took it – but if he signed to go with Tom and presented himself at training camp as a recruit, he had a chance of life. If he did a runner he would be a deserter and shot on sight, and if he stayed to face a trial for a crime he had already been found guilty of in the minds of his judges, he could go to prison for a long time, or they might shoot him.

Tom thought he knew which one the man would choose.

* * *

'We've got two at the moment, both hard cases, Major Gilbert,' the officer in charge of the remand cells told him. 'An Australian and a New Zealander; the Australian went for one of his so-called friends with a knife. Strange business because you couldn't wish for a nicer chap to talk to – and the other one is a murderer. We know he cut the brake lines on Lieutenant Armstrong's car. Not right through, but they were primed to go suddenly when he was at speed. Ironic that the car just went into a ditch and he'd have been fine if he hadn't fallen on a bit of metal – off a plough, so I've been told.'

'Nasty business,' Tom replied. 'Pity that metal was there – might still have been alive otherwise.'

'Oh, certain to be,' the officer said with a grimace. 'A little crash like that wouldn't have killed him if it hadn't been abandoned there. I blame the idiot that left it there in the first place. It was a hazard, even for kids playing nearby.'

'Yes, I agree with you,' Tom said. 'It must have been a nasty way to die, poor chap.'

The officer looked at him with respect. 'I've heard about your lot, sir. Brave men.' He glanced at Tom's arm. 'That looks painful...'

'It was,' Tom agreed pleasantly. 'Shall we beard the lion – so to speak?'

'Oh, yes, sir – we've got them in separate cells or they would end up killing each other. Who do you want to see first?' He gave Tom their names.

'The one with the knife, I think,' Tom said. 'I believe my brother spoke about him once – said he was known for throwing knives at doors, but a nice chap...'

'As long as he isn't directing his knives at you,' the lieutenant said and laughed. 'You wait in here, sir, and I'll bring them to you, one at a time.'

Tom walked into the small interview room and sat down. He placed a packet of cigarettes and matches on the table and waited. After a few minutes, he heard the sound of voices and then the officer returned with his prisoner. He was wearing cuffs, his hands behind his back.

'I think we can do without the handcuffs, lieutenant,' Tom said after one look into the prisoner's eyes. 'Sit down, corporal. I'd like to hear your story.'

The lieutenant took up a stand by the door.

Tom motioned for the prisoner to take a cigarette, but he made no move to do so. 'You may smoke, corporal.'

'Don't smoke, sir. Don't drink alcohol.'

'Really, why is that?' Tom asked.

'Not interested. I keep myself to myself, sir. I like fruit and chips – and chocolate.'

'Interesting.' Tom smiled. 'And why did you try to kill a fellow officer, Corporal Zeeman?'

'He called me bad names, sir – and he tried to maul my girlfriend. No one does that, so I threatened him with a knife. I didn't try to kill him, sir. If I had, he would be dead.'

'That good, are you?' Tom asked with a raised brow.

'Yes, sir. I can kill a snake with a knife before it can strike or bring a bird from a tree.'

'I see – so how would you like the chance to use that skill on the enemy? I am putting together a dirty squad and inviting you to join. If you do, you will come close to death, but you may escape, with skill and luck – and if you do, you can choose to remain with your squad or go free.'

Corporal Zeeman grinned. 'Yes, sir. Thank you, sir. I've heard about your lot and I'd like to join.'

'Very well,' Tom said. 'You will be given a pardon at the end of your term of service. When you leave here, you will have tickets, money and instructions – but if you run, you will be a deserter and you know what happens to them.'

Corporal Zeeman smiled, showing his perfect white teeth. 'I won't run, sir.'

'Good. I'll ask them to include some chocolate with your rations, corporal.'

Tom saluted as the man was led away, without the cuffs and with far more respect than he'd been given when he entered the interview room. Taking out his silver case, Tom extracted a cigarette and lit it. He took a few puffs and then put it out as another man was led in.

'Lieutenant Regan, sir,' the lieutenant said and took up his place by the door.

'Please sit down, lieutenant,' Tom invited. 'Have a cigarette if you wish.'

'I prefer to stand, sir.' The prisoner saluted smartly. 'I won't smoke until I am released. I am innocent of any crime – except calling Armstrong a bastard, which he was, and hitting him. Yes, we had a fight, but that's it – I didn't cut his brakes.'

'I'm not here to judge you,' Tom said. 'I'm here to offer you a chance to escape from the situation you find yourself in.'

'I am not guilty and a court will find me innocent. If the brakes were damaged deliberately, it was not by me – and I believe it to be sheer neglect. Armstrong drove as he lived, putting his foot down hard.'

'I am inclined to believe you,' Tom replied. 'Unfortunately, I doubt many others will when you had been heard to tell Armstrong that you would swing for him and there is evidence of foul play. It appears that you may – unless you would prefer to accept my offer?'

'I know about your lot,' the prisoner hissed. 'Why should I throw my life away, because of some trumped-up charge that any competent mechanic could disprove?'

'If that is your reasoning, it is your choice entirely,' Tom replied. 'I've been given a job to do to recruit enough men for a special mission—'

'A suicide squad,' Lieutenant Regan snapped.

'Yes, quite possibly,' Tom admitted. He gathered the cigarettes and put them in his pocket. 'That will be all, lieutenant...' He nodded to the officer on guard at the door.

'Hang on!' Regan said, clearly startled that the interview was over. 'I haven't said no...'

'I thought you had.' Tom looked him in the eyes. 'I don't

want men who will cause more trouble than they are worth. If you feel you are unjustly accused, take your chance at a trial.'

'They've already judged me,' Regan said bitterly. 'I'd have killed him in anger, but I'm not a murderer.'

'A pity,' Tom said coolly. 'You'll need to be if you want to survive. If you wish to accept, you will be given instructions, money, a ticket and a pardon at the end of your service – but if you run, you will be a deserter.'

'I know,' Regan muttered. 'I won't run. I'll show the bastards and one day I'll prove my innocence.'

'That is your choice,' Tom said and nodded. He took the cigarettes out of his pocket and handed them to Regan. 'I know you're dying for a smoke.' He looked at the officer guarding the door. 'Give him his belongings, lieutenant. He's made his choice.'

'Yes, sir.' The officer saluted, but the look on his face told Tom just what he thought. If it was up to him, he would have had Regan lined up for a firing squad and be done with it. Regan was clearly a known troublemaker and would need watching.

* * *

Tom was thoughtful as he drove back to the farm. He had two new recruits so far. One he would trust with his life and the other he wouldn't trust as far as he could toss him. If it hadn't been for what Tom knew, Regan could have sat in that cell and rotted for all he cared – but he'd felt compelled to offer him his chance. It was something he might well come to regret one day…

33

'So, according to you, it is all over and we just get on with our lives,' Artie said and stared at his brother in disbelief. 'You've fixed it, so that's the end of it?'

'Isn't that what you want?' Tom asked in a cool, calm voice. 'Or would you rather I just went to the police and told them the truth? Then they can lock us both up – or maybe I'm useful, so they'll just send me on another mission and throw the book at you?'

'It's what I should've done at the start,' Artie said, sounding bitter. 'They might have believed it was an accident then.'

'Perhaps. Even if they had, you would still have gone to prison for assault and grievous bodily harm – and Susan's reputation would be ruined, because people always blame the girl. Jeanie's heart would be broken – and all for what? So that you can keep your conscience clean? Grow up and be a man, Artie. This is what happens in life. There is a war on and men are killing each other every hour of the day.'

'That is not the same and you know it!' Artie challenged with his eyes.

'Yes, I do – but I couldn't let you go to prison. What about the farm? Mum is relying on you. It is your duty to look after things and *you* know it.' Tom met his brother's angry gaze with his own iron look. For a moment then Artie glimpsed the man his family never saw but was familiar to many a soldier. 'If it makes you feel any better, they reckon someone tampered with his brakes and he would probably have had an accident at some period – I just thank God Susan wasn't in it when it happened.'

'Bloody hell! Is that the truth?' Tom nodded. The brothers' angry looks clashed for a moment, and then Artie's shoulders slumped and his face crumpled, as if he might weep. 'I know you are right, Tom. I had to stop that bugger hurting Susan. I meant just to hit him a few times and then tell him to clear off – but he just kept coming back at me, wouldn't leave it. I was tiring, losing if I'm honest, and when he heard you coming and turned, I just shoved as hard as I could. I thought he would fall in the ditch and we could face him together – scare him off when he climbed out, but I never thought it would kill him.'

Tom's face relaxed into a smile. 'It was an accident. We both know it. We both know you had to stop him, Artie. You saved Susan – be glad of that and forget him. It is hard to do that. I know that as well as any man – but it has to be done. Put it out of your mind. You are not a murderer. That man died because he did a bad thing and fate decreed that he die. You have to learn to live with what you did – just as I do...'

Artie looked at him then, hearing something in his voice that struck a chord. 'Does it haunt you, Tom – all the things you've done?'

'Sometimes. I did them because I had to, because it was my duty, and because I'd be dead if I hadn't. So I think about it and then I dismiss it and think of all the good things. If you try, it will come – just don't inflict your guilt on others. Mum, Susan, and

Jeanie do not need to know – and I shall not be telling Lizzie, though she guessed something happened, but hasn't pieced it together yet. If she did, she would accept it as being what we had to do for the best. She knows what it's like to be in Susan's shoes, but she wasn't lucky enough to have someone there for her. I'd have gladly killed that bugger if I'd known – but she never told me it was rape, not until long after. In the end, he got what he deserved.'

'Too late for Faith, though,' Artie said and nodded. John's girl, Faith, had been killed by her Uncle Ralph, the same man that had forced himself on Lizzie. He'd died driving like a mad thing down a narrow road and meeting an oncoming tractor. 'That bugger the other night – I'd bet Susan wasn't the first he'd tried it on...'

'She wouldn't have been his last, so you've done a few girls a favour,' Tom said. 'Come on, Artie, let it go. You know I'm right.'

'Yes, you are,' Artie admitted. 'Thanks Tom – you've done a lot for me lately, and I haven't always deserved it.'

'Don't be so bloody daft,' Tom retorted. 'You are my brother. I reckon you'd do the same for me.'

'I owe you, Tom.'

'Well, one of these days you can pay me back,' Tom joked and offered his brother a cigarette. 'Look out for Mum and Lizzie while I'm away – and if I shouldn't come return—'

'You'll be back. Take more than a few bloody Jerries to kill you, Tom.'

Tom chuckled. 'They've tried a few times,' he admitted. 'So far they haven't quite succeeded, though I've got a limp and a wonky arm to show for it.'

'You'll manage,' Artie said with a wry smile. 'I haven't seen you fail at much.'

'I haven't got the reflex or the speed I had, and I can't lift heavy weights,' Tom said, 'But I shall cope. I don't give up easily, Artie.'

'Luckily for me,' Artie said. 'I mean it, Tom. I owe you...'

'Buy me a pint and we're quits,' Tom quipped. 'I shall miss the farm when I return to the army, Artie. I'm fine once I get back into the swing of things, but I had hoped they might let me go this time.'

'We all thought they might,' Artie said as they turned and walked towards the pub for a last drink together before Tom had to return to his duty.

Tom just nodded. Honourable discharge had been offered, but Tom had realised the offer he'd been made, of setting up his own squad, was the way to keep his family safe and so he'd taken the chance to recruit and train his new men. He was a bit uneasy with the choices he'd made so far, but at least there would be no further investigations into the death of Lieutenant Armstrong. Soon he would be back at work and Artie would continue on the farm as normal, carrying on from season to season. The passage of time would ease his guilt. Tom's family was safe and he would live with the consequences of what he'd done, whatever they might be.

34

In another few weeks, Lucy's tour of duty would be over. The months had flown in a blur of work and suffering. It was early November now and on Cyprus the darkness fell early. Lucy hated winter nights back home in England, but even more so here, where the light seemed to vanish in seconds. One minute she could still see the sun and the next it was almost dusk, or that was how it seemed to her, because she was working from early morning until after dark each day, her hours long and tiring so that she normally just fell into bed and slept once she had eaten.

'Nurse Lucy…' She turned guiltily as sister spoke, aware that she had been wool gathering, her thoughts far away. 'Ah, you are still awake, I am pleased to say. No, nurse, I am not angry. It amazes me that you have given so much these past months. I am recommending that we send you home for a rest.'

'I would rather stay—' Lucy began.

But sister shook her head. 'No, my dear. You've given more than we ought to have asked, but we have twenty new nurses coming out. Their ship arrives next week. It will take you, three more nurses, who are in desperate need of a rest, and some of our patients, when it returns to Britain. However, after Christmas, if you feel able, you may apply to return to us. I shall recommend that you are sent back in the New Year – should you wish it.'

'Oh – then I thank you,' Lucy said and smiled at her. 'It would be lovely to be home for Christmas. It is a long time since I saw my parents...'

'I am sure they will be delighted to see you,' sister said. 'Very well, that is the end of your shift. I am officially standing you down – so you are free to visit a few friends before you leave Cyprus.'

'Thank you, sister. You've been very kind to me and I've really enjoyed my work here.' Lucy smiled shyly. 'Do you ever take a break from work, sister?'

'Now and then. As a matter of fact, I am finishing my tour of duty here next spring. I shall be reluctant to leave, but I am being promoted to the matron of a small hospital near my home in Sussex. It is for men so badly damaged by the war that they can never return to normal life.'

'Oh, that is wonderful,' Lucy replied involuntarily and then blushed. 'I mean, you deserve it, sister.'

'Perhaps I do,' sister said, her eyes twinkling. 'However, I shall miss my patients and hands-on nursing. It is the best thing for me, I believe. I intend to make nursing my life and it will be a settled job – and I do believe that the tide is turning in this awful war, Nurse Lucy. It won't be immediately next year, but I've been given to understand that it is the beginning of the end.'

'I do hope you are right, sister,' Lucy said and sighed. 'I'm not sure what I want to do, but I might stay in nursing, make it my life as you intend.'

'If that is your decision, please come and see me in my new

post whenever you're ready. I think you should take your exams to become a ward sister. You would do very well in the position.'

'Yes, I might do that. I had planned to marry and go into district nursing but now...' Lucy shook her head. 'I will remember you always, Sister Jane – and thank you for your kindness.'

* * *

Lucy spent the next couple of days visiting the beach and the friends she had made. Luigi and his family were sad that she was going and begged her to return and visit them one day.

'I might come back next year if they will have me,' Lucy said, smiling because they were such friendly folk.

'They would be fools not to,' Luigi said and beamed at her. 'After the war, you must bring your family and visit Cyprus. You can stay with us whenever you wish. We shall never forget you, Nurse Lucy.'

Lucy thanked them and was hugged and kissed. She felt subdued after she'd left them and was back in her billet, packing for the return to England. It felt very strange to be going home after so long, but, in a way, she was pleased. She would just go home and enjoy Christmas and do nothing, then she would make up her mind what to do with the rest of her life.

The memory of her love for John was still strong in her mind and heart, though the pain had eased from its first tearing sharpness of bitter grief, into a softer sense of loss and regret. She would never forget the man she'd loved, hopelessly at first. Lucy had known that his love for her was not the flaming passion he'd felt for Faith, his first love, but she'd been content to know that he did care for her in a gentle, thoughtful way. She was sure it would have been enough, had she been given the chance to be his wife, but cruel fate had snatched that chance away.

Lucy decided that she would take the time spent on the voyage home and a family Christmas to decide what she wanted from life, and then she would put her unhappiness behind her and get on with whatever life gave her.

35

Pam heard the pounding feet on the stairs, then a small scream and sat up in bed. Throwing off the bedcovers, she jumped out and snapped on the light. It was the end of November and Jeanie's baby was due any day now. She pulled her old dressing robe on over her nightdress and went out on to the landing just as Artie came rushing back upstairs.

'Mum, you're up,' he said, looking distracted. 'I was going to wake you – I've rung the doctor, but he is out on a call already. His wife is going to send the midwife as soon as she can.'

Smiling, Pam nodded to her son. 'Don't panic, Artie. It will be a while yet before the baby comes. Plenty of time for the midwife and doctor to arrive. In the meantime, you can make up the range for me and put three big pans of water on to boil – and the kettle to make a cup of tea.'

'I couldn't drink tea...' he protested. 'Jeanie is suffering...'

Pam nodded reassuringly. 'Of course she is and she will for a while. She is having a baby and that's what happens. I shall be with her and, believe me, a cup of tea will be good for her. She might feel like a bite to eat and you can bring one of those pasties I made yesterday and a piece of cake, just in case.' She saw Artie's expression. 'She will need all her strength... Oh, I've just remembered. I've got a big bar of Cadbury's chocolate. I was saving it for Christmas, but that might be just the thing...'

'Mum...!' Jeanie let out a wail of pain and Artie went dashing into the bedroom. 'Are you all right, love? The midwife is coming and the doctor later...' Artie said.

'It hurts... Mum...' Jeanie's gaze went to Pam. 'Should it hurt as much? Owww—' She screeched. 'That was like a kick in the back and—' She sent an agonised look at Pam.

'That's good, it means you're getting there,' Pam smiled at her. 'Artie, go and put the kettle and pans on please – now! I want to help Jeanie...'

Artie left the room reluctantly.

Pam lifted back the bedcovers. 'Have your waters broken yet, love?'

'I think they just did... all over the bed,' Jeanie wailed in distress.

'It was going to happen and it's good,' Pam said. 'Don't worry about the mattress. You try to put on a clean nightdress, and sit in that comfy armchair by the window for a moment – unless you would rather pace a bit? I did a lot of pacing with Tom, as I recall. It does get easier with the next one...'

Jeanie did as she was told, pulling on a fresh cotton nightgown and discarding her wet one; then she walked over to the window to look out at the night sky while Pam whipped the wet covers off the bed and replaced them with sweet-smelling fresh sheets and a clean wool blanket.

'That should be more comfortable. You don't want anything heavy over you and you can kick them off when we're ready to get down to business... so get in when you're ready.'

Jeanie gave a reluctant laugh. 'You make it sound as if you were getting ready to make lunch...'

'Panic never did anyone any good,' Pam replied calmly. 'Just let it come, Jeanie, go with the pain. Scream when you feel like it. If Artie can't take it, he can go down the road to Lizzie.'

Jeanie laughed properly. 'I'm so glad you're here, Pam. If we'd gone to live in our own house, I'd be terrified. Artie has no idea what to do, except telephone for the doctor...'

She flinched as the pain struck again and sat on the edge of the bed, holding herself round the middle and rocking back and forth.

Pam touched her head lightly. 'I know it's bad, love,' she said as Artie came back bearing a tray with all the tea things, plus a generous slice of cake and two pasties. 'Do you fancy a bite to eat?' Pam asked and went over to the chest of drawers, where Artie had set down the tray. She poured the tea and brought Jeanie's cup and a plate with a piece of fatless sponge. 'Good thing I made these yesterday. We shall all need something to get us through the night...'

'How long does it go on?' Jeanie asked, biting her lip to hold back another gasp of pain as she took her cup.

'Hopefully, not too long now the waters have broken,' Pam replied. 'Every woman is different, but I was in labour for ten hours with Tom – but a lot of that was before my waters broke. Have you been having pains for the past few hours?'

'A little – just warning pains, I thought. They only started for real about an hour ago.'

Pam nodded. 'Perhaps you'll be one of the lucky ones.' She reached out and rescued Jeanie's cup as she gasped with pain and hunched over. 'Get back in bed now, love, and let's have a look at you.' She handed the cup to Artie. 'Close the curtains, please, love...'

As Artie obeyed, Pam lifted Jeanie's nightgown as she leaned back against the pillows, her knees up to her chest.

'Yes, you look as if that's coming on nicely. I think baby might surprise us by beating the midwife here...'

Artie swung round, alarm in his face. 'It can't come until she's here,' he said, a note of fear in his voice. 'I mean—'

'Baby will come when baby is ready,' Pam said with a reassuring smile. 'Don't worry, Artie. I've had five of them. I think I know what to do. Ah...' She cocked her head. 'I heard a car. Why don't you go down and see who it is?'

As Artie started down the stairs, Jeanie screamed. 'Mum...' she cried. 'It hurts... ahhhh...'

'Right now, push,' Pam told her, lifting her nightdress clear. 'Yes, baby is coming... Push a bit harder now, love. Yes, you can do it... that's right. I can see the head. Baby is coming the right way... it won't be long. Breathe, Jeanie. Pant... harder... Now push again – and yes, here he comes...'

And even as the midwife entered the bedroom, the next young Talbot came into the world with a little woosh and a whimpering cry.

'Done it without me, I see,' the midwife cried, smiling with delight as she took over from Pam, who retreated to a position where she could witness the birth of her third grandson. 'And we have a beautiful boy with a powerful pair of lungs.' The youngest Talbot screamed his disgust at having been thrust so unceremoniously into a cold world. 'What a clever thing you are, Jeanie. He is absolutely perfect, as he should be.'

'Oh, let me see, let me see,' Jeanie cried, tears of happiness on her cheeks. 'Yes, he is lovely. He has Artie's eyes... Oh, but his hair looks red...' She pouted her disappointment. 'I wanted him to be dark like his father.'

'He will be a redhead like you,' Pam said. 'He is gorgeous,

Jeanie, and you're right, his eyes are like Artie's, even though not the same colour... but all babies' eyes change as they get older.'

The midwife had done everything necessary and she wrapped the new baby in a large towel that Pam had brought from the airing cupboard; it was still a little warm and the howls stopped miraculously as he was placed in his mother's arms.

'What are you going to call him?' the midwife asked as she watched mother and baby for a moment.

'We thought Winston for Mr Churchill if he was a boy – and Elizabeth for a girl.'

'Winston. My, that's a posh name,' the midwife said, sounding a little disapproving. 'Still, I suppose it is in honour of a good man. I don't know what we'd have done without Mr Churchill. His speeches send a shiver down my spine – when he talks about fighting them on the beaches. Thank God it never came to that...'

'We were lucky we weren't invaded just after Dunkirk,' Pam said as she tidied up the bloody cloths and took away the bowl of warm water baby Winston had been washed in. 'I think this next year might see a difference – 1944. Surely the war will end soon now?'

'Well, it looks that way,' the midwife said comfortably. 'We're on the attack and the enemy are getting some of what they handed out to us now.' She nodded with satisfaction as she finished making Jeanie comfortable and, together, she and Pam slid another clean sheet under her. 'There – all shipshape and right again.' She nodded as Jeanie held the baby to her breast and he latched on immediately. 'Good instincts from mother and baby,' she approved. 'I think you'll do. Any questions?'

'I think we're fine for now, thank you so much for coming out at this hour, Mavis.'

'You're welcome. It's my job,' the midwife replied. 'I know

you know what you're doing around babies, Pam. I'll leave you to it, but I shall call in the morning to make sure mother is doing all right. I will tell the doctor to come tomorrow rather than tonight... or later today might be more accurate.' She turned to Artie, who was hovering in the doorway. 'You can come in, Dad. Winston doesn't bite – well, not you, anyway. I can see myself out...'

'I'll come with you,' Pam said and followed her out as Artie went to the bed to kiss his wife and marvel with her at the beautiful boy they had created.

'Well, she is a strong sensible girl and I'm sure she'll go on fine,' Mavis told Pam as she prepared to leave. 'You've had five, so she only has to ask you if she isn't sure. You know where I am if there are any problems, but I don't anticipate any. Nice baby. Congratulations, Grandma – your third, isn't it?'

'Yes. I have three grandsons,' Pam said and smiled at her. 'I am a very lucky woman.'

'How is Jonny doing? He sleeps well – haven't heard a peep from him.'

'Yes, he is pretty good at sleeping through the night, but if young Winston keeps on like that, he will probably wake...' Winston had just let out a great wail.

'He's still annoyed he isn't safely tucked up in mummy's womb,' Mavis said and chuckled. 'Good luck if he wakes Jonny. I think you're going to find life interesting for the next few months —' She broke off as they heard a fresh cry from upstairs, but a different one. 'Ah, that will be Jonny. I shan't keep you, Pam. Just a word of warning, don't wear yourself out. Ask those land girls to help out if things get tough.'

Pam nodded and smiled as she left, then quickly made her way upstairs to Jonny's room. He was standing up in his cot, staring through the bars, clearly wondering where the crying sound was coming from.

'It is all right, darling,' Pam comforted, taking him up into her arms. 'Would you like to meet your new cousin? His name is Winston Talbot... Oh, what a mouthful.' She laughed to herself. It wasn't a name she would have chosen, but she understood why Jeanie and Artie had. Winston Churchill was a great man and very respected now, though he hadn't always been. His conduct of the war had put heart in every man and woman in the country and Pam – like her son and daughter-in-law – felt they owed a huge debt to him for somehow keeping the invasion at bay when it had seemed so likely to happen.

* * *

As Pam entered Artie and Jeanie's bedroom, she stopped and smiled. Artie was lying beside his wife and their baby was between them, Artie's arm protectively over Jeanie – and all three of them were asleep.

'Ah, bless them,' Pam said and carried Jonny back to her bedroom. She would introduce the babies at another time. Tucking Jonny in beside her, Pam closed her eyes, though she did not immediately fall asleep. Her mind travelled back to the birth of her own children and the happy days when Arthur had been so proud of his wife and their family.

A little tear trickled down her cheek, but she didn't wipe it away. The memories were happy ones. Pam knew herself to be fortunate in her growing family. Three grandsons already. How many more would she have?

'Aunt Pam...' Her eyes opened as she heard George's voice near the bed and then the tentative touch of his hand on her face. 'Is everything all right? I woke up and heard screams, so I hid under the bedcovers.'

'Oh, poor George,' Pam said and opened her covers, inviting him to get in next to her. 'Jeanie had her baby. It hurts when a woman has a baby, so she screamed – but she is all right now. She has a little boy and you can meet him tomorrow.'

'That's all right then.' George snuggled up to her. 'I'm glad I'm with you, Aunt Pam. I like being on the farm and helping with the cows. Can I work for you when I leave school?'

'If it's what you want,' Pam said and ruffled his hair. 'I'm glad you're here, too, George. Most of my children are growing up. I know they will leave home one day, so it is nice to have you here – you will be with me for longer.'

'I'll never leave you while you want me,' George told her. 'I love you – you're better than a mum.'

'Am I? Well, that's good, love.' Pam kissed the top of his head. 'Let's all go to sleep while we can. You've got school tomorrow – though it won't be long until Christmas, so I don't suppose you're doing much work.'

'Mostly Christmas stuff,' George said, yawned and promptly fell asleep.

Jonny was asleep on her other side, curled into her and half lying on her chest. Between them she was snugly warm and Pam soon found herself drifting into a peaceful sleep.

Her last thought as she fell asleep was her wish that John could be home for Christmas. It would be the best present ever…

36

'You will help me with the bazaar, Lucy?' Lucy's mother smiled at her fondly as they sat eating breakfast together. 'I do it every year for the church, as you know – but it would be lovely to have my daughter with me this year.'

'Oh, Mum...' Lucy looked at her reluctantly. It wasn't truly what she wanted to do with her day. After an almost uneventful sea voyage of nearly three weeks, when the only sign of the enemy they'd seen was a lone plane tracking them, she'd only been home two days. She was just getting used to being back and she'd hoped to go out Christmas shopping for a few presents. 'All right, if you really want me to – what do I have to do?'

'You'll be on the white elephant stall...'

'But that is always just rubbish,' Lucy objected. 'Why not tea and cakes?'

'Because they are always busy and your pretty face might sell a few bits and pieces. Last year, I had to box almost the whole lot up again and store it. Please, Lucy?'

'If you want me to I will,' Lucy said. 'Why do you do it year after year, Mum? Why not let someone else have the bother?'

'Because they won't,' her mother answered simply. 'I do it because, however little we raise, it all helps – especially now. People don't have much money and the church roof needs urgent repair. We have to try or the congregation will get soaked when it rains.'

'Poor Mum,' Lucy said and laughed. 'Will Nick get leave for Christmas?' she asked, changing the subject. Her brother, Nick, was fortunately stationed not far from home and got frequent leaves.

'Yes, he will, and he has asked to bring a friend, so of course I said he could...' She smiled at her daughter. 'If you wanted to bring a friend to Christmas dinner you may, my love.' She sighed. 'I am hoping one of your father's grateful flock will bring us a nice big chicken; it has been promised, but things are still difficult, even though more food is getting through now and I do have some nice tinned fruit.'

'There isn't anyone I want to ask, Mum.' Lucy's face clouded for a moment. 'I am sorry to disappoint you – but there isn't anyone else.'

'Not yet,' her mother replied. 'I know you loved John Talbot, Lucy, but sadly he has gone. I know you will find someone else if you open your heart, my dearest, because you are too lovely and too generous not to.'

Lucy smiled and touched her mother's hand. 'I will one day perhaps,' she said. 'I am getting over it, but it is too soon.'

'Well, you have plenty of time,' her mother said and Lucy sighed inwardly. Why did everyone think she should be looking for a new love? Why couldn't she just be allowed to live her live as a single woman and do whatever she fancied? Her family loved her and she loved them, but they all kept telling her she would find someone else. Lucy wasn't at all sure she wanted to. She could surely find a life of fulfilment in her nursing, but her family and particularly her mother felt nursing was just for the war. Afterwards, she would be expected to marry and have a family. That would have been fine if she could've married John, but now... she just wanted to be left in peace.

* * *

The bazaar was just like every other event Lucy had helped her mother with while she was growing up. The stalls were so predictable: paperback books and the occasional nice hardback bound in leather, puzzles and small toys. The second-hand clothing stall – everything had been washed and ironed by a small band of volunteers and it was popular now that people were rationed on new clothing. The hoopla stall where people tried their skill for small prizes; the beans in a jar, the hand-knitted stall, loaded with pink bootees and blue mittens – and the cake stall. Every kind of hand-baked cake you could think of, done up in cellophane, and the tea and refreshment stall, tiny sandwiches, cakes and sausage rolls. The queue there stretched the length of the hall. Food rationing meant that people didn't often see these kind of luxuries at home these days and everyone wanted a share of the cakes and sausage rolls. A lot of people had contributed bits of their rations to provide them for the benefit of the church funds.

Lucy's stall, the white elephant stall, was piled high with nothing but rubbish. All the bits that folk stored under the stairs and then offered when the vicar's wife came collecting for the bazaar. An old shooting stick, the chair half-rotted away, a pair of rusted roller skates, a leather football with a patch on it, some worn-out football boots, and a pair of heavy leather gloves that might be useful if you were cutting a barbed-wire fence. There was actually an elephant's foot umbrella stand that some enterprising person had brought home from India. Beside that stood a brass tray with a beaten copper coffee jug, milk jug and cups – who would drink coffee from that? Then there was a silver-plated kettle on a stand, the silver had worn away in patches from being cleaned too hard, a brass toasting fork, a set of steel fire irons – actually, they weren't too bad – and a set of copper jugs: also, a fender, a fire screen and a huge and very ugly jardinière. Among all these items were many smaller pieces, jumbled in together, none of them worth more than a penny or two if anyone could be persuaded to buy them.

Lucy surveyed her stall with a jaundiced eye. Who on earth would buy anything from her? She certainly wouldn't! Perhaps she should put a pound in the kitty and call it a day. She'd been standing here for ages and no one had even stopped to look. Lucy was sure they all knew it was just the same stuff as they'd ignored the previous year.

She turned her head to look enviously at the cake stall; they were doing a brisk trade and she would far rather have been helping there than standing here with nothing to do.

'Hello,' a man's voice said, bringing her head back. She stared at the man in uniform, his scarred face vaguely familiar. 'You are Nurse Lucy, aren't you?' he asked, sounding a little dazed. 'I couldn't believe it – but it is you...'

'Captain Rossiter?' Lucy gasped as recognition suddenly came. 'Oh, but you look wonderful – your burns have healed so well.'

'They grafted some skin,' he said and smiled. 'It helped, as you can see...'

'They did a good job for you, captain, and your eyes – how are they doing?'

'Pretty much the same as when I left you,' he replied. 'I can see really well with one and not much with the other – but I get by. It means they've got me doing administrative work, so the war is more or less over for me.'

'Good.' Lucy beamed at him. 'So what are you doing here?'

'I came home to visit my folks – my uncle and aunt. My parents died some years back, but my Aunt Jenny was good to me, so I visit whenever I can. I'm staying over Christmas.'

'I'm staying with my parents,' Lucy said. 'I was given a long leave, so I have time to decide what to do next...'

'Great. Perhaps we can go somewhere? What about for dinner this evening?' He smiled at her. 'I owe you a dinner. Didn't I say I would take you somewhere nice?'

'Yes, you did – but then they sent you home and I didn't get to say goodbye.'

'I didn't want to say goodbye.' His eyes met hers. 'I knew it wasn't, Lucy. It couldn't be – because you are too special to me. I did try to tell you but...' He shook his head. 'They sent me home in a hurry. We didn't get the chance to say goodbye.'

'No, I was sorry about that.' Lucy felt a little flutter somewhere in her chest. It was a just a tiny flicker, but it was there. The look in his eyes was infectious, making her laugh.

'You really are as beautiful as I remembered – not some fevered dream.'

'I think you are flirting with me, Captain Rossiter.'

'Flirting isn't the right word, but it is a start,' he said and smiled. 'So that is a date – this evening?'

'If I can get away from here.' Lucy made a rueful face. 'I haven't had one customer and my mother is counting on me to sell at least some of this junk.'

'It is mostly junk,' he agreed. 'Some of the metal could go to the scrapyard.' He looked round the hall and saw a young lad and beckoned him to them.

'Yes, mister?' the lad said and saluted, because he was addressing an officer. 'What yer want?'

'Could you clear all the metal junk on this table to the local scrapyard for me? I'll give you ten bob.'

'Yeah! Me and me mate will have it done in a tick, captain.'

'Right.' Captain Rossiter took his wallet out and extracted two ten-shilling notes. 'Clear everything from this stall and there is ten bob each. Take it all to the junkyard and they might give you an extra bob or two.'

'Thanks, captain, I'll fetch me mate...' He went off at a run.

Captain Rossiter took two white five-pound notes from his wallet and handed them to Lucy. 'That is a donation to the church funds... Now will you come and have dinner with me?'

'Oh yes,' Lucy said and tucked the money into her jacket pocket. 'Mum has been wanting to do that for years but couldn't bring herself to junk it all. She thought it might raise something – and now it has.'

She went round the counter to take his arm and was stopped by a woman in a black hat with white roses. 'Oh, are you going? I wanted that big copper jug.'

'I am afraid it is all sold, madam,' Lucy said. 'Sorry – come back next year. I am sure my mother will have found another to replace it by then.'

She took Captain Rossiter's arm, hardly controlling her giggle as the woman went off looking highly annoyed.

'Can we get a cup of tea, please? I've been dying for one all afternoon.'

He glanced at the queue. 'Let's go to that nice tea shop up the road. They might be glad of some customers since they all seem to be in here...'

* * *

'Well, didn't I say you would bring me luck?' Lucy's mother said, looking at the two white five-pound notes later that afternoon. 'Your Captain Rossiter must be very generous if he paid all this for that load of junk.'

'He gave the boys a pound to clear it all, as well,' Lucy said, smiling at her mother. 'He was just grateful for the way I looked after him in Cyprus. I was his special nurse while he was really ill and patients do remember us.'

'Yes, so you say...' Her mother looked at her speculatively. 'So he took you for a cup of tea and he is taking you to dinner this evening...'

'Actually, I paid for our tea because he'd spent all his money. He will get some more for this evening, so he says – probably have to borrow it from his family, but since it was for the church, I didn't offer to give it back.'

'Does he live in Hastings? I don't know the name... They may not visit your father's church, so I probably don't know his family...'

'His parents died when he was young. His aunt and uncle looked after him and may not have the same name. Anyway, he is visiting them and that's why he came to the bazaar.'

'And then you took all his money. Poor Captain Rossiter,' her mother said with a little laugh. 'Five pounds would have been quite sufficient for that junk.'

'No. He gave the ten pounds to me for the church,' Lucy said. 'I wasn't giving it back after I'd stood there all afternoon. I'll offer to go halves tonight, though, just in case he is a bit hard up.'

'So I should think,' her mother said, then, 'You've got enough money, Lucy – and something nice to wear?'

'Yes. I have a pretty blue dress with a halter neck. I don't think you've seen it.'

'That is good...' Her mother nodded. 'And this Captain Rossiter – does he have a first name?'

'Yes, it is Jack,' Lucy told her. She could see the way her mother's thoughts were going. 'Stop making plans for my wedding, Mum. Jack is just a friend. He wants to take me out to say thank you for what I did when he was so ill.'

'Yes, if you say so,' her mother said and went away singing to herself.

Lucy shook her head and smiled inwardly. Her mother was so easy to read and she did so want to see Lucy happily married. It was a pity that it wasn't likely to happen for a long, long time...

* * *

Jack took her to the best hotel in Hastings that evening. There wasn't anything very special on the menu, but when the head waiter learned that he had been shot down and Lucy had nursed him, he went away with a thoughtful look and came back smiling with a different menu.

'We happen to have a turkey this evening, sir, miss,' he said. He glanced round the room. 'We can't offer it to everyone, so we save it for our brave fighting men and their young ladies. I don't know if you would fancy it instead of the Spam fritters you were thinking of?'

'Wouldn't we just,' Jack said and grinned, looking at Lucy, who nodded. 'That is very kind of you – and we'll have something nice to drink if you happen to have a special bottle put by... like champagne?'

'We might just have for a special occasion...' The waiter

winked and went off again, returning with an ice bucket and a bottle of what looked like costly French wine.

Lucy looked at it, whispering as the waiter went off again. 'Are you sure, Jack? I mean this is expensive – and you gave me all that money for the church...'

Jack laughed. 'Don't worry, Lucy. A few pounds and some champagne won't break the bank... Well, Uncle Philip's bank actually. He's in the manufacturing business and the war has been kind to him. At the moment, I am his blue-eyed boy and he'd give me the moon if I asked.'

'Oh. I'm afraid my dad is a cash-strapped vicar,' Lucy replied and laughed. 'Mum was very grateful for the money, though she regretted you had her hoard sent to the scrapyard. She will have to collect something different for next year.'

Jack's eyes twinkled with amusement. 'Your mum and dad sound wonderful, Lucy – just like their daughter.'

'Jack...' Lucy met his eyes across the table and the words she'd been going to say died. Suddenly, she didn't want to tell him that her heart belonged in the grave with John. In fact, her heart was fluttering, as if it was slowly returning to life, and she was smiling. 'This is really nice here. I'd never been.'

'We will come again, make it our special place – for anniversaries and things...' He reached across the table, touching her hand. 'You can tell me it's too soon if you want, Lucy, but I'm not going to waste any more time. Time has a habit of running out. I am in love with you and I have been since I first heard your voice and felt the touch of you hand – your soft gentle fingers that made me want to cling to life...' He held her hand tight as it moved in his. 'I know a lot of patients fall in love with their nurse and then forget them when they leave hospital – but I didn't forget you, not for one minute. I wrote a lot of letters to you but didn't send them, because I knew I needed to see you again first. I thought I might be making too much of my feelings and that perhaps it was just gratitude.'

Jack paused, looking at her, waiting for her to speak, but she said nothing, so he went on, 'I asked about you at that hospital and I found out that you lived in Hastings. I couldn't believe my luck when I discovered it was close to my aunt and uncle. It was no coincidence that I turned up at your stall this afternoon. My aunt told me you might be there. She knows your mother runs the bazaar for the church.'

'Oh, Jack...' Lucy breathed deeply, feeling she was being sucked into a whirlpool and out of her depth. This was crazy. They didn't know each other – except that for weeks when she'd nursed him, they'd been as close as two people could be without being lovers. 'Jack...' She paused unsure of what to say, because her heart was doing strange things and she didn't understand what was happening to her. 'I... do like you very much...'

'That's enough for me. I will teach you to love me,' Jack said. 'Every day of our life, I will make you glad you married me – because you are going to, aren't you, Lucy?' He paused, his intense gaze holding her captive. 'I know you lost someone you loved, but I believe there was something special between us – wasn't there? Tell me I'm wrong – tell me you feel nothing for me if it is so.' His hands were holding hers and she felt the strength of his passion, his love for her. It was, of course, too soon to think of marriage and yet... she needed to be loved so badly. All the empty aching need inside her cried out for love. She must tell him to wait... of course she must. It was foolish – and yet...

'I...' Lucy faltered. Why should she say they must wait? What was the point of holding back when she felt as he did that they were drawn together? Life was too short and even though Jack was no longer on active service anything could happen. She'd lost one man she loved, but she couldn't risk it happening again.

And she needed him. She needed to feel his arms about her, loving her, protecting her, healing her. 'Yes,' she said at last. 'I believe I am going to marry you, Jack...' and then she was smiling, laughing as she saw the delight in his eyes.

The waiter returned with their starter – a prawn cocktail, no less. 'I guessed it was a special day,' he said as he looked at their faces. 'May I be the first to congratulate you, captain.'

'Yes, you may,' Jack said and grinned like a Cheshire cat. 'She just said yes... What is your name?'

'Vincent, sir.'

'Well, Vincent, please open that champagne and join me in a toast to the most beautiful, kindest and wonderful girl in the world.'

'I'll take a sip with you, sir,' Vincent said beaming. 'And I'll bring a new glass for you, miss.' He popped the bottle, poured a half glass for Jack and a mouthful for himself. 'To a beautiful young lady – and a lucky gentleman.'

Having toasted Lucy, he whipped the used glass away and replaced it, before refilling Jack's glass and giving Lucy what was her first taste of champagne. She sipped gingerly, but liked the taste and the bubbles that seemed to go up her nose.

'We'll buy your rings tomorrow,' Jack said. 'I'll arrange a dinner for our families to meet each other and then we'll marry by special licence. It will raise a few eyebrows but who cares?'

'I don't,' Lucy replied, swept away now by excitement. 'The tabbies can count all they want; it won't help them.'

'Oh, Lucy, you darling,' he said and got up, coming round the table to kiss her lightly on the lips. 'If it weren't for the promise of that turkey, I'd whisk you off somewhere private so that I could kiss you properly.'

She laughed. 'There's no way I'm missing this prawn cocktail and my turkey dinner. I haven't had either for years.' She twinkled at him. 'You can kiss me when you take me home – and we'll take the longest route...'

Jack gave a shout of laughter as he sat down again. 'Oh, Lucy. You made me laugh when I wanted to give up – and you make me laugh now. I hope we shall still be laughing together when we're ninety-three...'

'What happens after that?' Lucy asked. 'I fully intend to be a hundred – and you'd better do the same or I'll haunt you.'

The sound of his laughter made other diners turn to look at them, but neither Jack nor Lucy cared.

A warm glow was spreading throughout Lucy's body. It might have been the champagne and the good food, but she thought it was something more. Lucy would never forget John Talbot. Her love for him had been real, but John was dead and she was alive. She deserved to be happy.

It was good. Lucy had let go of her dreams. Now she had a new one and she smiled across at the man who would hold her heart for the rest of their lives. She believed he would be a careful custodian and she would give him all the love that was in her. As she looked into the eyes of love, she knew that she had found her home at last.

37

'More cards and letters,' Artie announced, bringing in a pile of post. 'These are all for you, Mum. Jeanie, these are yours and ours... from your family, I think...'

Artie handed over the post and then went to the sink to wash his hands. The smell of streaky bacon and bubble and squeak filled the kitchen, making his stomach rumble. It was cold out, frosty, and he was hungry. As he turned, his mother placed a loaded plate on the table for him and he smiled his thanks as he sat down to eat.

Pam sat down in her chair with a cup of tea and started to open her cards. 'Oh, this is from Mrs Murry...' She shook her head. 'I didn't send her one, but there is still time.' It was another three days until Christmas.

'Who is Mrs Murry?' Artie asked, pausing with a forkful of delicious food.

'She lives in Chatteris and I used to meet her when your father took me to the dinner and dance for the farmers each year... Not your generation, Artie. I hadn't heard from her in ages, but I was told she lost her husband. She suggests that I visit her for lunch one day... as if I ever have the time.'

'You could, Mum.' Jeanie had been nursing a sleeping Winston but she placed him in his carrycot and picked up her pile of cards. 'Oh, this one is a letter – for you, Mum.'

Pam looked up from her cards, then reached out and took it. 'Wonder who that is from?' she murmured as she opened the envelope. 'Oh, it is from Lucy. She... writes to say she is back home and has met someone she nursed... She is going to marry him...'

'Lucy – that's the girl John wanted to marry...' Artie frowned. 'Well, she didn't take long to find herself someone else, did she?'

'It's nearly eight months,' Jeanie murmured. 'You don't know her circumstances, Artie.'

'Sounds like indecent haste to me,' Artie growled. 'Supposing she'd married John and had charge of his son? Lord knows what would happen to him.'

'Lucy wouldn't have harmed him,' Jeanie said mildly. 'I quite liked her – not that I knew her well.'

'Well, I'm inclined to agree with Artie this time,' Pam said. 'I would've hated my grandson to pass into a family I didn't know.' Artie nodded, but Jeanie looked away. 'I think it is a bit soon – not that I wish her to be miserable and lonely. If she's found someone else to love, well, good luck to her.'

'Yes, it's a good thing she's found someone,' Artie said. 'But I'm thinking of how John would feel... To my mind, she has betrayed him. No one knows for certain that he didn't survive.'

'Tom said we shouldn't give up hope,' Pam agreed with a sigh. 'No more of that now – we should be looking forward to Christmas. Susan will be home this evening. It will just be family this year. The girls are going to their families for a few days... Well, to Betty's family. She invited Olive to stay with her. I know it makes more work for you, Artie, but George is off school and he loves helping. I told him he would get paid the same as them and he's over the moon.'

'I can help with the milking,' Jeanie put in and smiled. 'Yes, I can, Artie. I'm fine now and if you think I'm going to stay in bed half the day, you're wrong. The sooner I start work again, the better...' She patted her tummy. 'I want to get this weight off and I shan't do that sitting around.'

'Winston will be fine with his granny if Jeanie wants to help,' Pam said. 'I was back to my normal jobs within a week after having my babies, Artie – and some women carry on as if nothing happened.'

'Romany women,' Artie said. 'I've seen them give birth and then carry on the next day, but Jeanie is my wife – not a gypsy.'

Both Pam and Jeanie started laughing.

Artie glared at them and then chuckled. 'Go on, laugh your heads off. I'm outnumbered.' He looked up as the land girls entered the kitchen, having finished their work for the morning.

'Oh, something smells good, Pam,' Betty said.

'We're having a special breakfast because you won't be here for Christmas,' Pam told her. 'Bacon, scrambled eggs and bubble and squeak.'

'Lovely,' Olive said and smiled. 'You spoil us, Pam.' She looked at Betty who nodded. 'We both appreciate it so much, so we clubbed together to buy you something nice.'

She left the room and they heard her run up the stairs. A few minutes later, she was back with a parcel wrapped in silver tissue paper, which she handed to Pam.

'We've got a little something for the children, too, but we thought you'd keep that for the day...'

'Have I got to open it now?' Pam asked with a little flush of pleasure as they nodded. She carefully untied the ribbon, because she would save that and the paper. Everything was saved and reused that could be these days. Opening the package, she discovered a beautiful cream silk blouse with a frill down the buttoned front and long sleeves with buttoned cuffs. 'Oh, this is lovely! Thank you so much, girls. It must have cost you all your clothing coupons, as well as being so expensive.' Tears stung her eyes as she turned to them and opened her arms. They both ran to hug her and everyone laughed.

'You deserve it. You are so special,' Olive said.

'Yes, you do,' Betty echoed. 'You've made us so welcome, Pam. We both love being here.'

'This is the nearest I've come to having a home of my own,' Olive announced and looked as if she wanted to cry. 'You're all so nice...'

Artie gave a snort of laughter. 'I bet you don't say that when I tell you I want that load of muck in the yard spreading before you leave...'

Betty looked at him in protest, because they had only two hours before their train left, but he was joking and she grinned as she saw his smile. 'Speak for yourself, Olive,' she said and stuck her tongue out at Artie. 'Everyone but...'

'Now you've been told, Artie,' Jeanie said. 'We've got some gifts for you girls, too. I'll give them to you when you leave – but you're not to open them until Christmas Day.'

Artie pushed back his plate with an exaggerated sigh. 'I suppose I'll just have to shift that damned muck myself then.' He was grinning as he went out. It was Christmas and his mood had lightened as everyone seemed to be happier this year. There was a feeling that things were beginning to go the way of the Allies. It had been a hard-fought war and it wasn't over yet, but things were easing. More merchant ships had got through recently and

Pam had actually been able to buy enough dried fruit to make some puddings.

Archie had managed to get hold of six turkey eggs early that year and three had hatched under the brooding hens; they had three turkeys, plucked and ready for cooking. Pam had the largest of the three to cook for her family's Christmas dinner, and Artie had sold the other two to people he knew. Pam had told him he ought to give them away, but he'd said he would sell them, though in actual fact he'd bartered them. His mother didn't yet know that she now owned two ewes, both of which were in lamb. It was her Christmas gift and Artie was rather pleased with the bargain he'd made. A little effort on his part might bring in quite a nice sum for his mother.

He hummed a little tune as he set to work loading the trailer with the muck he intended to spread on his fields down the fens. His conscience troubled him from time to time, because, accident or not, he'd killed a man and that wasn't easy to live with. However, Artie had listened to Tom. It was done. Nothing could change what had happened and he knew they'd been lucky. Tom had taken a huge risk if anyone had seen – but they hadn't and Artie had to live with it. God might not want him in Heaven when the time came, but he wasn't particularly religious and didn't quite believe in Heaven or Hell. The here and now was all that mattered in Artie's opinion.

He frowned as he thought about the girl John had brought home and told them he wanted to marry. It was only a few months, damn her! His mother and Jeanie might be pleased she'd found happiness but what if... Artie shook his head. With each month that passed, it became less likely that they would hear anything more of John. Men thought to have died did turn up months later, lost either in hospital or some prison camp.

There had been something in the paper recently about an escape from one of those camps...

Sighing, Artie shook his head. John had come back after being missing once before. It would be a bloody miracle if it happened again.

'Well, why not?' Archie muttered aloud. 'We're due some blooming luck, God. Why the hell not?'

* * *

Lizzie was tired when she got in that evening. Because it was Christmas, she'd been busy all day, and Arthur hadn't made things easier. She'd taken him with her, because her customers enjoyed seeing him. He would toddle from one client to the next and stand on his still wobbly legs looking up at them so curiously.

'He's wondering what these things are stuck on my head,' one of her regulars had said as she bent down to pick Arthur up and sit him on her knee. She'd produced a flat red lollipop and showed it to him. Arthur had clamoured for it naturally and ended up with a sticky mouth, face, hands – and a sticky gown for the customer, which had to be put in with the washing. At busy periods, there were so many towels needed that Lizzie had begun to take them to the laundry instead of boiling them herself. If only there was a machine that would wash, rinse and dry them! No such luck. It was in the copper or wash by hand, so at busy times, they went to the laundry instead.

She had found a small property for rent just three doors down from her hair dressing salon, on the corner of the High Street, and, on the spur of the moment had seized her opportunity and opened her little dress shop in time for the Christmas trade, and so far, the takings were keeping up with her own, though it might not be that way once the festivities were over. Lizzie was pleased with it at the moment, but it meant that she had more to do, of course. Accounts had to be kept and wages paid, and she made it her habit to check on stocks and supplies once a week. So by the time she had bathed and got a tired little boy into bed, all she wanted was to sit down and eat.

She wished a meal was all ready for her, but Pam was busy enough these days without another mouth to feed, so Lizzie didn't take advantage, though she knew she would always be welcome at Pam's table. A cup of tea and a sandwich, Lizzie thought. She popped the kettle on the range after giving it a poke to make it heat up a bit more, then she took the large fresh loaf from her basket and made herself a Spam and pickle sandwich. There was enough for lunch the following day, unless she made fritters of it for breakfast.

It was nine o'clock when Lizzie sat down in a comfy chair and reached for her post. She had a pile of Christmas cards. People hadn't sent many the previous year, but this year everyone seemed to have done so and there were several friends she would need to send cards to that hadn't been on her list. A lot of her customers had sent cards to the shop, but a few knew where she lived and so she had quite a pile to open. It wasn't until she got to the bottom of the pile that she saw the letter from Tom.

Lizzie smiled as she picked it up and opened it. She loved Tom's letters. They were always a treat. Although she knew he wasn't expecting to get leave this Christmas, she always hoped it might happen.

My darling Lizzie,

I hope you and Arthur are well, my love, and looking forward to Christmas. I know you will have bought something nice for him, but I wish I could get him a present. Unfortunately, things have been hectic here. We've been working our socks off, something big coming.

No more of that. I shall be thinking of you all over Christmas and wishing myself with you, my darling – but I have some news and I'm not sure what to do. As you know, I've made a lot of enquiries, badgered a lot of people, and at last... there is news. It might be John. Before you run to tell Mum, it isn't certain, Lizzie. At the moment, it is just a maybe.

A man was found by some monks living on a Greek island – some distance from where John's plane crashed. If it is him, he must have been in the sea for a couple of days and drifted with the current. When he was fished out of the water, more dead than alive, the monks planned to care for him until he died and give him a Christian burial. He had no clothes, no papers, nothing. The sea had taken it all, so they didn't know who he was – and he was ill for a very long time, not expected to live. When he finally became lucid, he said he was British and his name was John...

I know. I know. I can't help being excited, though John is a common enough name. The monks couldn't speak much English. When he was well enough, a fisherman took him to Cyprus and that is where he is now. In the hospital. On the voyage, he became sick again and, so far, he hasn't told them his full name, if he knows it. John lost his memory last time he was badly hurt...

But this isn't the fabulous news you are thinking, Lizzie. This man, whoever he might be, has been badly burned on his face and body. He is likely to be ill for some time – and may not recover fully. So, this is my problem. Do we tell the family? What do you think, Lizzie? If we give them hope and it isn't John... And even if it is him... supposing... well, you see my dilemma.

I had to tell you, but I can't decide whether we should tell Mum. Will you hate me if I say it must be your decision, Lizzie? If I could get leave, I would tell her and warn her of being too excited yet. I am afraid I have no chance of that, much as I wish it.

Perhaps you should ask Artie what he thinks? I'm just not sure. Mum has suffered enough and I don't want to raise her hopes for nothing – but there is a chance that it is our John.

Lizzie sat with Tom's letter in her hands as the tears ran down her face. Her heart felt as if it had been torn apart and then put back together again, but with a great big stitch in it. Could it be the miracle they'd all longed and prayed for? Pam hadn't thought it could happen twice. She'd been certain that John was dead, said she felt it. The man the monks rescued had been close to death – perhaps still was. He was badly burned on his face as well as his body... A little shiver went through Lizzie.

Was it even right to hope with all her heart that it was John Talbot in that hospital bed? What kind of a life would be his if he survived and came home? Lizzie shook her head. Lucy – would she still want him if she knew how badly injured he'd been? Lizzie knew she would still want Tom, no matter how severely he was hurt, but it was John – might be John – and she didn't know Lucy well enough to judge.

Lizzie glanced at the clock. It was too late to walk up to the farm now and Arthur was in bed, and this certainly wasn't news she could convey over a phone. She would sleep on it, Lizzie thought, though whether she could sleep now was another matter.

As she undressed and got into bed, Lizzie thought that

perhaps she ought to involve Artie, as Tom suggested. If he could come home, it would've been easier. Tom could always talk to his mother and judge her mood. The problem weighed on Lizzie as she crawled into bed, but she was so tired...

Sleep took her much sooner than she might have expected, her body weary from a full day's work and care for her child. She slept until six the next morning and then woke with a start as a yell from Arthur's room brought her wide awake. Lizzie went to him, lifting him up to discover a wet nappy.

After she'd made him comfortable, she took him down to the kitchen and put him in his high chair, making tea and then scrambled egg on fingers of toast for his breakfast. Arthur grabbed for it, feeding himself, even though much of it went on the floor.

Lizzie watched him. She'd made up her mind. As soon as she'd had breakfast, she would find Artie and tell him – but she was going to tell Pam, whatever he thought. If it was Lizzie's husband or son, she would want to know, even though it would hurt.

38

Pam was already hard at work baking when Artie walked into the kitchen, followed by Lizzie, who was carrying Arthur. Smiling, she told them to sit down.

'I've got the kettle boiling,' she said and then her heart caught as she saw their serious faces. 'What's wrong?'

'You'd best sit down, Mum,' Artie said. 'Lizzie and I – we have something to tell you.'

'John? Is it John?' Pam asked, sitting down hard with a bump. 'I had a dream last night. He was in hospital and calling for me...' Her breath seemed to stick in her throat and she couldn't go on.

'Tom wrote to me,' Lizzie said. 'He has had news, Mum, but it isn't certain – a man has been found and is in hospital, but they don't know it is our John, not yet. It might not be him.'

'Tell me...' Pam mumbled. Her head was whirling and her heart felt as if it would burst from the effort to remain calm when she wanted to shout, because she knew. She knew it was her John. She'd seen him and heard him – such a vivid dream.

'He was picked out of the sea by monks, no identification,

and very ill,' Lizzie said carefully. 'They saved his life and got him to Cyprus in a fishing boat, but he became ill again. Apparently, he has told them his name is John and he is British—'

'It will be him,' Pam said and burst into tears. 'It has to be, Lizzie...' Her joy stilled as she saw their faces. 'What... what haven't you told me?'

'The man in the hospital has been badly burned on his face and his body,' Lizzie said. 'He is still very ill and may not recover.'

Pam gasped and bent over double, feeling as if she had been punched in the stomach. So close to getting her son back and yet so far...

'No...' she said and raised her head, looking at Lizzie. 'He won't die. God couldn't be that cruel – to give him back to us after all this time and then snatch him away. It can't, won't happen...' She saw Lizzie nod, but she still looked grave. 'The burns – yes, that's bad. Very bad. I know—' she gasped, snatching at breath. 'He must be in terrible pain. It is why he called out for me – and he did. I felt it. The dream wasn't like any other dream I've had, Lizzie. It was as if I was there, looking down at him, and I saw the bandages. I really did...' Pam straightened up and wiped her face. 'I thought he was dead, but I was wrong. If they can get him home to us, we'll look after him, whatever it takes and for however long it takes. This is his home, his family. He is my son despite the scars.'

'It might not be that easy,' Artie said. 'How is John going to feel – that girl... would she still want him? Bugger! I'd forgotten...' He looked stunned. 'She's getting married...'

'She was married yesterday,' Pam confirmed, looking at him. 'She wrote to tell me. She didn't wait long enough...'

'And how is John going to feel about that?' Artie asked. 'It is going to be hell on earth for him, Mum. He lost Faith and now

Lucy... and by the sound of it, he doesn't have much chance of finding love again.'

'Lucy couldn't have loved him, not enough anyway,' Pam said. 'He will be scarred, perhaps horribly so, but he is my son, and he will be welcome here no matter what.'

'I didn't mean it like that,' Artie said, looking awkward. 'I'm thinking of how he may feel. If he is badly scarred, he might not want us to see him.'

'Please, don't upset yourself, Pam,' Lizzie said as she saw anger flare between the two. 'We don't know all of it yet. Tom's letter arrived yesterday. Things may have changed – he won't have got the news immediately. You will have to wait and see, Pam. We all must – and then it is John's choice.'

Pam nodded, sagging back in her chair as it hit her. 'He took a while to get over it last time he was badly wounded. He will need time. I think they can help burns patients at special places – they will send him there first.'

'*If* it is him,' Lizzie reminded, but it was obvious to everyone that Pam fully believed John was alive and in hospital.

'I can wait until they contact us,' Pam said and took a deep breath. 'Thank you for telling me, Lizzie – that wasn't easy for you.'

'I'm so sorry it wasn't better news, Pam.'

'John is alive. That is all that matters to me.'

'What about that girl?' Artie asked. 'Are you going to tell Lucy?'

Pam raised her head to look at him. 'Why? She doesn't need to know now. She got married to someone else. Why upset her by telling her that John may be alive but badly burned? It would make her feel guilty. No, I shan't tell her.'

'I think she would want to know,' Lizzie said, but Pam shook her head.

'No. I shan't write to her – after all, we aren't certain.'

Lizzie looked at Artie and he shook his head but said nothing.

'Shall we have that cup of tea now?' Pam asked as Jeanie came downstairs and into the kitchen. She was carrying Winston and had Jonny by the hand. He pulled clear of her and ran to his granny, pulling at her skirts. Pam bent down and picked him up, holding him on her lap and stroking his hair.

'I have work to do,' Artie said. 'I'll be home at four.' He went out, clearly wanting to get away.

Jeanie looked at Lizzie. 'Is something wrong?'

'John has been found,' Pam answered before Lizzie could. 'He is in hospital in Cyprus and badly burned – but he will get better.' She nodded to herself as if that settled it. 'Are the children ready for their breakfasts? It seems odd without the land girls, doesn't it? Too quiet.'

Jeanie raised her eyebrows behind Pam's back. Lizzie mouthed, 'Later,' at her and she nodded.

Pam kept up a flow of chatter as she made breakfast for Jonny, and Jeanie fed Winston a bottle. Arthur saw them having toast and jam fingers with the crusts cut off and clamoured for his share, so she put a slice nicely cut up into soldiers in front of him, even though Lizzie said he'd been fed.

'It won't hurt him,' Pam said. 'I fancy some myself – what about you?'

Lizzie declined and drank her tea before she left. She wasn't going to work until the afternoon when Dot Goodman had promised to fetch him, and she took Arthur home so that she could do some cooking. Christmas was almost on them.

* * *

Pam sat alone in her kitchen and wept. She'd been too stunned by the news to know what she felt at first, hardly knowing what she said or did, but overcome with her joy that at least there was a chance she would get her son back. Artie's objections had sunk in later and she knew he was right. John had always been a sensitive lad. There was no way of knowing what he would want to do next... But, in her heart, she knew he had to come home. Only here was there a chance for him to be healed inside, in his heart and his mind.

39

Susan was waiting for Artie when he got back that afternoon. She caught him as he switched off the tractor, pulling at his arm, leading him away from the house to the cowsheds. He looked down at her, saw her worried face and sighed. He'd been expecting this since she got home the previous evening. She'd given him a few significant looks and Artie had known what was coming.

'Is it true?' she asked in an urgent low voice. 'That man – is he dead?'

'Who told you – what have you heard?' Artie asked, watching her face. She looked worried and distressed and he hesitated, then knew he had to stick to the story Tom had given her, because Susan must never know the truth; it would haunt her. Artie was still haunted himself, but he was learning to live with it and he didn't want his sister to feel in any way guilty. After all, that rotter had tried to rape her!

'He was found dead in the ditch not far from here...' Susan looked at him fearfully. 'Artie, you didn't?'

'I tried to give him a good hiding but he was better than me, but I managed to wind him with a lucky punch – and then he saw Tom coming and he jumped in his car and drove off. He was drunk, Susan. He would have beaten me, but when Tom turned up, he decided it would be one too many and he cleared off – driving like the devil was after him.'

'Thank goodness,' Susan said and then burst into tears. 'Oh, Artie. I've been worried that you'd done something terrible and might get in trouble – and it would be all my fault because I went out with that man. I didn't know him well enough and I never thought. I don't care about him, but I do care for you...' She gave a sob. 'And now Mum is crying and John is badly hurt...'

Artie put his arms around her and she wept against his chest. He hesitated, then stroked her hair. 'It's all right, love. Never feel guilty over that scum. He got what was coming to him – they say he'd been fighting with some of the men at the airfield previously and that one of them may have tampered with his brakes.'

'I'm not glad he's dead, but he wasn't a nice person,' Susan said and drew back, rubbing her eyes. 'I'll just forget him, but I'll be more careful who I go out with in future. At college, I'm sticking to going out as a group with other girls and blokes together.' She wiped her face, swallowing a sob. 'Do you think it is John in that hospital?'

'Not sure. He was missing a long time, but then he would be if he was on some island where only monks lived, because they wouldn't have many visitors. I'm not sure what to hope, Susan – if it is him, his life is ruined... Poor man, whoever he is.'

'Yes.' Susan gulped and then kissed his cheek. 'I'm glad you're here, Artie. I do love you – you know that? I'm grateful for what you did that night and I always will be.' She smiled at him mistily. 'We all need you here to look after us, Artie.'

With that, she turned and ran back to the house.

Artie stared after her. He watched as she went into the house and then turned towards the milking shed. Suddenly, he felt lighter, the shadow that had hung over him for a while lifting. She was right. His family did need him to look after them – and that's all he'd been doing. Looking after his family. An accident was an accident.

He began to whistle. Life was good and it was Christmas; they would put the tree up that evening and Artie had a few presents to wrap. The sale of the piggery land was still going through, so he hadn't got his money yet, but he'd saved enough to buy some nice gifts for his family. He'd made up his mind to give Tom a few hundred pounds when he got his money, to say thank you for all he'd done for him, finding a buyer for the land – and making sure he didn't go to prison for grievous bodily harm.

A little shiver went down Artie's spine as he thought of what might have happened. Instead of looking forward to Christmas with his family, he could have been sitting in a cold cell regretting what he'd done. There were times when Artie resented his elder brother, but he understood now that Tom had been a good friend to him. Their disputes were mostly Artie's fault. It was time he grew up, put childish disputes behind him and pulled together for the sake of the family.

Susan's show of love had made Artie realise how much he had, so much of it he'd always taken for granted – and all that could have been lost. A little prayer for forgiveness and gratitude left his lips as he started to milk the cows and he counted his blessings. A beautiful wife, his lovely little son, a loving family – and after Christmas he would be a landowner. It would be the start of a wonderful new life…

40

Sister Jane bent over the burns case at the end of the ward. He had been in and out of his fever for so long that she'd almost despaired of him. She'd nursed him herself, because he needed special attention and she didn't trust any of her nurses to go that extra mile. If truth be told, she was missing Nurse Lucy and had regretted sending her home, despite the card she'd had to tell her Lucy's good news. She was happy for Lucy, of course, but she would be missed as a nurse. She'd been so very good with the young men who had been badly burned and feared for their futures.

About to turn away, she felt a light touch on her arm, 'Lucy... is it you?' a weak voice asked. 'Oh, Lucy, I do love you so. I never told you... not enough. It wasn't just for Jonny—' A little choking sob came from him as Sister Jane bent over him and lightly stroked the back of his hand, one little bit of him that had escaped the flames of the burning plane before it crashed.

'It's not Lucy,' she said. He'd said the name so many times in his fever, calling for her over and over. 'It's Sister Jane. Can you tell me your name – is it John? You've been so ill and we were not sure who you were, though you tried to tell us several times...'

'Where am I?'

'You are in a special hospital in England. I brought you with me when I returned from Cyprus on the hospital ship, but you fell ill again. This place is for men who have been badly injured and may need to stay here a long time. I am in charge here, though I am still known to my patients as Sister Jane.' The intelligent eyes that looked at her from behind the white bandages were a clear blue just then. Mercifully, he had not been blinded by the fire that must have engulfed him. 'Hello, Sister Jane,' he said, his voice stronger now. 'I thought you might be my girl. She is a nurse, too, and her name is Lucy Ross... My name...? Yes, I do remember now. My name is John Talbot and I live at Blackberry Farm in Mepal, England...'

'Good, you have remembered,' Sister Jane replied. 'We can arrange to let your family know what happened to you now.'

John's hand had moved up to his head, his fingers moving over the bandages, exploring. He looked down at his hands and then at her. 'I've been burned, haven't I? Is it bad?'

'We don't know how bad it will be yet,' she said calmly. 'Time heals a lot and the skin will get less red – it will probably be mottled and brown after a while. They may be able to do some grafting if you want and if it proves necessary...'

'You've seen my face without the bandage – how much is affected?'

She hesitated, but honesty was best. 'All of the left side, across your forehead and all your chin. Your eyes and right cheek were not caught by the fire.'

John was silent for a long moment, then he inclined his head. 'Thank you, sister.' He caught her hand as she turned away. 'My family – you should tell them I am alive, but not Lucy.

I would prefer that she didn't know. She would stand by me, because she is that sort – so she mustn't be told the truth. Please,' he held her wrist strongly. 'Make sure they know not to tell her. Let her find her own life and be happy.'

'Yes, I will write to them myself. Rest now and later you can dictate the letter yourself and I will send it for you.'

He thanked her and lay back against his pillows. John's eyes closed so he didn't see her anxious look as she walked away.

* * *

Sister Jane thought of the letter from Lucy Ross in her pocket. Ought she to tell John that the girl he loved had married someone else? He didn't want her to stand by him, but all the men felt like that when they realised that they would be terribly scarred.

It was a dilemma and one she would rather not have had, but there was time enough to decide. She was not sure what it was about the young airman that had touched something in her heart, but Jane felt an affinity for him that she'd not felt towards any man since her husband had died. He was a stranger to her, in his early twenties, Jane was past thirty and dedicated to her work – but she was determined that he should get well and feel able to face his life again. With most of her patients, Jane retained a cool, kind efficiency, but there was something different about this one that aroused her fighting instincts. She would do all that she could to see that he was able to face his life once more.

In the meantime, John's family would be relieved to hear that he was alive and making good progress and he certainly wasn't going anywhere just yet. He needed to get strong again. It would be weeks, even months, before John had to face his family and his life. There was time to tell him that Lucy was married when he finally went home...

* * *

MORE FROM ROSIE CLARKE

A Family at War, the first instalment in Rosie Clarke's brilliant wartime saga series, *The Family Feud*, is available to order now here:

www.mybook.to/AFamilyatWarBackAd

ABOUT THE AUTHOR

Rosie Clarke is a #1 bestselling saga writer whose books include Welcome to Harpers Emporium and The Mulberry Lane series. She has written over 100 novels under different pseudonyms and is a RNA Award winner. She lives in Cambridgeshire.

Sign up to Rosie Clarke's mailing list for news, competitions and updates on future books.

Visit Rosie's website: www.lindasole.co.uk

Follow Rosie on social media here:

- facebook.com/Rosie-clarke-119457351778432
- x.com/AnneHerries
- bookbub.com/authors/rosie-clarke

ALSO BY ROSIE CLARKE

Welcome to Harpers Emporium Series

The Shop Girls of Harpers

Love and Marriage at Harpers

Rainy Days for the Harpers Girls

Harpers Heroes

Wartime Blues for the Harpers Girls

Victory Bells For The Harpers Girls

Changing Times at Harpers

Heartbreak at Harpers

The Mulberry Lane Series

A Reunion at Mulberry Lane

Stormy Days On Mulberry Lane

A New Dawn Over Mulberry Lane

Life and Love at Mulberry Lane

Last Orders at Mulberry Lane

Blackberry Farm Series

War Clouds Over Blackberry Farm

Heartache at Blackberry Farm

Love and Duty at Blackberry Farm

Family Matters at Blackberry Farm

The Trenwith Trilogy

Sarah's Choice

Louise's War

Rose's Fight

Dressmakers' Alley

Dangerous Times on Dressmakers' Alley

Dark Secrets on Dressmakers' Alley

The Family Feud Series

A Family at War

Standalone Novels

Nellie's Heartbreak

A Mother's Shame

A Sister's Destiny

Sixpence Stories

Introducing Sixpence Stories!

Discover page-turning historical novels from your favourite authors, meet new friends and be transported back in time.

Join our book club Facebook group

https://bit.ly/SixpenceGroup

Sign up to our newsletter

https://bit.ly/SixpenceNews

Boldwood

Boldwood Books is an award-winning fiction publishing company seeking out the best stories from around the world.

Find out more at www.boldwoodbooks.com

Join our reader community for brilliant books, competitions and offers!

Follow us
@BoldwoodBooks
@TheBoldBookClub

Sign up to our weekly deals newsletter

https://bit.ly/BoldwoodBNewsletter